WHAT WE DO IN SECRET

Christina Graves

try, it just grips you right back in. I couldn't get enough! This seriously should be a movie!"

ARC Team Review

"Thriller fans, buckle up, because this one is a ride, y'all! Wtf did i just read? Christina delivers an unforgettable, edge-of-your-seat experience with *What We Do in Secret*. It's got everything a thriller fan wants: mystery, betrayal, jaw-dropping twists! From the very first page, I was hooked. Graves wastes no time pulling you into her dark little world, where nothing is as it seems and trust is a dangerous game.The pacing is absolutely relentless in the best way. Just when you think you've figured out what's going on, she flips everything upside-down. The twists are smart, well-placed, and keep you guessing right until the very end. I read this in one sitting, completely unable to put the book down! What really stands out is Graves's writing style. It's sharp, immersive, and filled with emotional depth. She builds tension, crafts complex characters, and keeps you invested in every secret that's revealed. It's the kind of storytelling that sticks with you long after you've turned the last page. Honestly, I need this to be a movie! It reads like a psychological thriller film already, one you'd want to watch over and over. If you're into dark secrets, shocking betrayals, and expertly written suspense, this book needs to be at the top of your list."

ARC Team Review

ALSO BY CHRISTINA GRAVES

Still, Dark Places

ALSO BY HORRORSMITH PUBLISHING

The Devil Came Down the Mountain
Still, Dark Places
Dark Things Crawl Out
What We Do in Secret
Lake of Secrets
Haint Blue
The Taste of Tiny Bones
A Light on the Bayou
Haunted Halls
Their Hearses
Three Garden Village
Hidden Children
Angie Baby
Crepuscular
Blood Ground
His Shrill Song

WHAT WE DO IN SECRET

A Domestic Thriller

CHRISTINA GRAVES

HORRORSMITH PUBLISHING

An Imprint of Horrorsmith Publishing

For information about special discounts for bulk purchases, please contact Horrorsmith Publishing at lsmith@horrorsmithpublishing.com.

Cover Design by The Cover Collection
Editing by Lyndsey Smith, Horrorsmith Editing
Interior Formatting by Lyndsey Smith

ISBN 978-1-967163-98-4

For my girl friends, Sarah, Autumn, and Memory. You're the reason I have this book instead of a plea deal. I love you.

PROLOGUE

For my girl friends, Sarah, Autumn, and Memory. You're the reason I have this book instead of a plea deal. I love you.

PROLOGUE

Flames roar against a clear night sky littered with stars. The stray sparks take to the darkness like fireflies. It would be beautiful in a way, if there weren't three bodies burning inside.

By morning, the flames will have eaten them, along with the house. The truth just has a way of consuming beautiful things.

It is almost poetic. But it shouldn't be so easy to erase someone's entire life like that. To have all those memories, all that history, reduced to a smoldering pile of ash.

Like it never existed.

This place was supposed to be a fresh beginning for my family. A chance to start over with the one I loved, who loved me, even though they were never very good at it. Everything felt so safe. For a moment, nothing in the world could touch us. But I was terribly wrong.

I *wasn't* safe.

And I don't know that I ever was. I am reminded of this with each crash and pop sounding from within the furnace of my former life.

A detective in a crisp white shirt approaches me in the ambulance, pulling me from my thoughts. When I notice him, I instinctively pull my son closer to my side.

We met before, when he first arrived on scene. The detective is a boulder of a man, stone-faced and hardened in a way only someone who has confronted real evil would understand. You have to build a wall around yourself to keep it from getting inside. I know that now.

"Ma'am." His timbre is even, and he scribbles something down on a small pad.

With one hand, I wipe the tears from my eyes and grip my son's shoulder with the other, preparing for more interrogation. I understand, of course. He is just doing his job. But that doesn't stop me from feeling like I am going to choke on my words if I have to relive this awful night...again.

"You doing okay?" he asks.

Relief floods my body. What a gentleman. He is just inquiring about my well-being. I open my mouth to answer, but he isn't speaking to me at all.

The detective is focused on Bodhi.

"He's still in shock," I offer in a shaky voice when Bodhi doesn't answer. "He hasn't spoken since the fire started."

"That's understandable. You've been through a lot tonight, buddy." His voice is soft. Kind. Not the emotionless hard-ass who grilled me for almost an hour while my entire life was burning to the ground. He even offers Bodhi a smile which reaches his eyes.

Bodhi doesn't return it. He doesn't react at all.

When the detective turns to me, his tone stiffens. "Did EMS complete their evaluation?"

"They did. Just a few scratches and some bruises. We're so lucky." I give Bodhi a kiss on the top of his head.

The detective nods, studying my son and me for a moment.

"Any idea when I can get him out of here, Detective? He doesn't need to keep seeing this."

The detective looks at me for a moment longer than I think necessary, then back to Bodhi. His shoulders relax, and an expression of sympathy washes over him.

"We've got your statement. We can put you up in a hotel if you don't have other accommodations."

"That's very kind of you, truly, but we'll be all right. We've got some family I can call to help."

"I understand. I'll need an address and phone number...in case we have any more questions." He hands me a notepad without waiting for me to agree, and I take his pen without hesitation.

I can't let him know I am lying.

We have no other family. That bitch made sure of that. All Bodhi has is me. I have to be strong for him. For my son.

All I want to do right now is get this place as far in my rearview as I can. So I scribble a random address from the next town over, one which will take a while for him to verify, and I make up a phone number. The detective gazes down at it for a moment before raising his eyes to mine.

I don't like the way he is watching me. Like he is trying to find some reason to make us stay. To question me further. But I have told him everything I can. What else does he want?

"We'll be in touch, Ms. Cole," the detective finally says, releasing the vise on my gut. Luckily, the detective didn't notice it. With one last gentle glance at Bodhi, he turns and walks back to his SUV.

"Come on, kid. Let's get you out of here," I say.

Bodhi doesn't look at me, even as I strap him into the back seat of the Altima. When I close the door, he rests his forehead on the window and stares off into the crackling dark. He stays like that, unmoving, while we pass through the awful iron gates surrounding our quiet little community.

I am not who he wants. If he had been given the chance, if things could have been different, it wouldn't be me sitting in the driver's seat. But for now, I will have to do.

Bodhi just needs time. He will understand how much I love him. That everything I had to do, I did for him. To keep him safe.

Safe from *her*.

CHAPTER

ONE

Secrets don't stay secrets in a place like this. It won't take them long to find me. To find everything.

The tiny pills click lightly against each other while I pour them from one hand to the other and back again. A light shock ripples through my nerve paths when the pills brush against the curvature of the scar tissue on my hand. I stare at myself in the mirror.

Such a pretty girl. It's a shame about her.

The words play on a loop in my mind—a single soft voice at first, before multiplying rapidly into a crescendo so loud they become a droning hiss of static.

I look away, silencing them, and turn my attention to the little tranquilizers in my palm.

"Take one every night. They'll help with all the thoughts that scream together in your head. These will quiet them down so you can sleep," my doctor said at our last appointment.

She means well.

In a sense, she's right. They *will* help me. Just not in the way she intended.

I bring them to my lips. Just when I am about to pour them down my throat, a set of headlights wash across the room, subsequently followed by the sounds of car doors slamming shut.

I return the pills to their bottle and make my way to my bedroom window facing the street. It's one a.m—odd for anyone to be up at this hour. This is a nice, quiet neighborhood. Most of the residents here take their Ambien by eight and are knocked out next to their snoring spouses by now.

A U-Haul sits beneath the light pole directly in front of the house. I strain my eyes in the dark, attempting to catch a glimpse of the kind of people who do their business while decent humans are trying to sleep...among other things. A light flicks on in the main room, and I can just make out the silhouette of a woman who is most definitely *not* mean old Mrs. Lowe. The old woman who lived there must have finally gone to meet the savior she was always rambling on about.

Before I went away, she had to be wheeled around by an aid if she wanted to leave the tomb which had become her bedroom. I remember watching her from my window while the nurse took her for her daily stroll down the street, her head bent off to the side like her neck was broken. She looked more dead than alive, even then.

Funny...I hadn't seen a For Sale or Rent sign out front when I got back.

The shadow woman wanders from room to room, flicking lights on and off again, like a ghost. What is she doing? When her silhouette returns to the kitchen, another form joins her, this one taller. He raises both hands to his head. The shadow woman moves closer, placing her palms on his face. For a moment, their shapes merge.

She's kissing him.

They move together out of sight, and moments later, the light flicks off. The house is once again enveloped in darkness. If it weren't for the U-Haul sitting out front, I could almost convince myself I dreamed them into existence.

Before finally returning to my bed, I walk past the bathroom, where the bottle of pills is still waiting for me on the counter. I don't acknowledge them. My thoughts cling to the ghosts across the street. Where did they come from? What kind of people are they? The couples I know from this neighborhood are painfully boring. Certainly not the type to roam around in the middle of the night.

I finally drift off to sleep and dream of a silhouette couple dancing above Mrs. Lowe's grave. Except Mrs. Lowe isn't dead. She's in her coffin beneath them, her screams silenced by the earth surrounding her, her fingertips bloody stumps scratching frantically at the top of her coffin.

Before I wake up, gasping, Mrs. Lowe has become my own mother.

"Such a pretty girl. It's a real shame..." she whispers, before she pulls me into the earth by my ankles.

CHAPTER

TWO

One thing I know for certain: my new neighbors are not from around here.

New Haven is Stepford with a Southern charm. Or at least, that's how *Better Homes and Gardens* magazine described it. When I read the article, I laughed out loud, knowing if they had actually read the book they would reconsider that analogy.

I guess they aren't entirely wrong in some ways. Our quiet little community is about five square miles of oversized houses, manicured lawns, and more manicured people. There's even a community-run grocery store so we don't have to leave the safety of our birdcage to do our guilt shopping for alcohol and ice cream.

A stark contrast from the people I've been watching unload the U-Haul all evening.

On paper, they're the all-American family. A mother, a father, a little boy who looks to be about six or seven, with a mop of messy brown hair, and a golden retriever. That's where the banality ends.

I waited all morning by my bedroom window to catch sight of

them, but the first signs of life don't appear until close to four in the afternoon. What kind of person starts unloading a U-Haul that late in the evening?

The kind who moves into a residential neighborhood under the cover of night, I suppose.

The mother comes out first. She's wearing ripped dark jeans, combat boots, and a graphic T-shirt which has some kind of lewd band name across her breasts. Her long hair falls just below her shoulders in loose waves of black and red. Not natural red like mine, but deeper. The color of bottled blood they sell on the generic aisle at the supermarket. She raises an inked arm and wipes the sweat beading on her forehead.

The father blends with her in every way. He's wearing a long-sleeve T-shirt which fits loosely on his lean body. It's so tattered it is more rags than a shirt. If I wore that, I would look like I had been mauled by a wild animal, yet somehow, it works for him. His hair is dark, like hers, and hasn't seen a brush in days. They have so many tattoos it's hard to tell if they have multiple small ones or large ones running the lengths of their bodies.

The couple is intriguing individually, but together, they are surreal. Like a Dali painting. Sure, they are ridiculous against this pastel backdrop, like a couple of rock stars playing house, but I picture them in the city somewhere, in a studio apartment. The kind with the pipes exposed and the bathtub in the same room as the bed. In that environment, they are perfect.

They share a kiss for the hundredth time when they pass each other, carrying boxes in and out of the house. So public with their intimacy. I've never seen anything like it. They are all touch and tongues if they are so much as five feet from one another. More than once, I've had to look away, my face flushed.

It is during one of these displays that I grab my phone and snap a photo of them. She wraps her arms around him from the back, and he leans into her, his eyes closed. I don't know why I do it. They just seem so at peace in that moment. I want to remember it.

"I know what you're thinking, but this isn't like last time," I say, placing a tray of oatmeal and fruit on the small table beside Mother's bed.

She doesn't respond. Doesn't even look at me anymore. She doesn't need to. The disappointment in me is permanently painted across her face. It always has been. The only difference is that now her vile comments are trapped inside her body, like a tomb.

Part of me pities her, but a larger part enjoys the peace and quiet. Still, it's important to engage with her when I can.

"I've got it all under control."

I tell her everything I've observed so far. How their little boy played carelessly in the front yard with the dog until she called him in for pizza around six. About the endearing way she fluffed his hair playfully before shutting the door behind him.

"The front window isn't open anymore. At some point in the night, she hung not a curtain, but a black and red mandala tapestry. Can you believe it? The homeowner's association is going to have a field day with that. Remember when they tried to tell you that the white rocks you placed in the garden weren't neutral enough?"

I spoon some oatmeal into her mouth.

"I've been trying to learn their routine—or lack of one, rather."

This is, of course, an understatement, but I try to paint as vivid a picture as I can when I talk to Mother. It's her only glimpse of the outside world anymore, and I want it to be a colorful one. So, I watch their lives from my window seat, like a movie. I make up stories in my head about them to fill in the gaps. Imagine conversations they are having while eating takeout for the third day in a row. Conjure up backstories for them. Families. How they met.

I don't tell Mother everything going on in my head, of course. Full disclosure is never the best route to take with anyone. The last thing I want is for her to worry about me.

I tried to let it go at first, but each day I find myself in my usual seat by the window in my bedroom. They fascinate me.

People in general are captivating. Not the version you meet for brunch or have a minute-long conversation with at the grocery store. Those people aren't real. I want to know who they *really* are. Who they become when they think no one is watching.

If you want to know the truth, you have to witness the things they do in secret.

CHAPTER

THREE

My little hobby is slightly unorthodox. But burglary is certainly not for the small-minded.

I hate that word so much. *Burglary*. It's not like I am some kind of hardened criminal, for goodness' sake. I only *look*… mostly. Who someone is behind closed doors is the most interesting thing about them. I just like to get a peek—and perform the old switcheroo on occasion to keep things fun.

Once, I grabbed Mrs. Baughman's diamond bracelet and placed it in her fishbowl. When I was seventeen, I took the Williams's family cat and put him in their dryer. Their housekeeper found him a few days later, poor thing, a little dazed but alive and well. They fired the housekeeper shortly after that. I guess she wasn't doing the washing once a day, like she claimed she was.

The naughtiest thing I have ever done was kiss one of the pastor's collared shirts with Mother's red lipstick. I wish I could have been a fly on the wall when his wife discovered it. Church that Sunday was the most entertaining it had ever been.

A little chaos now and again keeps things interesting, but I never do any *real* harm. I have to follow the rules. Granted, they are all rules I made up, but for the most part, they allow me to move around without being noticed. However, just by being here, right now, I am breaking Rule #1: Never go out after dark. Especially in a neighborhood like this.

Unfortunately, my new neighbors are only ever out of their house for any extended amount of time at night. If it weren't for the occasional late evening sighting, I would swear they were vampires.

It is risky. More so than usual since I never really know where they go or how long they will be gone. I assume night jobs, but they don't dress for any career I am familiar with. What kind of decent workplace allows that much leather in the uniform? Strippers, come to mind, but I have a hard time placing the husband in a club as a dancer. The wife, perhaps.

Tonight, for example, he left in a black band T-shirt, leather jacket with studded shoulders, and ripped jeans. His hair was its normal amount of disheveled, like he just rolled out of bed. He won't be back until 2:00 a.m, if not later, and she didn't go with him this time, like she sometimes does.

Not long before he left, she stretched beneath the streetlight in her usual workout attire—black yoga pants with a cropped top—preparing for her semi-regular night run. She is either the bravest person I have ever seen or she is completely insane. Jogging anywhere at night is probably the most dangerous thing a woman can do. There are creeps out there!

She should consider herself lucky that I have been watching, keeping an eye out for her return. And that is a task in itself since there is no rhyme or reason to her comings and goings. If I had to guess, it would be two or three times a week? But the nights are sporadic, so most of the time, I simply have to watch and wait for her to appear beneath the streetlight, her preferred starting point. The only constant is that these night runs can usually last an hour or more.

It's not ideal, but it is what I've got. I am tired of waiting.

My usual outfit, a pastel jogging suit, would be virtually impossible to hide and would immediately sound alarms. No one would suspect a woman jogging in the middle of the day of any wrongdoing; the opposite is true at night. The slightest movement of shadow is seen as a threat, especially in a neighborhood like this. It's another reason I find her practices odd.

It took forever to find something dark enough to wear, but after some thorough digging, I managed to find a navy sweater in the back of Mother's closet. She wouldn't mind my borrowing it. It's not like she is going to be wearing it anytime soon.

Getting into the house across the street is easy enough. I haven't noticed a security company poking around, installing cameras, just yet. It's something I learned to watch for early on. Usually it takes several days, weeks sometimes, for new residents to install a system, giving me ample time to have my fun without much inconvenience.

I run my hands along the top of the lattice. My stomach does a happy little flip when I find Mrs. Lowe's spare key in its usual place. I turn the key in the door with a satisfying click.

Once inside, the dog I've come to know as Ollie runs over to me, his tail wagging in anticipation. For the last few weeks, I have been sneaking treats to him on my daily "jog" while he plays in the fenced-in yard. This is Rule #3: Always make friends with the family pet first.

I remove the dog biscuit from my pocket and hold it out to him. He slurps it up gratefully and remains quiet. I reward him with a quick belly rub and go about my business.

Inside, it's too dark to make out my hand in front of my face—another inconvenience I don't have to worry with during the day. Luckily, the streetlight out front offers just enough illumination into the main room and the kitchen.

The house is still bare for the most part. Cluttered, but void of any intentional arrangement. Everything is just sort of...everywhere.

There is a coffee pot and a blender, a dirty pan and a sink full of dishes with hardened food stuck to them, clothes piled on the counter tops, long ready to be folded, next to takeout boxes from various restaurants. She isn't much of a housekeeper.

Piles of unopened mail lay scattered in disarray, covering the kitchen island. I lift one of the envelopes and hold it up to the light. Stevie Cole and Simon Lowe. Different last names. I wonder if they aren't married after all or if Stevie is one of those feminists who refuse to take their husband's name because they believe it removes something from their identity. The latter is possible. She seems...alternative...in that way.

A small TV is perched on a table in the corner, older than any television I have ever seen before. On the other side of the massive living room is a mountain of unopened boxes almost my height. I can't help myself.

One has already had the tape cut, so I lift open the lid and have a look inside. It's a hoarder's dream. They're filled with papers, art magazines, and odd little trinkets which don't seem to go with any particular aesthetic.

In one of the boxes are dozens of VHS tapes. It explains the ancient TV, at least. Who watches VHS anymore?

In one of the smaller boxes are three framed photographs individually wrapped. Only three. It strikes me as odd. If there is one thing the middle class wants to boast about, it is how beautiful their families are, whether it's true or not. They use their walls as a shrine of sorts.

There is also something else I find a bit strange about them. These photos aren't the polished snapshots of a professional photoshoot, which line the halls, desks, and entryways of the other houses around here. Everyone always seems stiff and perfect in those, with smiles that never reach their eyes. These are candid shots, unfiltered and blurry. Not like mine, from a lack of experience and knowledge. These flaws—if that's what you want to call them—appear intentional.

One is of their little boy, Bodhi. I conclude that's his name after spotting the words "Bodhi's Shit" scribbled on one of the opened boxes filled with games and toys. In the photo, he is running along a grayscale beach with a much smaller Ollie, straight into a colony of seagulls. The birds are frozen, taking to the sky in a whirlwind of wings and claws.

The middle photograph is of a baby Bodhi, no more than two years old at most. I can tell it is him by the mop of brown hair. He and a younger, less inked Simon are cross-legged on the floor, stacking blocks. Bodhi isn't looking at the toys, though. His chunky arms are raised to the sky, and he is laughing with his entire body at something the photographer is doing off-camera. Simon is smiling at them as well, adoration in his eyes. It had to be Stevie.

The last one, and most interesting, is a black and white snapshot of a couple standing in the blur of a party. Every person in the photo is indistinguishable in the haze, aside from the couple in the center. Simon and Stevie in another life. One which suits them much more than the one they are living in now.

Where the rest of the shot is shaky and unfocused, they are the exact opposite. I can make out every detail. Every strand of hair. Every thread and spike and rip of their clothing. A joint rests on Simon's lips, and Stevie holds a lighter in her free hand, frozen in the act of sparking the flame.

Something about it keeps me from looking away. She isn't facing the camera, but up at him, her long hair several shades lighter here, almost white, hanging over one shoulder. Stevie is laughing as if he has said something ridiculously funny. Simon looks back at her, equally enthralled and so close that, if his lips had not been otherwise occupied, I am sure he would have kissed her.

It isn't anything really. A casual moment of intimacy between two lovers in a crowd. Yet something about the atmosphere makes me feel like I am witnessing something I shouldn't be. They seem tragic in the most romantic way. As if their very essence is trapped there in that ocean of faceless people. They shouldn't be walking around in the real world, doing mundane things like buying houses in the suburbs and shopping at Trader Joe's. The two should be here in this moment, unusual and timeless.

Like a photo taken before a tragedy only you know is coming. Like those black and white photos of Sid and Nancy before she was found dead in that hotel room. It is an uneasiness I find difficult to explain, but I feel it in every nerve of my body.

Ollie nudges me with his head, begging for another treat, and I nearly jump out of my skin. I drop the photo frame with a sharp crack.

"Shoot!" I reach into the box.

There is the tiniest crack along the side of the frame. Surely, it's small enough that it can be explained away as a moving casualty. I seal the box back and turn to Ollie.

"Bad dog," I whisper.

He tilts his head to one side and looks at me, perplexed.

"Go on!" I command, shooing him away.

He walks to a dog bed in the corner of the kitchen and lays his head down.

Rule #6: Don't break anything! If there is a quicker way to alert someone to your presence, I don't know of one.

I have to be more careful, I think, making my way up the stairs.

CHAPTER

FOUR

The water from the rainfall showerhead feels like God licking my entire body. I don't want to get out, but I have been here entirely too long already. A sudden wash of cool air nips at my skin when I turn the water off, so I pull the towel from the hook and wrap it around myself. It's black—no surprise—fluffy, and glorious on my skin. I have to remember to get some just like this.

At the marble double sinks, I wipe away the condensation from the mirror.

Such a pretty thing. It's such a shame about her, says a singsong voice in my head while I take in my reflection.

I quickly look away toward the chaos on the counter. Like the kitchen, it's an absolute mess on one side—the telltale sign of someone trying to get ready in a hurry. Makeup palettes, brushes, tweezers, lotions, and perfumes litter the surface. The other side is tidy for the most part, aside from a few stray beard clippings in the sink.

I open one of the lotion bottles on Stevie's side and lift it to my nose. It smells expensive. I squeeze a generous amount onto my fingertips and rub the cream into my neck and shoulders. It feels delicious going on and turns my skin to velvet. When I have covered my body in a layer, I pat my hair with the towel and make my way into the primary bedroom, leaving it on the hook.

I have to admit, when I first came into this room, it was like walking into another house entirely.

It is massive, to start, almost a quarter of the entire floor plan. At some point, they must have had the wall between two of the bedrooms removed to create one huge primary. A four-post bed wide enough for four people backs up to an exposed brick wall. Also new. The brick is painted matte black, and as boring as I find that color to be, there is something elegant about the way they have it.

The bed has a woven lace canopy draped over it, adorned with a string of soft decorative lights. In the half-dark, they almost appear like little stars in the evening. The only signs of color are a few maroon pillows lining the headboard—drops of blood in a void.

I crawl inside the sheer curtains and sink into the soft feather blankets, allowing every inch of my skin to be enveloped in them. When I turn onto my stomach, I bury my face into one of the lush pillows and inhale the scent of the couple in the threads. God, I could die and be buried in this bed.

After a moment, I flip onto my back and lift myself onto my elbows to survey the room.

Unlike the rest of the house, it is sparse but seems to be completed, except for a few paintings leaning against one of the far walls. They are massive, but she certainly has the wall space for them. Their size isn't what drew my attention to them, though. It's all the color.

To contrast the neutral palette which seems to be the preference for the rest of the house, the paintings are vibrant splatters that remind me of a mix of Van Gogh and Pollocks. I kneel in front of one of them.

Up close, I can make out the form of a woman in the chaos of reds, oranges, and blues. She is nude, her head thrown back, her hair dancing around her body, her arms gripping her throat. The strokes of the brush make it look like she is dancing, caught in a moment of pure euphoria. She appears feral and beautiful and serene all at once. They should hang her above the bed.

I tip-toe over to the his-and-her closets, being careful not to drip on the hardwood floors and leave any prints. His is an immaculate grayscale with pops of white, organized from darkest to lightest. Between this and the "his" side of the sink, I conclude Simon to be the neat one.

It makes sense now. If I lived with someone as chaotic as their downstairs would indicate Stevie is, I would need to have a few clutter-free spaces to escape myself.

I close his closet and walk over to the second one. Definitely Stevie's. It's like a box of clothing exploded inside. I manage to remove one of the black cocktail dresses and drape it over my body, then step in front of the full-length mirror. The dress wraps around me so perfectly I don't think I could have picked a better fit if I had bought it myself. Maybe black isn't so bad after all.

That's when I hear it.

The unmistakable thud of shoes on pavement.

CHAPTER

FIVE

I peek out the window overlooking the driveway, and my heart sinks into my gut like a stone. Stevie is making her way up the driveway, heading straight for the porch. She's back early.

How long has it been? I pull my phone from my pocket and curse myself. It has been an hour and a half. I must have lost track of time.

She makes it to the stairs by the front entrance, and I duck. Their bedroom window would be perfectly visible from that spot, even at night. Hopefully, she didn't see me.

Ollie, who has been waiting curiously at the bedroom door this entire time, darts down the stairs at the sharp click of the lock turning. The hinges whine when the front door opens. There is no way I will be able to get down the stairs without being seen. Stupid open floor plans...

I am now annoyed with the lack of clutter in this room. If it were even half as messy as the main floor, I could easily slip behind one of the mountains of boxes without Stevie noticing. In here, there is literally nothing. I am completely exposed.

The closet is an obvious no. Everyone immediately goes for that. I could hide in the primary bath, but she would certainly find me if she went in. Aside from the mess on her side of the vanity, it is more open than the bedroom.

The front door closes with a muffled click. I don't have much more time to decide.

"Stay," I hear her say, minus the baby speak. "You know how Daddy gets about you being upstairs in the bedroom."

It's the first time I have heard her real voice up close. It isn't the high-pitched Southern drawl, like most of the women around here. Hers has a rasp in it, like a smoker's, yet it's still soft somehow. I like it. But I can't linger over something so trivial when I am in such a compromising position.

Seconds later, her footsteps echo against the wooden staircase, rhythmic thuds gaining momentum, like a heartbeat growing louder while she ascends. With no more time to find something less cliché, I crawl underneath the bed.

The ice-cold floor against my skin reminds me that I forgot to take off the skimpy dress, not that I would have been able to. And all my clothes are...still on the bed!

I reach up to grab them, but it's too late. Stevie enters the room so swiftly that I am sure she must have seen my hand outstretched. I snap it back underneath, relieved when she moves past the bed and begins tossing items around in one of the nightstands. Ollie obeyed and stayed downstairs, which I am grateful for. He wouldn't have been fooled for a moment and would have given me away immediately.

Items knock against each other inside the drawer in a cacophony of sound. It shocks my system after how quiet I have been trying to be for the last hour. What's the saying my mother used to use? A bull in a china shop? She called me that a lot when I was younger. It's why I made it a point to soften myself. My movements, my voice, my demeanor...Destruction was never what I wanted. Stealth is all one needs to get the upper hand.

I watch Stevie's feet dart around the room frantically, going from one nightstand to the other, then the desk, and finally to the small table in the corner. She displaces items in her wake. When Stevie disappears into the primary bathroom, I reach up and yank my clothing underneath the bed with me. My panties come loose from the bundle and fall to the floor, just beyond the bed frame.

My breath catches in my throat. I reach for them again, but just as I do, Stevie reenters the room, and I freeze.

If she glances toward the foot of the bed at this exact moment, there is no way she won't spot them. The bright yellow of the material sticks out like a sore thumb, even in the darkness. If she reaches down to pick them up, she'll see me. There is no way she won't.

I imagine what she will think, finding a strange woman under her bed, wearing her clothes. Her husband...boyfriend...whatever he is, isn't even here for an affair to explain it away. There is no good reason I can come up with that would force this to remotely make sense. I don't want to think of the fallout from that. Luckily, she crosses the room and instead goes straight for the closet.

I take the opportunity of her back being turned and snatch my panties in one swift motion. Even if she notices the missing dress, there is a chance I can still make it out without being seen if she leaves the room. Stevie rifles through some boxes at the top of the closet, and then I watch her grab the empty hanger the dress had been on. She considers it.

There's no way she knows...

How could someone who allows the downstairs to get in such a mess notice one dress missing that quickly? It's one empty hanger among dozens of others, for goodness' sake!

I hold my breath and wait for her to figure it out, bracing myself to run. She shakes her head and continues digging in the shelves and drawers of the closet. What could she possibly be looking for?

"Where the fuck is it?" she says, her tone sharp.

She is still digging in the bottom of the closet when something vibrates near my foot. The glow of a cell phone screen pierces the dark, and Simon's face gleams back at me. This must be what she is looking for. Of course, it would be right here...with me.

Thank God it fell where it did, tangled in the fabric of the canopy. Otherwise, the vibration on the hardwood floor would echo throughout the room, giving away its location...and mine.

The screen goes dark again. He hung up.

Stevie walks over to a small computer on the desk and powers it on. She types something in, and ringing comes from the monitor. I can't see her face, but I can just make out the computer screen. She is video calling someone. I stiffen.

Stevie's back is turned to me, but I would be perfectly visible to whoever she is calling if I so much as move an inch while they are watching.

Simon answers. Background noise from wherever he is drowns his voice so badly that I can barely understand what he says.

"Did you find it?" he yells over the crowd.

"No! I'm on the laptop. My watch says it's here at the house, but I've looked everywhere."

Well, not *everywhere.*

"I'm sorry, baby. I'm sure we'll find it."

"Yeah. It just sucks. I..." She trails off.

"What's wrong?"

"Did you take a shower before you left?"

"You think I'd dare show my face in public without getting pretty first?"

"The floor is soaked."

"I'm sorry, baby. I thought I cleaned it all up. I'll clean it when we get in."

"It's fine. I dried up what was left. Just be careful. I could have killed myself."

"We can't have that now, can we? The life insurance policy hasn't even gone through yet."

"Shut up!" Stevie laughs. "Also...have you been in my closet?"

My stomach twists, and I feel like I'm going to throw up. Of course, she noticed.

"Why would I be in your closet?"

"I don't know...I just...I think someone's been in my closet. One of my dresses is missing." There is a tinge of doubt, even as the words tumble from her lips.

Doubt is good.

"I don't see how you find anything in there."

"It's an organized chaos, okay? Don't start."

"You started with me. Which one's missing?" Simon asks.

"The little black one. You know, the one with the slit in the side. I was going to wear it tonight."

"Oh yeah...I remember that one." His tone is flirtatious.

"Stop! I'm being serious!" She laughs.

"I really hope we find that one because..." His voice trails off, and he makes some kind of gesture.

"You are such a child," Stevie says.

"Babe, I'm sure it's still packed up somewhere. We'll find it. And

your phone too."

"I just could have sworn I hung it up."

"It's been pure chaos. Maybe you just thought you did."

"Yeah, maybe." But she doesn't sound convinced. "I'm about to head out. We still meeting at Donavan's after the show?"

"Yep. Sam and Kristin are coming. Wear the red dress instead. You know, the one with the uh...swoop at the top."

"The off-shoulder one? Why?"

"Easy access."

"Perv. I love you."

"I love you too, babe. Hurry up," Simon says.

"Love you too." She closes the laptop and exhales.

I expect her to head back down the stairs, but she doesn't. She stands at the laptop, unmoving. It's almost eerie how still she is.

My heartbeat pounds in my ears. I try to slow it by taking small, quiet breaths. That's when I realize she isn't *just* standing there. Stevie's gaze is fixated on something across the room. The expression in her eyes...it's unsettling.

For a moment, I wonder if I have left something out and blown my cover. But she walks over to the painting of the wild-haired woman. Stevie stares at it for a moment longer before she does something odd. She takes the painting and turns it around so the image faces the wall.

Without another word, Stevie returns to the closet, rifles through it, and pulls out a red mid-length dress with an open top. She kicks off her running shoes and removes her clothing right then and there, leaving only her underwear. The items fall to her feet in a crumpled pile.

She has even more tattoos than I thought. They run almost the entire length of one side of her body, sparing her stomach and breast.

I've never seen another person this naked before now. Most of my encounters have been fully clothed, hurried. I was never very attracted to any of them anyway. But Stevie...she's like looking at a work of art. There's so much to take in.

I don't have time to linger on it because, as if my prayers are being answered by the divine themselves, she slips on a pair of black boots which had been sitting by the closet door and disappears back down the stairs, her steps more heavy than hurried.

What was that all about?

I don't move. I couldn't if I tried. Not until the hum of the engine outside breaks the silence and the crackle and pop of wheels on the concrete fade into the distance.

When I'm sure she is gone, I roll out from under the bed and throw my jacket over Stevie's dress. Rule #7: Don't take anything—one of the most important. I'm breaking it, but I can't risk staying in this house for a moment longer, even to change.

With her lack of organizational skills, maybe Stevie will chalk it up to another casualty of moving. Things go missing all the time while relocating, or so I've heard.

I consider scooping up the phone as well. My curiosity at what could be on it is almost too much to resist. But no. The phone would be going *too* far. With technology these days, there's no telling what kind of location services she has. It is a chance I can't take.

I make my way for the door, and with each step, I feel a little lighter. Or lightheaded—I'm not sure which. I will just be so happy to be out of here.

When I reached the bottom of the stairs, something catches my eye. A twinkle of light coming from the shadowed space between the kitchen, stairwell, and the living area.

I move closer, straining my eyes in the dark. My curiosity momentarily trumps my urgency to get out before Stevie returns, having forgotten something else. When I reach it, I realize it is a door. A locked door. And not just any locked door.

A stray beam of light filters through the makeshift curtain at just the right angle, revealing not one, but three locks secured to the frame.

From previous escapades in this house, I know this particular door leads to the basement. Mrs. Lowe used it mostly for storage. Toward the end of her life, she was certainly in no condition to be climbing up and down the basement stairs, but that is no reason to lock it up with not one, but three padlocks. This is new—the work of someone who has something very important to keep secure.

The sensation of eyes on my back causes me to turn.

Ollie sits at the base of the stairs, watching me, tail wagging. I leave the basement fortress and give his head a soft scratch, then head to the door I entered through. Before I disappear into the darkness of the side yard, I glance back at him, a seed of an idea fleshing out in my head.

His head is cocked to one side, tongue hanging out of his mouth in anticipation, as if waiting for me to make a decision.

I smile and pull another dog treat from my jacket pocket.

CHAPTER

SIX

llie!" she calls again. There's a quiver in her tone which comes as no surprise to me.

The fight started almost immediately when they arrived home. I know because I was waiting eagerly at my bedroom window to watch the events unfold. But I hadn't anticipated an actual fight. Maybe a considerable amount of fear and worried discussion, but not an all-out brawl.

And a brawl is exactly what I was witnessed at the house across the street. It wasn't physical or anything like that, thank goodness, but only just. The shouting was muffled by the distance, so I couldn't make out much of what was being said, but I didn't need to hear the words to know they were venomous.

I felt a twinge of guilt while I listened to the scene unfold. But it was too late to do anything about it. The damage was done, and I had no choice but to witness the fallout.

Thankfully, most of the fight took place in their bedroom. Since curtains remain a low priority for them, I was able to watch some of it play out. Simon's hands flew to the air in fury, and for a moment,

I was afraid he might hit her. He didn't. Instead, he turned his back on her, running a hand through his hair.

Stevie withered beneath the weight of something he said. Whatever battle she was waging, she had lost. He left her standing in the bedroom, alone. Moments later, he exited the house, climbed into the ugly black van—with spray paint on the side—I've grown to associate with his presence, and tore out of the driveway, sending dust and rocks flying in its wake.

Stevie remained there for a moment, one of her hands on the back of her neck, the other resting on the bed frame. Then, as if back from a trance, she disappeared from sight. Moments later, the porch light switched on and the door opened.

I glance at myself in the mirror one last time, making sure I appear just the right amount of bothered, before venturing out and waiting until she gets slightly past the house next door, so as not to be too obvious.

"Ollie! Come here, boy."

"Is there something I can help you with?" I flick my porch light on and step out so she can see me.

"Oh, shit! I'm a fucking idiot." She comes closer. "I'm so sorry. I didn't even realize how late it was. I didn't wake you, did I?"

"I was just doing some reading, and I heard you yelling. Are you okay?" I am impressed with how smooth the lie rolls off my tongue. Especially since my knees are shaking.

"God, I'm sorry. I just...I left in a rush earlier, and I must have left the door open, and my son's dog got out. You haven't seen a Golden Retriever wandering around tonight, have you? "

"No, I haven't. I'm sorry. There are a few dogs that run loose around this area. Harmless. I'm sure he took up with one of them."

"You're probably right. It's just...my son will be back tomorrow, and he'll freak out if I don't find him." The quiver in her voice returns, as if she is on the verge of breaking down.

When she steps closer to the light, her eyes are swollen and bloodshot. As I suspected, she has already been crying tonight. I don't respond right away, so she continues.

"I'm going to look for a while, but I'll try to keep it down." Stevie turns to continue up the street, and my stomach twists.

No. Don't go yet.

"Well, hold on a moment, and I'll help you look." I reach inside to shut the door behind me.

"Oh, no...I can't ask you to do that!" she protests.

I ignore her and lock my door.

"It's no problem at all." I wave her off casually. "We'll cover more ground this way."

She looks at me for a moment, as if she is really seeing me for the first time since we started talking. "I'm Stevie."

No last name. Interesting. I also detect the slightest flash of discomfort.

"I'm Karla Cooper. I should have introduced myself a while ago, but I wanted you to get settled before bothering you. I know how chaotic moving can be."

"Chaotic is an understatement," she says.

I offer a small laugh in response, even though I don't know the first thing about it. The last time I moved, I wasn't allowed to take anything except the clothes on my back. And they didn't let me keep those once I arrived at the hospital.

"I'll take the next road over and circle around. We can meet back here. I'm sure we'll find him," I offer in the same cheery pitch I've heard the other women in the neighborhood use when speaking. The tone of Southern pleasantries.

"You are a lifesaver. Seriously!" With a quick wave, she jogs back up the street.

I turn to walk around the corner until I'm sure I am out of sight and call the dog's name a few times, just in case Stevie is still within earshot. When I am confident she is far enough that she won't notice, I sneak back into my house through the side door and let out a breath. My stomach twists until it's tangled into a tight knot.

I have been practicing that exchange right up until the moment I stepped outside. In spite of my nervousness, I am quite pleased with myself. I glance in the mirror long enough to smooth my hair and straighten my cardigan.

My basement can only be accessed by a small red door located in the kitchen—the stomach of the house. I don't prefer it down there. It reminds me of a grave. It's deep and dark, and the air is thick, making it difficult to breathe. I avoid it when I can.

When I turn the handle, claws scrape against the splintered wood. The creature ascends the steps.

Ollie hits the door like a brick, and I almost fall back from the force of it. He darts past me, but I grab his collar just in time to yank him back. Ollie whimpers and snarls, trying desperately to break loose of my grip. I pull the collar tight until I am sure he is having trouble breathing.

He continues struggling for only a moment more before going still. When he does, I loosen my hold.

"See! That's all you have to do," I snap.

I listen for movement upstairs. The last thing I need right now is Mother waking up and ringing that blasted bell.

"Are you going to stay calm?" I say, then feel silly for anticipating a reply.

I pull Ollie through the house to the side door without any more fuss, but I can still sense his hesitation. Being locked down there for so long probably hasn't made me his favorite person, but then again, I've always been more of a cat person anyway. At least they're quiet. I can't have Ollie barking and alerting the entire neighborhood to his whereabouts.

The night remains still. Once I'm confident I won't be seen, I open the door, clutching Ollie's collar a little tighter as a warning so he won't get any ideas. I drag him across the street until we are directly in front of Stevie and Spencer's front gate.

Ollie whines, recognizing his house, and tries one more time to break away from me. I twist his collar again. He growls and snaps at my hand before I can get a good grip. I cry out, releasing his collar, and he runs toward a figure coming around the corner.

"Ollie!" Stevie yells. She kneels, and the dog runs into her outstretched arms. Stevie fusses over him while I examine my hand.

I am bleeding. Not bad enough to need stitches, but just enough to make me feel dizzy. I hate the sight of my own blood. It's familiar. Wounds hold memories in that way. I am lost in the echo of one when Stevie speaks

"I saw everything!" she snaps.

My heart sinks into my stomach. I look up at her, but she has already closed the distance between us.

"He's never done that before. I'm so sorry!"

The bite. She saw him bite me. That's all.

"It's okay...really. I'll be fine," I reassure her. Relief washes over me.

"Like hell you are. We need to get that cleaned up. Come inside."

She doesn't wait for an answer. Stevie takes my non-bleeding hand in hers and Ollie's collar in the other. He follows happily beside her, and a twinge of heat rises along my neck.

I hate that fucking dog.

What We Do in Secret

CHAPTER

SEVEN

Being in Stevie's house by invitation seems starkly different from my secret conquest.

The house is identical to how I left it earlier: All the loose papers blanket the counter, dirty dishes rest in the sink, and the mountain of boxes stand like a monolith in the far corner of the living space. It is the same, but while I sit on the side of Stevie's garden tub and she cleans and bandages my hand, an uneasiness hovers over us. A puzzle piece doesn't quite fit.

On occasion, Stevie smiles up at me. It's strange being this close to her. She looks like she's had a long night. In this light, her eye makeup is smeared, and her hair is coming loose from the ponytail. Her bangs are sticking to her forehead in stringy clumps. Still, somehow, she is probably the most beautiful person I have seen up close. Even more beautiful than my mom used to be in her prime.

My mother put a lot of effort into her appearance, as do I. But Stevie isn't trying at all. She just…is. And the way she smells—the scent of her perfume, mixed with sweat and alcohol—is surprisingly sweet in such a small space. I lean in closer and breathe her in.

"I can't believe he did this. I'm so sorry," she repeats for the hundredth time, working on my hand.

"I'm sure he was just scared. I'm a stranger to him. I'm just glad we found him."

"Where was he anyway?"

"Not far. A block or so over," I answer quickly.

"Well, you really saved my ass. Seriously. I owe you one." With that, she secures a gauze bandage and stands in front of me. "I'm gonna get us some drinks."

"Oh, no! I couldn't impose," I say. It's almost 3:00 in the morning, after all.

"If I'm going to have you running around in the middle of the night, the least I can do is get you a drink. Plus, it'll take the edge off the pain."

"I suppose my hand is a little sore." I rise to my feet as well and follow her into the kitchen.

Stevie is already clearing off the counter and replacing the paper and pizza boxes with two glasses and a bottle of aspirin.

"What's your poison? Whiskey or...whiskey?" She laughs, pulling a bottle from the freezer. "I don't have everything unpacked yet, so we'll have to improvise."

"Whiskey is perfect." I place the aspirin in my mouth.

"That it is, my friend." She offers up a toast.

With a clink of the glass, I pour the burning liquid down my throat. I've never had whiskey before, and from the taste of this, I wasn't missing much.

"Burns good, huh?" She giggles, pouring herself another shot and swallowing it before I can get the words out of my mouth.

My eyes are watery.

Stevie adds maple syrup and lemons to the table with hand movements that are on par with a magician's sleight of hand. She pours and mixes the ingredients together with such showmanship that I'm sure she is going to pull a rabbit out of one of the glasses. When she's done, she slides one of them to me.

I take a cautious sip, slower this time. The bite of the whiskey lingers, but the syrup smooths it out enough that it almost tastes good.

"Better?"

"Much," I say, finishing off the drink. "How do you know how to do all of that?" I gesture vaguely toward the ingredients on the counter.

"I bartend at O'Keefe's on the weekends."

So, she's a bartender. Not a stripper. I nod.

"The house is lovely. Your decor is unique." I glance at the tapestry over the window.

"You are very kind, but you don't have to lie." She cocks an eyebrow. My stomach seizes, and she laughs. "I know we've been here for over a month and everything should be unpacked already. It's just a lot. And with Bodhi and working...We have a window company coming on Tuesday to size the windows for blinds since your HOA is such a pain in the ass. They told us we need to call a blind guy. I've never even heard of such a ridiculous thing."

"Yeah, they are pretty ridiculous about everything. If there's anything I can do to help with the unpacking, I'm just right across the street."

"You've done enough. I can't ask you to unpack my shit too."

"It's fine, really. I've got more time on my hands than I know what to do with."

"Well, I appreciate the offer. I may take you up on that one of these days."

"So, what does your husband do?" I think back to the tattooed man I have been watching over the last few weeks. Surely, there aren't many jobs available to someone who looks like him.

"Simon? We aren't married." She practically scoffs. "He's a musician. He does tattoos on the side sometimes for extra money... when the band stuff is slow."

"You two aren't married?"

"No. God, no. We prefer to live in sin." Stevie winks. "What about you? Surely, you don't live in that big house all by yourself?" She leans on the counter, studying me, and I squirm in my seat. "You got a man?"

"Nope. Never married." I smile politely.

"Really?" She seems genuinely shocked. "I didn't take this neighborhood as a singles-friendly kind of place."

"Oh, it definitely isn't. Almost everyone is married here, except the occasional widow...and us." I laugh. "My father left when I was eight, and I lived with my mother until..." I pause to consider the amount of information I want to offer. "She...had an accident a while ago and had to be put in a facility, so now it's just me."

"I'm sorry to hear that." Stevie covers my hand, resting on the counter, with hers. It is warm and smooth.

I try not to stiffen beneath it.

"It's okay. I'm managing. She's better off where she is now." I take a sip of my drink to keep from meeting her eyes. "I have to be honest with you…It's just nice to talk to someone that's not a lawyer or a nurse."

"I can imagine. Simon's grandmother passed away recently. That's partly why we're here. She left him the house."

"Mrs. Lowe?"

"Yeah. Did you know her well? If you grew up across the street, you had to have met at some point. She lived here for, like, a hundred years."

"Not well, no. But she and my mother were friendly. I'm sorry to hear she's passed. She was always very kind to me," I lie.

Mrs. Lowe was an old bitch who constantly threw fits about me being too near her flowers.

"Simon has been really messed up about it. But we'll get through it." She slides another shot toward me. "To healing." Stevie raises her glass, gesturing for me to do the same.

"And new friends," I add.

With a smile, we each toss our glasses back.

A set of keys dangles from the hanger just over Stevie's shoulder. I dare a single glance at the door beneath the stairs. All three locks are firmly in place.

What We Do in Secret

CHAPTER

EIGHT

"Wait, so you're, like, a real-life photographer!" I slur, looking through the book of photos in my lap.

In just under an hour, Stevie and I have made our way to the bottom of the bottle of whiskey, and she has managed to dig up a second we didn't even bother mixing. You get used to the burn after a while. We are sitting on her area rug with a cardboard box between us as a makeshift table, laughing hysterically at everything. I can't remember the last time I felt so feather light and girlish. This must have been what the sleepovers I was never invited to were like.

The photo album she calls a "portfolio" is filled with the same type of shaky, grainy snapshots I saw in the frames. At first, I thought they looked like the work of an amateur, but the closer I examine the contents, the more they reflect a distinct style. They are all black and white candids of everyday things: her family, of course; people at diners; and random strangers she finds interesting.

In one, a girl of about fourteen stands against a wall of graffiti, a skateboard in one hand and a pack of American Spirit in the other.

Her eyes are blackened with eyeliner, and she's looking at something off in the distance, her face pinched in concentration.

In another are two older businessmen sitting at a bar, their ties loosened, thick cigars resting between their lips, with two glasses of scotch in front of them.

My favorite of them all is of an elderly woman who appears to be homeless. She is sitting on an outside bench, wearing a patchwork dress, her skin the texture of old leather. The woman is running her wrinkled hand across the back of a stray black cat that has jumped up onto the bench beside her. Her smile is warm and lights up her face. It shifts something in my chest.

I catch myself grinning back at her, wondering where she is now, where she got her next meal from. If she found many reasons to smile like that. They are the people you see every day and never notice. But Stevie did.

And not only that, but she managed to capture them in a way that makes you wonder how you missed such beauty in the first place.

I think of my own candid snapshot of Stevie and Simon from that first day. His head resting on her and Stevie embracing him in a second of intimacy. My photo is nothing compared to hers, but I imagine the impulse to capture the moment is the same.

"I just like to take pictures." She shrugs the compliment off.

"Yeah. *Just* pictures," I say sarcastically.

"Okay, pictures some people were willing to pay a lot of money for once upon a time. You happy?"

"Were?"

"Yeah. I don't do that anymore."

"But why? You're so talented!" I insist, placing the portfolio to the side and finishing my glass.

"I needed this." Stevie ignores my question. She leans back and closes her eyes.

"What's that?"

"I don't know. To just relax. I've been...I'm just not good at all this." She gestures vaguely around the room.

"At what?"

"I don't know. This house. This neighborhood. The fences. Your damn cardigan."

"Wait! My cardigan?" I feign offense. "What's wrong with my cardigan?"

"Nothing! You just have this whole domestic goddess thing going. Like a '50s pinup."

"Domestic goddess?" I scoff. "Is that even a thing?"

"You know what I mean. You just seem to have it all figured out."

"I'm drunk at 6:00 a.m. on your living room floor. None of us have it figured out! I have to wonder, though, why someone like you wanted to move to a place like this in the first place."

"Someone like me?" Now she is the one feigning offense.

"You know what I mean. You're...cool." The slur in my speech is painfully obvious. It's so unladylike. I'm glad Stevie is the only one around to witness my misconduct. She has no room to judge.

"I am not!"

"Not like country club cool either. Like, really cool."

"What does that even mean?" She laughs.

"Ask me in the morning when I'm sober. I can't elaborate right now."

"It is morning!"

"Cool." I repeat the word, and we both crack up. The room is spinning again, so I join Stevie and lie down on the rug.

"It's better for Bodhi, you know, since his mom lives nearby." Her tone is suddenly serious.

"His mom?"

"Yeah...Bodhi is actually Simon and his ex's."

"Ah." I think back to that photo of Simon and baby Bodhi looking up adoringly at the photographer. While I assumed it had been Stevie, it could have been Bodhi's biological mother. "So, she lives nearby, then? His biological mom?"

"Oh yeah. Six fucking blocks from here, on Chestnut."

"Fancy," I say, remembering the humongous houses in the next neighborhood over. They are certainly larger in that area and more expensive than this side of New Haven. It's nice over here, but those are homes of doctors or lawyers with their own practices, not widows and upper management.

"Yep," she snips.

I open my eyes, and she is sitting up, pouring herself another drink.

"I take it there's some hostility?" I ask.

"I mean, full disclosure?"

"Of course."

"I don't know how living this close to her is going to go. It's good for Bodhi. It really is, and I'm so happy he can just get on and off the bus at her house if he wants. But that woman is a fucking nightmare."

The way Stevie grits her teeth when she talks about the woman intrigues me.

"Oh really? How so?"

"She's perfect. Like literally suburban royalty. At least, that's what she wants everyone to think. Underneath, she's vile as fuck. Hold on." Stevie rises to her feet and stumbles to one of the half-opened boxes. She digs out a laptop and crawls back over to me, then sets it up on our box table. "I lost my stupid phone earlier, but look."

When she turns the laptop toward me, she has a website pulled up. It features an article with a perky blond woman donning a Miss America smile. Bodhi is beside her, his mop of messy hair combed back and sleek, so unlike the messy kid I witnessed running around the yard that first day. Miss America's hand is tenderly perched on his shoulder.

The headline reads: "Melissa Van Lowe : Millionaire 'Mommy Blogger' Talks Healing and Happiness Post Divorce."

The article is dated two months ago. I already read every word earlier, after returning from my little snooping session.

Truth be told, I know most of what Stevie has confessed from my shallow dive into her social media. Fortunately for me, most of her dirty laundry is a simple Google search away. It took some digging to get beyond the headlines of Melissa's blog, but in her own right, Stevie is a bigger deal than she is making herself out to be. A household name in certain circles. The few photos featured on her photography website are of her shining like a stained glass window with big brand advertisers and gallery owners.

In one photo, she stands proudly in front of a massive black and white image the size of a mural. I don't even need to read the caption to know it is one of hers. Stevie has a distinct style that is recognizable if you are familiar with it.

The girl featured in the image can't be more than fourteen or fifteen. Her clothes are dirty, and her face is sunken from malnutrition. She sits along the brick siding of what appears to be an abortion clinic. Picketers surround the entrance, frozen mid-scream, with homemade signs held high above their heads that read various versions of the same thing.

Save the Children! Pro-Life! Abortion Kills!

Saving innocents is a worthy pursuit by any standard, and their intention is almost honorable, if it weren't for their convenient unawareness of the child right behind them, in desperate need of saving.

It is a powerful image that, from the looks of it, Stevie received a lot of recognition for. She is talented. Vibrant. Engaging with her audience online. Stevie built a name for herself and cared about the community she created. Then it just stopped six months ago. That's when Melissa's blog posts began.

No matter how much weight her name held, apparently, this Melissa person's was heavier. A salacious story of infidelity will always trump a human rights piece. No matter how talented a woman is, once people know who she's sleeping with, that's all they care about. People want to be entertained, not informed.

The comments were lethal. I don't blame her for backing away after reading a few of them. In fact, I would have disappeared from social media as well.

"She added the 'Van' after they got married." The way Stevie says the word practically drips with resentment.

"Oh wow. This is Bodhi's mom? She looks…" I start but stop myself.

"Perfect. Right? I know. It's so infuriating."

Perfect is not the right word for Melissa "Van" Lowe. Celebrities pay a lot of money to look like her. To be fair, I'm sure she did too.

"What exactly is a 'Mommy Blogger'?"

"Apparently, it's someone who takes their children and uses them as clickbait so they can ruin people's lives by blasting their private business all over the fucking internet." Stevie shuts the laptop with a little more force than necessary. Her smile is gone, and for a moment, I think she may cry again. Or scream.

"That sounds violating."

"It is. Extremely. But what are you going to do, you know?"

"I take it she wrote about you?" I already know the answer. At least, I know the version in the exposé Melissa wrote, but it doesn't feel like mine yet. I need her to tell me, to offer up the information freely.

"Simon and I didn't exactly have the most honest start."

"What do you mean?"

"I mean, they were still married when we…met."

"Oh!" I say in my best faux surprise voice.

"It's not a chapter in my life I'm very proud of. Anyway, she found out and announced that they were filing for divorce. And naturally, everyone in the goddamn world wanted to know why the domestic power couple decided to call it quits. Enter Stevie," she says with a half bow from her sitting position on the floor. "I didn't even know he was married the first time we had sex. I'm not exactly the target audience for their brand, so I didn't know who the hell she was."

"But the second time, you did..."

"And the third. And the fourth." She sighs, placing her head in her hands as if warring with the admission.

I don't know how to respond.

"What can I say?" Stevie laughs. "I fell in love with him. Fast. We're the same in so many ways. Maybe the worst ways, now that I think of it. But isn't that what everyone wants? Someone who sees the ugly in you and loves you anyway?" It doesn't sound like she's asking me as much as telling herself.

"It all sounds very chaotic," I reply, trying to cut through the tension.

"Oh, it was. *Still* is. And life started catching up to us. The divorce went through quickly. She basically got everything. The one thing she did give him was shared custody of Bodhi, but it's all a show. She just wants to write about how she's such a good co-parent on her blog."

"I see. That's a lot to unpack."

"Hell yeah, it is. But get this...Bodhi is a package deal with the fucking dog. She gave him the damn thing when he was a baby, and they have almost never been apart. And our first month with them alone and I've already fucked that up. I can't believe I left the damn gate open." She puts her head in her hands again.

"You messed up. It happens." I place my hand on her back.

"I think you and Simon will disagree. He got so mad at me earlier. I'm surprised you didn't hear us screaming at each other."

I keep quiet.

"I feel like she's always waiting for reasons to punish Simon with Bodhi. That dog would have been just another thing for her to hold over us."

"It's going to be all right. I promise." I keep my tone even, though my words come out in a drag. "You aren't the worst decision you've ever made."

"I feel like I am sometimes." Her voice sounds small.

I almost feel bad for her. But then again, she *did* sleep with another woman's husband. I offer a smile I hope appears genuine.

"My God, what time is it?" She wipes her wet eyes, and I glance at my phone.

"It's almost 7:00 a.m."

"I shouldn't be keeping you up with my sob story."

"You needed to tell someone. I'm glad you trust me with all of that." I pull myself to my feet. It's clumsy, but I manage, and she does the same. "But I should be heading back while I can still walk on my own."

I wobble a bit but am able to catch myself. This is more than I've had to drink in...well, ever. Stevie laughs and agrees, mumbling something about making it up the stairs.

We say our goodbyes, and before I step out the door, she pulls me in for a hug. It takes me aback for a moment. I haven't been touched like this by another person in I don't even know how long. It feels...dizzying. Or maybe that's the alcohol.

I breathe in the scent of her mixed with the whiskey and assign it to memory, with the warmth of her skin on mine. When she lets me go, I turn to walk down the path on shaky feet. The porch light goes out, and I am enveloped in darkness, besides the orange glow of the streetlight.

Something catches my eye.

Their garbage bin is on the sidewalk. Trash pick-up is tomorrow, so that's not abnormal, but something catches the light in a strange way. It almost looks like...

I am seconds away from stepping through the gate to get a better look when a deep voice calls from somewhere in the dark.

CHAPTER

NINE

"Hello, neighbor," the voice calls again.

I turn, straining my eyes against the dark. That's when I spot an orange flare beneath the magnolia tree, which covers one side of the house. My observation skills are a little delayed from my inebriation, but I finally notice the ugly black van parked on the curb. Simon must have returned at some point during our drinking session and chosen to keep his distance.

"Simon?" I whisper, making my way to the small glow—the cherry of a cigarette, I realize.

"Shouldn't you be in bed?" He takes another hit. The light momentarily illuminates his face.

"I could say the same for you."

"Stevie doesn't like me to smoke in the house. Or at all really. Don't tell on me, okay?" He grins, and I can just make out the shape of it in the shadow. It's nice.

Whether it's whiskey courage or a moment of sheer insanity, I find myself grinning back. Slowly, I close the distance between us until we are both hidden beneath the shelter of the magnolia.

I reach up, take the cigarette from his fingers, and place it in my mouth, inhaling deeply. It's disgusting, but I don't let him know that.

This, I've done before. In lockup, little indulgences like this are currency. I exhale the smoke above us and watch it dance in the air until it disappears in a haze.

"I can keep a secret." I hand the cigarette back to him.

He is shocked. I don't need to know his type to understand that men need to be jolted on occasion. It builds character.

I don't wait for a response and, instead, make my way across the street.

Stepping back into my house feels like coming up for air. This entire day has been like a fever dream, one I will wake up from in the morning having no memory of. But I can't allow this. I can't let myself forget anything.

Every detail feels important somehow, like an incomplete mosaic. In pieces, it doesn't make sense. But once I find all the parts, I'll be able to see it more clearly. There is something about them, something so subtle I can barely make it out in the alcohol-induced haze of my mind right now, but I'm sure there is something I'm missing. Maybe *several* things. I'm as sure of it as I am aware of the beating of my heart in my ears.

And now I'm certain of one other thing.

The family across the street is hiding something.

Why else would the painting of the euphoric woman, the intricate piece I found in their bedroom just yesterday, be crumpled in their trash can? It doesn't make sense. Not yet. But I'm going to figure it out.

A sharp, metallic ring echoes from upstairs, yanking me from my thoughts.

Mother's bell.

I force myself to breathe slower, steadying my shaking hands.

"Coming, Mother," I call out, my voice cracking while I ascend the stairs. One step at a time.

When I reach the landing, a chill runs down my spine. The bell rings again, louder.

I freeze.

She never rings twice.

What We Do in Secret

CHAPTER

TEN

"You look well." Dr. Sarah McCoy seats herself in the oversized chair across from me, a notepad delicately in her lap. She pulls the pen from her shirt pocket, removing the tip before making eye contact with me.

"Thank you. I *am* well." I mirror her position, hands clasped, trying to seem as relaxed as I can. Even though it's the farthest thing from what I feel, I need to get this over with.

Dr. McCoy is all right, I guess. She's smart, and at least she doesn't talk to me like I am some kind of crazy person, like my last head doctor. It's just...Her office is so white. White furniture, white walls, and white lights. It reminds me of the padded room I was in for a while. Just existing here gives me a headache.

I try to focus on the few pops of color to give my eyes a rest.

Directly behind her is a massive Rorschach-inspired painting which resembles two snakes entwined. I don't know if that is what they are supposed to be. That's the point of the inkblot designs. It is how they tell if you're insane or not. Some people see ribbons, for example; others see snakes.

Across the room, a large, deep-green vase sits on the table in front of a floor-to-ceiling studio window overlooking the city of Birmingham. A lush plant with white flowers spills out of it onto the floor.

"You missed our last appointment. I hope everything was okay at home."

"It was. *Is*." I hate that I stumble over the simplest words while in this chair. "I've just been a little busy these last couple of weeks."

"Do I need to remind you that these sessions are a condition of your release?"

Or I'll be sent back to the hospital, whether I like it or not.

"I know. I'm sorry. With Mother's condition, it's just been a lot, you know?"

A flash of sympathy washes over her face. After all, it was my mother's declining health which convinced the board to reduce my sentence in the first place. Well, that and good behavior.

"Caring for an elderly parent can certainly be a challenge. How is she doing?"

"We're taking it one day at a time."

"You do have help at least? A home nurse, perhaps?"

"No. It's just me." I smooth the hem of my dress. Was the material this itchy earlier this morning? "Mother's insurance won't cover home nursing, and we really can't afford it, with all her other medical expenses."

"Karla, I know your situation is difficult, but I'm not sure it's the best thing to take on something like this alone? You could—"

"I don't have a choice…right now, at least," I blurt, tucking a lock of hair behind my ear. "I'll manage. I promise."

She studies me, her expression unreadable. I hate it when she looks at me like that, like I'm some kind of a zoo animal and she's the scientist trying to figure out how dangerous I am before she lets me out into the wild. She sighs, and her shoulders relax.

"I do have a few contacts over at St. Mary's. I can make some calls this afternoon?"

"No," I answer too quickly. I need to recoil. "I mean, I couldn't ask you to do that. You've done enough for me already. When I got released from the hospital, I got a second chance. I'd like to earn what I have."

She seems skeptical but satisfied. For now.

"That's very admirable, but everyone needs help on occasion.

How about I have Morgan get their contact information ready for you for when you leave? You don't have to call them, but if you do, just tell them I referred you."

"Thank you. You're too kind to me." I force through a smile, something I do a lot of here.

Smiling through my entire interrogation with Dr. McCoy. Smiling at her frumpy secretary, whose hair could use a good brushing and some highlights. Smiling at the other patients waiting in the lobby while they scratch at their skin and talk to people who aren't there. Smiling until my cheeks are sore, just so she will continue to report to the judge that I am not unhinged.

It's all so silly, really.

"Karla?" Dr. McCoy says. She has asked me something.

"I'm sorry?"

"I asked about your medication. Have you been taking it?" She seems suspicious, like she already knows.

"Of course," I lie. The bottle has been sitting in my bathroom ever since Stevie and Simon moved in. "They really help. Just like you said they would."

"I'm happy to hear it. So, no more night terrors?"

"Just your typical dreams. Teeth falling out...Being naked in public...That sort of thing." No need to mention my mother's corpse in her coffin, pulling me under every night.

She nods in response and scribbles something in her notepad. I wonder what she writes about me in that thing.

"Anything new you want to talk about today?"

If I don't offer up information, she thinks I'm hiding things. Luckily, I have been through enough of these sessions to know that half-truths are key to the art of lying.

"I made a new friend."

"Oh?" she asks, waiting for me to continue.

"Yeah. She just moved in across the street. I helped her find her dog." I pull my cardigan sleeve down over the bandage on my hand.

Dr. McCoy notices but doesn't say anything. "A friend that lives close by could be nice."

"She's a photographer. Well, more of an artist, really."

Dr. McCoy shakes her head, her expression even while I speak. This is the part where she wants me to keep talking so she can analyze every word I say. I know the drill.

"She even convinced me to get a camera."

"So, you've taken up photography?"

I don't like the way her neutral expression falters ever so slightly. She places her pen on her lap. I don't know which is worse: when she's jotting away about me or when she stops. Right now, with her leaning in ever so slightly, it feels like the latter.

"I'm not very good yet. There isn't a lot to photograph in New Haven. All of the houses are the same. The people too. I just thought it would be something fun to do."

I don't tell her that, the day after my nightcap with Stevie, the first thing I did was purchase over two thousand dollars' worth of camera equipment. It was easy enough to find. I noticed the logo stamped across one of the boxes in Stevie's house. If that brand was good enough for her, it is certainly good enough for an amateur like me.

Impulsive, I know, but seeing Stevie's photos inspired me. Plus, as much as I hate it down there, my basement is the perfect place for a dark room. More than anything, I hope it gives Stevie and me something to do together besides drink. I don't think I can stomach another night of that. The headache the next day was almost unbearable.

I also don't tell Dr. McCoy about the painting, about Stevie's weird interaction with it, or how strange it was that it ended up in the garbage bins shortly afterward. And I certainly don't confide how I waited for all the lights to go dark at the house across the street so I could creep back over and get it. Dr. McCoy wouldn't understand.

I don't know how yet, but that painting is important.

"Karla?"

I glance up at the sound of my name.

Dr. McCoy is looking at me, her eyebrows pulled together in concern. "Are you sure you're okay today? You seem to be somewhere else."

"I'm just a little tired. What did you say?"

"I just said getting out of the house on occasion could be helpful for you. I just...I want you to be careful."

"Careful?"

"I don't think either of us want a repeat of Emma."

I dig my nails into my palm, where the bandage covers the moon-shaped scar. A bolt of pain shoots up my arm, but I keep my hands firmly in my lap.

Keep smiling. Keep smiling.

"We both know how quickly things can get out of hand."

This isn't like last time. That was a long time ago. Stevie is nothing like Emma. Stevie is better than Emma. Stevie is good.

I want to scream the words at Dr. McCoy, to pitch them like a brick straight at her head. Of course, I can't do that. She would send me back to the hospital so fast it would make my head spin. So instead, I keep smiling.

"I understand your concern. This is nothing like last time. Stevie's different. I'm different. I'm getting better. I just want to move on with my life. I figured a new hobby would be a good place to start."

Half-truths are also the key to lying to yourself.

CHAPTER

ELEVEN

She hasn't seen me yet.

I take advantage of the little time before she does and adjust my outfit in the large front window of O'Keefe's. This is my best day dress—a robin's-egg-blue flare skirt with a Peter Pan collar and Mother's pearls. I tuck a stray lock of hair back into the knot at the nape of my neck.

Everything looks amazing. I just wish I hadn't ditched my favorite cardigan in the trash a block over. That might have been a bit dramatic, but Stevie didn't seem to like it the other night, and I can't afford any more points against me than I already have.

Simon told her what happened between us. I mean, I don't have any proof. It's just something I know. What other reason would Stevie have to avoid me to the extent she has since that night?

It's impressive, truly, considering our proximity. Four times now, I have knocked on their door and had no answer, even when I knew they were home. Once, I even saw that hideous mandala tapestry flutter like someone was on the other side of it, waiting for me to leave.

I don't blame her. It was a momentary lapse on my part. I don't even know why I did it, but it's not like I kissed him. Considering his history, I wouldn't have pegged him as one for full disclosure, but I guess I was wrong. I knew better.

Control the impulses or the impulses control you, Karla, says Dr. McCoy's voice in my head.

Now Stevie is shutting me out when I've only just been invited in.

"Karla?"

I whip my head around to the open door where Stevie hovers, a bar towel in her hand.

"What are you doing just standing out here?"

"I—" My throat feels thick, the words refusing to form.

She has been watching me, waiting. I must look like an idiot. Get yourself together, Karla.

"I was just in the area, and I remembered you mentioned working here, so I decided to come by."

"And stand outside the window, staring at me like a creep?" she spits, words so hot they may as well be a soldering iron.

"I was going to come in...but then you looked busy, so I—"

"We're about to hit the dinner rush."

"I'm sorry. I just left from visiting my mother."

Immediately, her expression goes from annoyance to regret.

"Thursdays are kind of our day. Mostly they're good, but today was a bad day. I just wanted to brighten my mood a bit, but clearly, you're working, and I've disturbed you. I shouldn't have come by." I turn to leave, but she speaks again.

"Wait." When I pivot on my heel, Stevie is kicking open the door with one of her boots. She gestures inside. "I'm an asshole. Come in. Let me make you a drink."

"Are you sure? I don't want to be—"

"You could use it! Now, come in before everyone thinks you're a theme hooker or something."

"I don't—" Before I can finish, she is ushering me inside, and I am hit by a scent wall of lemon cleaner, liquor, and wood polish. I fight the urge to gag.

"Everything okay?" This comes from a girl behind the counter I did not notice before. Though seeing her now, I wonder how I missed her. Her hair is blue and dreaded down her back. She is covered in tattoos, just like Stevie, and has more jewelry in her face than most of the women in New Haven have in their jewelry boxes.

"Yeah. It's just my new neighbor, Karla. Karla, Astrada."

The distinction. Neighbor. Not friend. Not acquaintance. Neighbor.

"Ah, that explains it, then." Astrada gives no further context.

"Explains what?" I ask.

For a moment, her eyes drop, taking me in.

Oh. Astrada blends in with the urban aesthetic of the bar décor, if you can call it that. I am the one who sticks out like a sore thumb and feels incredibly self-conscious. If they're friends, she probably knows about my moment with Simon as well. Maybe this was a bad idea.

"Nothing." Her eyes return to mine.

When she glances at Stevie, it feels like the two of them are sharing an inside joke and I am the punchline. Heat rises to my temples.

"That's a lovely name you have," I offer, a weak attempt to change the subject.

"Thanks. I made it up."

"I'm sorry?"

"I said I made it up. My slave name was Kate. When I moved out of my folks' house, I changed it."

"Oh. Okay, then. Well, it's lovely."

"You said that." She flashes a tight smile.

The impulse to reach up and scratch it off her face entirely makes my fingers tingle.

"Ash, why don't you go help Greg with food prep," Stevie says, sparing me.

"Sure thing, boss lady." Astrada turns a little too quickly and disappears through the double doors beneath a sign that reads: "Employees Only."

Once she's gone, I can breathe a little easier.

"Boss lady, huh?"

"Glorified babysitter more like it."

"She does have...character."

"Don't mind her. She's just a bit..."

"Candid?"

"I was going to go with insufferable." Stevie laughs, and in spite of myself, I allow a small grin. "She's good people underneath all the grit."

"I'm sure she is."

"So, is this a one-shot or two visit?" She places two glasses on the bar.

My stomach twists at the sight of them. "That's very kind of you, but I'm driving."

"Water, then?"

"Water is perfect." Anything is better than that vile stuff I threw up for two hours.

A few moments later, Stevie pushes a glass of water filled with various fruits toward me. I thank her and take a sip. It's delicious. I'm about to say this to Stevie, but she looks as if she would rather be anywhere but here.

She *has* to know.

"I'm sorry I'm interrupting your work."

"What? No, not at all." She waves me off, but it is obviously forced. "We open soon, but most of the grunt work is done. Stevie takes a seat opposite me at the bar and tries her best to look comfortable. "So, what happened?"

"With what?"

"You said you had a visit with your mom?"

"Oh, right." I quickly take another sip of my water. "I'm sorry. It's just been a trying day."

"You want to talk about it?" She leans onto the counter, her arms crossed in front of her.

"It's just hard, you know, seeing her like that." My voice softens.

Stevie's eyebrows pull together in concern—a sign that she believes me. If she did witness what happened with Simon, she is certainly a better actress than I thought. Or maybe I am just overthinking this entire thing. Nothing happened, really. "She barely even knows who I am anymore."

"That's got to be so hard." Stevie takes my hand in hers, much like she did that first night.

This time, I lift my palm up and return the grasp.

I ignore the way her fingers stiffen when I do so.

"I appreciate you letting me get my bearings before the drive back."

"You don't have to thank me for that."

"I do, though. You've been so kind to me. It's nice to have a friend to talk to."

Friend. Not neighbor. Not acquaintance. Friend. I wait for her response, but to my disappointment, Stevie simply smiles before letting go of my hand.

"I need to check up on the crew. Make sure everything is ready to open. You can hang out here as long as you need." Stevie rises to her feet.

"Thank you," I say, trying to mask my disappointment. Just as she is about to head toward the kitchen, I stop her. "Stevie?"

"Yeah?" She turns back toward me.

"Did I do something to offend you?"

"What are you talking about?"

It's risky being so bold, especially if she *did* witness my little moment with Simon, but I can't stand not knowing.

"Maybe I'm imagining it, but it feels like you've been avoiding me since the other night."

Stevie remains silent, so I continue, pouring the words out like a faucet.

"I just got the impression you wanted to be my friend. I don't have many of those, so maybe you were just being nice and I misunderstood. If I did or said something to offend you, I—"

"Karla, stop." Stevie closes the distance between us and lowers her voice.

I feel out of breath.

"You didn't *do* anything." She inhales and closes her eyes. "But I have been avoiding you."

"Oh." My head feels dizzy.

I don't know what to say to that. She doesn't really owe me any explanation.

"The truth is, I'm embarrassed."

This confession is not what I expected.

"Embarrassed?"

"I knew you for two seconds, and I told you almost every shady thing about me." Her voice drops to a whisper while she continues. "I told you I slept with a married man, for God's sake. Talk about oversharing. Who would want to be friends with someone like that?"

"Stevie—" I begin, but my mind is still playing catch-up.

So, she didn't witness my non-incident with Simon? She is ashamed of herself?

"That's just not something one should disclose when first meeting someone," she says.

"That's it? That's why you've been giving me the cold shoulder?"

"Isn't that enough?" She laughs.

"I told you that I've lived alone with my mother my entire adult life," I say. "That's the most pathetic thing ever."

"That's different. You were being a good daughter. I was just being..."

"A slut."

She looks up at me, shocked, and for a moment I am afraid I've said the wrong thing. Then her expression cracks, and she bursts out in laughter.

Relief washes over me, and I manage a small giggle for the sake of joining in. "And now you live in the suburbs, with a white picket fence and a Golden Retriever."

"What have I become!"

"It's only a matter of time before you start wearing pastel and join a Jazzercise class to combat your muffin top."

"If that ever happens, promise me you'll just kill me."

"Is everything okay here?" a voice calls to us from the kitchen.

We both look over. Kate—sorry, *Astrada*—is peering at us. We hadn't realized our laughter had gotten so loud. Stevie and I share a look, and the expression on Astrada's face is poisonous. Now she is the one on the outside looking in.

"Stevie, we could use some help with prep."

"I'll be right there," Stevie says.

Astrada disappears back into the kitchen.

Stevie turns to me with an apologetic look on her face. "I really do have to get back to work, but let me cook you food to apologize for being an ass."

"When?"

"Tonight, around seven? Bodhi and Simon will be there, so we can't get shit-faced again, but it'll be fun, I promise."

"Seven sounds great."

When she disappears through the kitchen doors, I make my way back to my car with a little more zest. Not because Stevie and I have gotten back on track, but because now I have a new curiosity.

She didn't know about my run-in with Simon, which means he did not tell her.

Now I want to find out why.

What We Do in Secret

CHAPTER

TWELVE

"I hope you like pizza. I burned the ziti," Stevie says in lieu of a traditional hello when she opens the door.

I start to tell her that I love pizza, but she doesn't stay to listen to the lie.

"And the damn breadsticks!" She leaves the door wide open, a light billow of smoke remaining in her wake.

The lack of etiquette isn't surprising, coming from her, and the smoke *is* a bit concerning, so I try not to judge too harshly. How does someone burn breadsticks anyway? They are the simplest thing in the world to bake.

"Is everything okay?" I call into the house, keeping my heels planted awkwardly on the welcome mat designed into a Ouija board, with the words "Go Away." My question is met with a stream of expletives, making my cheeks flame.

I feel a bit silly standing in front of the open door, so I step into the house, hesitating only for a moment, looking for Ollie. Seeing how he has already mauled me once, it would be the respectable thing to do to put him away before I arrived, but you never know how people think, and they aren't the most organized. When I'm confident the beast will not be making an appearance, I follow the smoke trail to the kitchen.

"Damn it!" Stevie yells, simultaneously slamming down a baking sheet on the stovetop. The metal echoes through the room.

The contents are charred and far from edible. Simon is feverishly fanning smoke out of the French doors I came through the other day. Their little boy—well, Simon's son—is sitting on the stairs, covering his ears with his hands. We make eye contact momentarily before his eyes dart back to Stevie, who has just released another expletive.

The poor thing. She really shouldn't be cursing like that in front of children.

"Is there anything I can do to help?" I try to keep my tone as calm and polite as possible, not needing those obscenities directed at me.

"What? No! Of course not. Well...Actually, could you take Bodhi upstairs so I can get all the smoke out of here? He has asthma, and I don't want him breathing all this shit in."

"Of course." I place my soup dish down on a spare oven mitt and turn to Bodhi.

He is still sitting on the stairs, looking completely overwhelmed. I cross the floor and kneel in front of him.

"Hi, Bodhi. I'm Karla Cooper. I live across the street."

He doesn't respond but removes his hands from his ears so I know he is listening. Up close, I notice how much he favors Simon. It's not just the soft waves of brown hair which dust his eyebrows. He has the same deep honey eyes and nonchalant stare, absorbing the world around him, not just mindlessly passing through it, like most. His cheeks are plump but no longer possess the roundness of the baby in the photos, yet his jaw hasn't taken on the sharp edges like his dad's either. He's perfect.

Someone crouches beside me. The sudden closeness is a shock to my nervous system, but I remain still, waiting. Simon gives me a reassuring look before turning his attention to his son.

"Hey, buddy. Do you have your inhaler?" Simon's tone is surprisingly soft for someone who appears so...rough.

Bodhi answers with a nod. He drops his hand to his front jeans pocket.

"Good. Keep it on you, just in case. Karla's going to take you up to your room while we try to get all this smoke out."

Bodhi glances toward me, then back to his dad. He still seems unsure.

"You can show her your sketches."

Bodhi sits up straighter with this new suggestion. I take the bait.

"You're an artist?" I ask, exaggerating the excitement in my tone.

He nods.

"I've never met a *real* artist before. Would you show me some of your work?" I offer my hand.

He hesitates only for a moment. As Bodhi pulls me up the stairwell, I glance back at Simon, who gives me the smallest smile before disappearing into the panic that has become their kitchen.

I never got a chance to check out Bodhi's room during my previous prowling session. Right away, I notice how much more imaginative his little setup is over Mrs. Lowe's sewing room—and the rest of the house, for that matter.

This room was once dreadfully boring and a little creepy, with stacks of fabric lining the walls, needles, bins filled with buttons on plastic shelving, cutting tables, and pegboards. Mrs. Lowe never made anything for real people that I am aware of. Just those dresses for her hoard of porcelain dolls.

She had hundreds. Mrs. Lowe told my mother once she sold them at flea markets, but I can't imagine why anyone would want them. Their eyes bore into me in every room in the house, watching me, like they knew something.

Thankfully, the creepy dolls have been replaced by Bodhi's tiny furniture and toys. The old, outdated wallpaper has been replaced with a fresh coat of black paint. An interesting choice for a child's room but not completely surprising, considering his parents' taste.

That's not what catches my eye. Little string tea lights and glow-in-the-dark stars make the room resemble the night sky. There are dozens of space-themed posters pinned to the walls. A cardboard rocket ship with a painted fire trail soars its way from the blue and green circle to a moon light above the bed, where a tiny American flag is being held up by an alien. The most intriguing thing about the entire spectacle is that it all appears to have been hand-painted or crafted together using various objects.

I am so captivated by the room that I hit my head on something dangling from the ceiling. Upon closer inspection, I find a solar system model with surprising detail. It hangs from the center of the room like a chandelier.

"That's my science project. I got an A minus, but it was because I didn't include Pluto," Bodhi says in a small voice when he catches my focus lingering on the various planets, meteors, and satellites. This is the first time I've heard him speak.

It's adorable, and I want nothing more in this moment than for him to keep talking.

"You forgot an entire planet?"

"I *didn't* forget." He sounds truly irritated that I would suggest such a thing. "Pluto is only a dwarf planet. It hasn't been classified as a planet for a long time."

"Oh. I didn't realize."

"Most people don't. I tried telling Mrs. Hatch that it didn't meet the criteria set by the International Astronomical Union to be a planet, but she deducted points anyway."

"I see. That hardly seems fair."

Bodhi shrugs without looking up from the desk drawer he is rummaging through. "To be a real planet, the celestial body has to orbit the sun and have enough mass to be almost round. Those aren't the problem. It also has to be the dominant gravitational force in its orbit."

"And Pluto isn't?"

"Officially, no. It has volcanoes and mountains like Earth does, but it's part of the Kuiper Belt of icy objects." He finally pulls a book from the drawer and places it in my hands.

It's a sketchbook filled with space-themed drawings. Rocket ships blast off with cheering crowds...Saturn and all its rings, only the rings are tiny rocks, and I wonder if that's really what the rings are made of...Little sketches of different-shaped objects with scribbled captions beneath them like "Asteroid," "Meteoroid," and "Meteorite."

The drawings are actually pretty good for a little kid. He must get his artistic flair from his dad.

"These are fantastic, Bodhi. You really like astronomy, huh?"

"Yeah, but mostly planetary science." He answers in a matter-of-fact tone.

I have no idea what the difference is, but something tells me he will explain it in no time.

"You really like them?"

"Of course!" I say. "Why wouldn't I? You're very talented."

"Some people think it's weird to love one thing too much."

Or one person.

"I'd rather pour my entire heart into one thing than scatter it thin across a dozen—" I can't finish my sentence. The words catch in my throat when I flip a page in his sketchbook to a drawing that is nothing like the others.

There are no planets or stars or super-kid-genius rock studies in this drawing. It isn't as detailed as the others either. They are intricate illustrations of things Bodhi clearly spent a lot of time studying. This one seems more like a hurried sketch of something glimpsed, a gesture. The way someone may recall a dream several hours after being awake.

The idea is clear, but the details are a bit fuzzy. And the idea shockingly resembles the crooked body of a person lying on the floor, with long, swirly scribbles for hair. It could have been completely overlooked if not for the heavy saturation of red marker beneath the person.

Blood?

"This one is—interesting," I manage.

He leans over the book to see which drawing I'm looking at but doesn't respond.

"What is this?" I coax.

For the first time since getting him to open up, with a surprising wealth of knowledge and strong vocabulary for a little boy, he is eerily silent. Bodhi looks up, his big brown eyes wide and inquisitive, like he is trying to figure something out about me. He opens his mouth as if to speak, but we both jump at the sound of a voice behind us.

"Pizza's here. Smoke's gone. Hope you guys are hungry," Stevie says from the doorway.

Bodhi grabs his sketchbook and tucks it beneath a few spiral notebooks in his drawer.

I consider bringing it up to Stevie. Kids don't just draw things like that from their imagination. I suppose it could have come from a horror movie, considering the VHS tapes I saw downstairs. But something about the careful way Bodhi conceals the sketchbook gives me pause.

Instead, I turn to Stevie and say, "Starving."

I glance at Bodhi and wink, which prompts a small smile from him. When I offer my hand, he takes it without hesitation this time.

CHAPTER

THIRTEEN

"This soup is delicious, Karla. What is it again? Zippa Tuscana?"

"Zuppa Toscana. Tuscan soup," I answer Stevie for the third time. I was hesitant about making such a heavy side dish for the ziti, but now that the options are limited to franchise-distributed frozen pizza and blackened breadsticks, I'm grateful I did. I ate a small slice to be cordial and politely declined when offered a second.

Bodhi, however, is working on his third slice. By twenty, he will have the arteries of a forty-year-old man if he's not careful. I clench my fists under the table, resisting the urge to swat the processed garbage out of his hand.

"Really good stuff. What's in it?" Simon brings another spoonful to his lips.

"This is actually one of my mother's recipes. Italian sausage. Garlic and spices. I get most of the vegetables from the farmers market in town, and I usually grow the spices myself. I will again once I get settled," I say with a touch of pride.

Simon nods appreciatively and leans back in his chair.

"I can definitely taste the difference. Just wow. I'll have to get you to teach Stevie a thing or two. This woman here can't cook to save her life—" His teasing is cut short by a playful punch to his arm from Stevie.

"I might not be a chef, but"—Stevie leans into him, eyes glinting, and smirks—"I have *other* talents."

The innuendo has the kind of intimacy which feels too private for polite company. I sip my water, allowing the moment to linger just a bit too long before slicing through the tension. "So, where did you two meet?" I ask.

There's a notable shift between them. I can't tell if it's intentional, but Stevie turns her body slightly away from Simon before grinning back at him.

"I don't remember. Do you?" He smiles back, but there is an undercurrent of unease in his body.

"Asshole." Stevie playfully punches him again. "It was a concert, and he knows that. He's just being a dick tonight."

Does every word out of her mouth have to be so brash? Did she cuss this much during our nightcap? Bodhi doesn't seem to notice this time. He has helped himself to a bowl of my homemade soup, and I watch him take a bite. Bodhi looks up at me and smiles in approval before returning to the bowl.

At least the poor kid will get some nutrients from this meal after all.

"Oh yeah, the concert." Simon squints his eyes at her.

Stevie lifts her eyebrows slightly, challenging him. I may not understand what kind of unspoken conversation they are having with each other, but I know the language. Whatever they say next will not be the full story.

"Bottles of water were, what?

"Seven dollars," they echo together. "And the band wasn't even that good."

"How great can a band called Gorphobic be anyway?" Stevie adds in a light tone.

I notice a slight slur in her speech. The wine she has been drinking like water is taking hold, no doubt. She seems to be a functioning alcoholic.

"They weren't as bad as Scalpel Rot."

"I don't know. 'Sutures of Sin' wasn't terrible."

"It's literally a song about a convent orgy!" Simon rolls his eyes.

"It's a metaphor!"

"Sure...A metaphor for why half the crowd left for overpriced water." Simon smirks before continuing. "Anyway, I ended up next to this group of wild girls—"

Stevie interjects with a mock cough.

"Sorry. This group of *sophisticated ladies* in crop tops and leather." Simon laughs.

"I'm assuming you were Leather Crop Top Girl Number Three?" I ask, attempting to join in on the banter.

"Absolutely not!" Stevie gasps, clutching her metaphorical pearls.

I bite my lip to keep from giggling.

Stevie doesn't seem the type to have ever owned a decent string of pearls in her entire life. Mother always said there were three things every true Southern lady should have: a string of pearls, a cast iron skillet, and a concealed carry license. Does Stevie own a gun?

I bring my own fingers to my neck and run a polished nail along the smooth orbs. My eyes drift to her neckline. It isn't a string of pearls, but she has a necklace too—a small gold chain with what looks to be a miniature origami bird pendant made into a clasp. Simon probably gifted it to her. Then again, her mother may have given it to her, just like my mother left this one to me.

"—then they laughed in his face, and he skulked away, like a kicked puppy. I felt so bad for him."

"I walked away like a *grown man*," Simon says.

I've missed a plot point in this story and scramble to catch up.

"Like a sad, injured stray," Stevie affirms. "So, when he came up to the stand, I gave him a water and a beer, on the house. Haven't been able to get rid of him since."

"I believe you asked me to stay, if memory serves. Isn't that what you said later that night, when I drove you home and—"

"Anyway...that's how we met. Anyone want a drink?" Stevie leaves the table before anyone can answer.

I guess the wine wasn't enough. Though I feel the urge to help her, I become aware of how alone I am with Simon...and Bodhi, of course. Simon watches me, and every nerve in my body fires painfully.

"That's quite a story," I say.

No mention of Melissa. I take a bite of the soup to give my hands something to do.

"It was quite a night."

"Sounds like it. It was love at first sight, then?"

"Love...ha." He laughs. "No, it wasn't love. She did shock me, though."

"How do you mean?"

"With her attentiveness. She always had so much going on, but she still saw me. It was like I was a ghost being seen for the first time in a long time, and it was...shocking."

"I see." I picture the scene again. This time, the noise of the concert is drowned out by a smokey-eyed Stevie at the concession stand, seven-dollar water in hand, like some kind of rock concert oasis.

"It's only happened twice," he says, breaking up my daydream.

"Twice?"

"You shocked me the other night." Simon brings the soup to his lips but keeps his hooded eyes fixed on me. His words linger heavy in the air between us.

I remember the taste of his cigarette on my lips, having just left his. My cheeks flame under his gaze. There's no mistaking his intention. I turn my head, smiling just enough for him to see it. With his track record, I shouldn't be shocked, but I am a little. Usually, I can sense it in men. Anyone can if they're paying attention. That restlessness that keeps them craving more.

My father had it before he left. A majority of men do in some capacity, but most of those men don't have girlfriends like Stevie. What more could he want? This is why he didn't tell her about our moment the other night. He is hoping there will be more of them. Maybe I do too.

I'm almost grateful when Bodhi drops his spoon in his bowl with a loud clang, disrupting the heaviness between us.

Almost.

"All done!" he announces.

"Good job, buddy. Let's see?" Simon shifts in his seat to peer into the empty bowl, and Bodhi tilts it so Simon can see the full scale of its emptiness. "You even ate all of the croûtons! Nice."

"Did you know that astronauts can't eat bread in space?" Bodhi directs this question at me.

"I did not know that," I say, tearing my eyes from Simon.

"The bread releases crumbs, which can float around and damage the space equipment or be inhaled. They use tortillas. They don't make crumbs and are easier to handle in microgravity. Do you think next time you make the soup you could use tortillas?"

"I'm sure I can." I smile.

He beams up at me with the same laugh lines as his dad.

"Do you want to see my meteorite? I got it from space camp last year!" Before I can answer, he leaves the table and disappears up the stairs.

"I take it he's shown you his collection?" Simon leans back in his chair again.

It's unsettling being studied this way, but also, I find it kind of nice.

"It's certainly impressive. Especially the drawings." I watch Simon's face for any indication he knows the strange sketch exists.

If he does, he doesn't give it away. His eyes momentarily drop to my lips, though. He's not even trying to be subtle.

"You must be extremely proud of him. He's a smart kid."

"Too smart for his own good sometimes."

Bodhi returns with the meteorite as Stevie enters with an assortment of liquor bottles. I make a fuss about the rock and let Bodhi tell me interesting facts about it while I hold it in my palm. He has just finished telling me that shooting stars—meteors—are simply bits of rock and metal which burn when they enter the earth's atmosphere, that they don't become meteorites until they hit the ground, when Stevie cuts him off.

"That's enough, Bo. It's getting late. Time for bed."

"But it's only 8:oo!"

"Come now, buddy. The boss has spoken!" Simon picks Bodhi up from the chair and throws him over his shoulder.

Bodhi doesn't protest this time. He laughs hysterically while his dad spins him around, all the while moving toward the staircase.

When he begins to ascend, Simon looks at me, eyes sparkling. "Tell our new friend goodnight!"

"Goodnight, Miss Cooper! I'll show you the rest of my collection later!"

Before I can respond, they both disappear upstairs.

I admit I'm slightly annoyed that Stevie sent Bodhi to bed early just so we could drink. Though I'm not a parent and I learned a long time ago that most don't appreciate the insight of non-parents when it comes to their methods, to be fair, Stevie isn't a parent either.

"So, what's your poison?" she asks, pouring herself a glass full of whiskey.

"Do you mind if I use your bathroom first?" I ask.

"Sure. Down the hall, past the kitchen on the left."

I'm barely listening while I make my way to the bathroom. After all, I already know where it is.

I need a moment to gather my thoughts. Between the processed pizza, the look Simon was giving me, Simon and Stevie's uncomfortable banter, the mere thought of drinking again, and that creepy picture Bodhi drew, my head is starting to do that thing it does when I'm around other people for too long. It all feels so...scripted. It isn't real.

Well, Bodhi is genuine. Children are different. They never pretend, and you always know where you stand with them. Adults are the liars. As nice as it is to have a normal dinner, by any standard, this isn't the kind of interaction I can maintain for any length of time. I'm smiling so much my cheeks hurt.

In the bathroom, I glance at my reflection in the mirror. If I didn't have a full face of makeup on, I would splash myself with some cold water to help calm my nerves.

Such a pretty girl. It's such a shame about her.

I turn away from the mirror and start making my way out to the dining area. Simon and Stevie are whispering in the kitchen. I slow my steps to listen to what they're saying, but something catches my eye.

It's the door to the basement.

And it's unlocked.

What We Do in Secret

CHAPTER

FOURTEEN

I normally wouldn't risk it.

Simon and Stevie are literally *right there* in the next room. Under normal circumstances, I would plan another visit while they are both out, access the keys, and be in and out before either of them knew I was here. But none of my usual methods seem to fit this family.

It is frustrating how many rules I've had to break already. Why can't they just be normal? Then again, I suppose they wouldn't be half as interesting, and I wouldn't care what is locked down in Mrs. Lowe's creepy little basement.

I consider my options for a moment, but it's not like I have all night. With their odd hours and sporadic returns, it feels less risky to just grab a quick peek now.

A glance around the corner shows an already sauced Stevie practically straddling Simon on his chair. I don't think my presence will be missed for at least a few more minutes.

I'm glad I took it easy on the pizza at dinner. The door is only slightly ajar, with just enough of a gap for me to slip through. It's pitch-black, other than the small trail of light coming from the door, illuminating the aged wooden staircase all the way down to the basement's cracked concrete floor. I step lightly while I descend the stairs.

It does no good. I'm painfully aware of every creak and groan of the old house. They may as well be land mines.

When I finally reach the bottom of the stairs, I pause, listening. The houses in this neighborhood are so well insulated, including the basements, that many of them are practically soundproof. I screamed for almost an entire day once when Mother locked me down in ours, and no one ever heard me. It was only when I was silent that she let me out.

When I'm confident they can't hear me any more than I can them, I take in what little of my surroundings I can. It smells like a grave down here, old wood and dirt, with the slight hint of mold.

My eyes have adjusted to the dark for the most part, but it's still almost impossible to make out anything specific. A shelf, maybe, in the corner...Some buckets of paint closer to the staircase...I walk out of the light spilling in from the door, and that's when something catches my eye.

There's a thin red rim glowing from the door beneath the stairs. I almost missed it. If I remember correctly, it's not a very big room, maybe five by six feet. It's more of a closet than anything. Mrs. Lowe used to keep her spare sewing machines and doll body parts in it.

I pull at the old wooden door, but it doesn't move. Along the edge of the frame is the lock. I yank the metal piece from its latch. The wood, swollen and distorted by age and moisture, still resists, but eventually, it gives way, scraping harshly against the basement floor with a grated shriek.

Inside, the room is washed in red. The area has been emptied of all the bulky sewing items and doll corpses, and they have been replaced with thin tables lining the three walls. A small space between the tables is just big enough for one person to fit, so I step inside the room for a closer look.

It's a dark room. I saw a dozen pictures of them when I was researching what camera to buy to impress Stevie. Of course, a real photographer would have one. I'm not sure why it would need to be protected by three locks, though. Seems a bit excessive for some photographs.

On the tables are four massive trays with some kind of liquid inside. They give off a chemical odor which burns my eyes. Various items ranging from tongs to rubber gloves litter the remaining surfaces.

There's a string pulled taut along the perimeter of the room, and about a dozen photos are clipped to the line in varying stages of development. Some are too fuzzy to make out in the low light, and others are crisp and vibrant, even with limited vision. Most are similar to the ones in Stevie's portfolio—black and white candid shots of total strangers. One is of Bodhi and Ollie in the front yard on moving day. The logo on the U-Haul, which was parked out front for over a week, is visible. I can even make out my house in the background.

If only she were to zoom in on the window to the far right, she might have seen...

Another photo catches my eye. This one is hung in one of the corners, almost entirely hidden behind a portrait of Simon. I move it down to get a better look.

The image is of a young girl, maybe fifteen or sixteen years old. She's wearing all black against a solid white background, frozen in a position so complex that only someone trained in yoga or dance could manage it.

The execution of the shot is different from Stevie's other work. This isn't some random girl seen dancing on a street corner. This is posed. Every detail, from the color palette to the form of her limbs and the way her wild hair seems to be dancing *with* her instead of being a part of her body, is intentional. It's beautiful and moving and shockingly familiar.

I think back to the painting in their bedroom. The one Stevie so angrily snatched up and I later spotted in their trash can by the road. I've studied that painting every day since I fished it out and hung it above my bed. The wild hair. The movement. Could this be the same girl?

I can't prove it, but something in the expression on her face tells me she is.

"What are you doing?"

Stevie's voice from behind me is like a bullet to my back. I spin around. My heart drops into my gut. The photo falls from my hands, but I don't see where.

She is standing at the door to the dark room, one hand on her hip. The other braces her body against the doorframe.

"I—I..." I start but can't finish. What am I supposed to say? I was just trying to find out why you have your basement locked up, so I decided to go exploring while you weren't paying attention? Even I know how that sounds. "The door was open, so I thought..."

When I can't finish, she crosses the small space and kneels. When she stands again, Stevie has the photo in her hand.

"So you just thought you could go snooping around?" She lifts her eyes from the image to me.

Stevie is dangerously close. So near I can smell the alcohol on her breath blending with the chemical smell of the room. Then she reaches around me with both arms, boxing me in.

I almost panic until I realize she is hanging the photo back up on the string. Her hair brushes along the skin on my neck and shoulder, and it smells like smoke, alcohol, and the crisp scent of her shampoo. I don't know what to do with my body. It's difficult for me to focus on anything other than how incredibly close she is.

The table behind me bites into the backs of my thighs. I can't move forward, even an inch, without colliding with her. When she finishes, Stevie steps back, but just an inch or so.

"I think you better go. It's late."

She shifts her body to the side, allowing me a path out. I don't hesitate.

Out of the darkroom, I am through the basement and up the stairs without checking to see if she is behind me. Simon is no longer anywhere near the kitchen, and I am relieved. If he doesn't already know what I've been caught doing, my face would have certainly given it away.

Tears wet my cheeks, and my throat burns with all the anger and frustration I'm struggling to keep contained until I am in the safety of my own home. Anger at myself for not following my own rules. Frustration with Stevie and Simon for putting me in a position where I considered breaking them to start with. Why can't they just be normal! Why can't I...

As rude as it is, I let myself out. I don't even grab the soup dish. Stevie can keep it.

I make my way across the street. A thought comes to mind. A story, actually.

Alice in Wonderland.

My mother used to read it to me. When little, I was fascinated with Alice. With how she became so fixated on that silly white rabbit that she abandoned her entire life in pursuit of it. She seemed selfish. Or maybe she just reminded me of my father.

He abandoned me in search of something more, after all.

I guess I understand her, and him, a little more now. Like I dove headfirst into my own rabbit hole. It happened before I realized what I had done.

The diving is the easy part. It's the coming back that's jarring.

Even when I close my own door behind me, I can't shake the feeling that I'm missing something. Or maybe something I've forgotten?

My father forgot me. I wonder what important items Alice left behind when she emerged from the rabbit hole? Did she lose something important, like her mind?

Or maybe it was herself she lost.

CHAPTER

FIFTEEN

I'm practically vibrating when I get back to my house. Once the door shuts behind me, the cap slips, and the heat boils in my chest. With my back against the front door and the lock secured in place, I erupt with a visceral scream.

It's not enough.

I pound my fists against the door again and again until one of the impacts makes contact at an odd angle, sending lightning strikes of sharp pain up my arm. With a gasp, I catch a glimpse of myself in the mirror to my left. The reflection stops me cold.

I barely recognize the person staring back.

My hair, so meticulously styled just a few hours ago, is flared out in every direction, and my makeup is smeared across the red balloon that has become my face. At some point, I started crying, marked by the rivers of mascara streaking down my cheeks. The drama of it all is practically theatrical.

I've always been accused of being intense, but this is just ridiculous. With one wipe, the mascara leaves a trail on the sleeve of my cardigan, and I immediately regret it. The stain against the white fabric rekindles the boiling rage in my gut.

It's a shame about her...She's such a pretty thing...such a pretty thing...pretty thing...pret—

One of my heels has been kicked off during my outburst. I grab it and slam the heel into the mirror. It shatters under the force. Shards of glass fall to the floor like splintered raindrops, catching the dim light in sharp, fleeting flints before settling into silence on the floor. That will definitely leave a scratch. I can't bring myself to clean it up tonight.

How could I have been so stupid, breaking all those rules like that? Why? *Why* did I do it? Stevie is never going to invite me over again. I'll be lucky if she even looks at me.

Considering the way she was glaring when she told me to leave her house, it's probably best. I hate that expression. I've seen it many times before. From the kids at my school. The neighbors the day they took me away in handcuffs. Even my own mother. The mouth slightly parted, as if in mid-gasp, and the wide, unblinking stare of uncertainty, like they aren't sure if I'm a predator or prey yet. And, if that wasn't enough, the undertone of pity, the slight dip of the brow and tilt of the head which inevitably follows, bites harder than hate ever could.

I even recognize that look in my own reflection if I stare at it too long. Like even *it* is mocking me.

I just got greedy. I know better. It's the last one, Rule #23: Don't get too close. No matter how much truth there is to find by peeking in on people's private lives, they are never as dazzling up close as they are from a distance.

From far away, you can build people into something they aren't. You can marvel at their potential, fall in love with their essence, but up close, the truth is always ugly. Up close, you find the cracks in the porcelain.

That picture in Bodhi's sketchbook is proof of that. Maybe it's a manifestation of a child's wild imagination, or perhaps it's something he saw on TV. I tell myself this, but something inside me knows it isn't true. There's a deeply rooted intuition screaming that something isn't right in that house.

It's the same feeling some people get about me. And they aren't wrong. There *is* something wrong with me. Eventually, everyone I get close to sees it, and they push me away, or they leave. From the moment I say hello, they already have one foot out the window, ready to jump.

But Bodhi is just a kid. A sweet kid. A smart kid. One who seems just as fascinated with me as I am of him. If something is wrong over there, can I really leave him to fend for himself?

Listen to me...*Fend* for himself...

Other than excessive cursing and burned breadsticks, neither Stevie nor Simon seem like the violent type, and Bodhi appears healthy. I'm allowing my imagination to run away with me again. Still, kids should be drawing things like spaceships and dragons, knights with banners. They shouldn't be drawing broken girls in pools of something that looks strikingly like blood.

For some reason, I think of the painting I found in Stevie and Simon's bedroom, which now hangs above my own bed. The eerie similarities to the photo of the dancing girl in her darkroom...

Why did Stevie toss it out in the first place? She seemed angry it was there. Is it possible it had been put there by mistake and she was just aggravated it was out of place? As disorganized as she seems to be, Stevie did notice immediately that her dress was gone from the closet. Maybe...

Let it go. Just for tonight. Let it go.

I ascend the stairs to my bedroom, attempting to abandon all thoughts of Stevie on the floor with the broken glass. Then, once inside my bedroom, I can't help it. The first thing I do is take my usual place by the window and gaze toward her house.

The lights are all dark except for one. It's the downstairs bathroom, barely visible in the farthest corner, almost entirely hidden by the branches of the magnolia tree in the side yard. But I can make out someone inside.

I pick up my camera I keep on the seat by the window for convenience and zoom in on the window.

It's Simon. Light is coming from a small lamp on the counter, just enough to illuminate his profile. I almost drop the camera when I realize what is happening.

His hand is down the front of his pants, his shoulders undulating, his head tossed back. His eyes are closed tightly, lost in some fantasy. Before the moment is lost, I snap a photo.

I instantly regret it.

The flash from the camera reflects off the window, and it may as well be a spotlight. I drop from sight, and the camera falls from my hands. Luckily, it lands on the cushion of the window seat and goes no further.

Maybe he didn't see.

I try and convince myself the flash was too far away for him to notice. And his eyes were closed. There's no way he saw me, the flash, the camera, or anything else tonight.

Though I tell myself this, the urge to confirm, to dare a glance out the window, is so strong I can't resist. I *have* to know. So I pull myself up on the window seat, camera in hand, and zoom in once more on the window across the street.

The light is off in the bathroom, and for a moment, I think it's empty. But my eyes adjust to the dark. The faint glow of the streetlamp outside catches his silhouette.

Not only is he still in the bathroom, but he's looking directly at me.

I dive below the window once again. This time, the camera falls to the ground with a sharp crack. I snap the blinds shut, pick it up, and carry it over to my nightstand, wanting to scream, wanting to throw it out the window.

Oh, who am I kidding? I want to throw *myself* out the window. And I consider doing just that when my phone chimes from my pocket.

It's an Instagram notification. I click on the alert, and my chest tightens. It's Simon. He is requesting to follow me.

I stare at the notification, allowing it to marinate before deciding what to do. He saw me. That part is clear. Did Stevie also tell him about my little expedition through their house? I can't think of a valid reason why she wouldn't. Didn't couples always gossip about their friends and neighbors when they weren't around? I can picture her stomping upstairs and spilling all the details of why I left so abruptly.

The heat of shame rises in my throat, and tears begin to well up. I've never wanted to disappear more than I do tonight.

How did he even find my social media? This is a new account, and it is as generic as they come. I don't even have a picture of myself on it, for goodness' sake. After all the vile messages I came home to on my old one, I deleted it and created this one, just to check out his and Stevie's accounts.

My finger hovers over the delete button, but at the last minute, I accept it. I instantly get another notification. It's a message this time.

Shouldn't you be in bed?

If there was ever any doubt he saw me, it is gone now. I should delete the message. Maybe I should delete the entire account, sell the house, and move away at this point.

Instead, I type: *I could say the same about you.*

The three little dots dance, indicating he is typing out a reply. I hold my breath until the message finally pops up.

Touche.

It is disappointing when the dots don't appear again. I'm not sure what to say to that, so I decide on something safe. Something I genuinely want to know.

How did you find my social media? Stalking me?

I decide to delete the last part, then hit send. His response is insanely fast.

I have my ways.

I see.

The typing dots waver, and another message pops up.

You won't tell on me, will you?

I don't know what he's talking about exactly. The cigarette on the first night we met? Being up alone? Or the fact that I caught him masturbating in the downstairs bathroom while his girlfriend and kid are in the house? I decide on a safe answer. One which mimics the energy from our first meeting.

I can keep a secret. Can you?

This time, I don't delete the last part. I allow the implication to linger. Then he says something that lights me on fire.

Open the window. I want to see you.

I return to it and twist the rod to part the blinds. The house across the street is dark, including the bathroom window behind the magnolia tree. I can't see him, but he's there. The weight of his eyes presses on me, even from this distance. It's a new feeling, to be the one being observed.

My phone buzzes again. There's another message from him.

Take your dress off.

He's certainly to the point. Nothing like the chatty man I met at dinner. His words are like hot stones on my skin.

Is this really happening? I wonder where Stevie is? If she were to glance out any of her front windows, she would notice the light on in my bedroom and me, blatantly undressing in front of it. In fact, any of my other neighbors could look out at any moment and see me as clear as day. I picture Mr. Griffin, with all his heart issues and breathing treatments, gazing out his window and dropping dead from a heart attack.

As much as the exposure should terrify me into closing this window and going straight to bed, it has the opposite effect. I place my phone on the nightstand and turn toward the lamp, away from the window. With a quick glance over my shoulder, just to make sure I still feel his eyes on me, I unzip my dress. I bend over and step out of it, taking my time for him to relish the view.

A notification pops up. The message reads: *You are so sexy.*

I'm not sure I've ever been called that by a man. Maybe an old orderly at the hospital, but never someone like Simon. Or someone who has a girlfriend who looks like Stevie.

The words are electric, and I use this newfound fuel to walk over to the window. I raise my arms, bracing myself against the frame, and arch my body toward him. What must he be thinking? What must he be *doing*?

I smile in the direction of the darkened bathroom and pull the curtains closed.

If not for the adrenaline, I am sure I would be a puddle on the floor. My mind is swimming, my body humming. Every muscle feels like I've just completed a full Tantric yoga flow. It's practically orgasmic.

But I have to be careful. I've been around men like him long enough to know they are used to getting anything—and any*one*—they want. They expect everyone and everything to fall at their feet. I'm ego food for him, just as much as he is for me, but it's not like it is with others.

There is always a power exchange between men and women. It becomes a game of chess. Or cat and mouse. Hunter. Prey. If I am going to hold his interest, I have to shock him. He said it himself at dinner. And I need to hold his interest.

At least for now, until I figure out what is going on in that house.

If Stevie is going to shut me out, I need another way in.

Nothing bonds people like a secret.

CHAPTER

SIXTEEN

Simon's van finally pulls away from the house across the street around four in the afternoon. It's not that I don't want to be around him necessarily, but he feels like a distraction. I've been disgusted all morning. With him, yes, but mostly for allowing myself to be so easily affected by him.

Self-awareness. Dr. McCoy says it's the only way to truly change patterned behavior.

I'm aware enough to understand that my reaction to his attention is not a reflection of my desire for him, but rather flattery that a man who has someone like Stevie could also desire me. Flattery is the most dangerous weapon to wield. Everyone wants to feel wanted. But it's rarely genuine.

His eagerness to transgress on his relationship is valuable information to have, I suppose, but I would be naive to rely on it. It is the primal pursuit of instant physical gratification he wants, not a shoulder to cry on. Not someone to tell their secrets to. He is a waste of time if I can still get back in Stevie's good graces. Nothing like that can ever happen again—unless I have no other options, of course.

The truth is, I feel a little bad for her. I can't imagine what it's like to love someone who is always craving the next best thing.

Her vulnerability that first night, the way she laid herself bare in front of me, to accept or judge…To give someone that kind of power over you, alcohol-induced or not, is the cry of someone desperately in need of a friend. People only overshare when they have nowhere else to pour their pain. It just builds inside us until, one day, someone asks if you're okay, and it may as well be the trigger of a gun, with how the confessions fire off in bullets.

I know what that's like.

Lonely can recognize the same in a crowd. It's in the way the eyes drift across the surface until they land on yours.

My now cracked camera is sitting in its usual spot on the window seat. I scoop it up and head toward the door.

"Now, don't you go anywhere. I'll be back in a little while," I yell into my mother's room.

The bite in my tone is intentional, but a pinch of unease twists in my chest. I normally like to keep myself from taunting her too much, given her condition, but I'm in a foul mood today. Plus, it's not like she doesn't deserve a little torment. Goodness knows she put me through enough of it.

I open her door slightly. The old wood groans on its hinges. I'll have to make a point to fix that soon.

It's so dark in her room all the time, but she claims the sun hurts her eyes. With the thick curtains closed tightly, the space is gloomy, like a funeral home. It even smells like one, with all the potpourri my mother likes to keep around.

I wait for my eyes to adjust to the dim light. Finally, they land on the small mound of blankets in the middle of the bed. The mass moves ever so slightly—the lazy rise and fall of someone sleeping. I inch the door open a few more centimeters, allowing a bit more of the light in, just enough to wash across her face.

Her sunken eyes are closed, her mouth slightly ajar. Her once well-kept hair is tousled around the translucent orb of her face, like a wild, white halo. The necklace she has worn since I was a child glints when it catches the light. The eye of a vulture. It suits her.

Well, it used to.

Now she's just a frail little body beneath a pile of blankets, lying in the dark all day. Maybe tomorrow I can talk her into letting some life in. A houseplant, perhaps. A few hours of sunlight shouldn't kill her.

I close the door as quietly as possible and adjust the camera strap on my shoulder. Outside, the air is heavy with the threat of rain, the kind which doesn't come all at once but teases, gathering thick in the clouds, waiting to split open when it will cause the most inconvenience.

Bothersome or not, the smell is intoxicating. I breathe it into my lungs and allow it to invigorate me for what I am about to do.

My heels click on the pavement in rhythmic little clips-clops while I make my way to the house across the street. It's so crazy how, just yesterday, the two-story craftsman looming closer felt semi-welcoming but is now like I am breaching enemy territory. I tap my fingers on the camera's plastic casing to soothe my nerves.

This is ridiculous. I just went snooping for five minutes in her basement. It's not like I ran over her dog, as much as I would like to. If anyone should feel weird about this friendship, it should be me after finding that drawing.

I quicken my pace, making it to the porch just in time to hear shuffling on the other side of the door.

I knock once, twice, and then wait.

Silence.

The shuffling comes to a swift halt.

"Stevie?"

Silence.

"Stevie, it's Karla. I was hoping to speak with you for a moment."

The porch boards creak beneath my shifting weight. I start to knock again but then think better of it, deciding instead to try something else.

Toward the walkway, several clay pots line the steps. Their once green occupants have wilted a little with the whiplash weather coming with the season, hot at noon and cold by the evening.

Perfect.

I take a careful step and give one of the bigger containers a slight nudge when I do, sending it cascading over and causing a sort of domino effect with two more of the planters. They each shatter loudly when they hit the concrete steps, and shards go everywhere. I take a quick leap back onto the porch and try to seem bewildered.

The door swings open, and Stevie steps out.

"What the fuck, Karla?"

I lift my hands in mock surrender. "It was an accident, I swear! My heel caught on the edge of one of those dang steps, and the pot just...took the others with it."

Stevie narrows her eyes, scanning the fragments like they are a murder scene and I'm holding the smoking gun. "Well, those shoes are super impractical. Do you normally launch garden ware to get someone's attention, or am I just special?"

I force a sarcastic smile. "Only for you, darling."

She doesn't return the sentiment, but she doesn't close the door in my face either. Stevie crosses her arms and leans against the doorframe, waiting.

This is my opening.

I swallow my pride and try to mold my voice into something soft and sincere.

"Look," I say. "About last night...I really am sorry. I shouldn't have gone down there. I just—" I pause, trying to find a half-truth to carry the weight of this lie. "My mom...I told you she used to be friends with Mrs. Lowe."

Stevie's eyes visibly narrow at where I might be going with this.

"Even back then, she kept the doll parts down there," I say. "At least, that's how I remember it. I used to sneak down there while they were gossiping in the kitchen. It was like my very own forbidden playroom. I would mix and match them. I felt like, one day, I'd create the perfect little doll. This one's eyes, that one's hair..."

I trail off, eyes searching the porch rail like it will help me find the words.

"Something about seeing that basement just kind of pulled me in. I forgot myself for a minute. I wasn't trying to snoop. I was just... somewhere else. In my head. Do you know what I mean?"

"Yeah." Stevie's posture hasn't relaxed, but her eyes have. A little. Just enough to allow a sliver of hope.

What moment does she get lost in?

"I'm sorry," I say. "It won't happen again."

She adjusts the strap on her backpack. "What do you want, Karla? I was on my way out."

I nod toward the camera in my hands. "I was hoping you could take a look at this. It's busted, and I don't really know what I'm doing yet."

This gets her attention. "You take pictures now?" The faintest smile tugs at the corners of her mouth.

"You made it look so cool. I thought it'd be good for me. Getting out of the house. Finding a...hobby. I thought I even had a friend who might show me the ropes." I glance up, catching her eyes, and watch them soften a little more.

She seems almost...guilty.

Stevie sighs and motions toward the camera. I pass it to her, and our fingers brush against each other lightly. I try to ignore it, steadying my breathing.

She studies the camera, turning it over slowly. "You really did a number on it."

I offer a half shrug. "I was trying to take a picture of a snake and dropped it."

"A snake?" she asks, arching a brow.

"Yeah."

"Hmm, well...this crack along the lens? That's going to cost a pretty penny to fix. You might be better off replacing the entire thing."

I nod, disappointed but trying not to let it show.

"But," she continues, handing it back, "if it were mine, I'd leave it. Damage like this can cause light leaks that could give you something pretty unusual. Sometimes, it's the damage that makes the art."

I take the camera from her and run my finger along the crack. "Thanks," I say, turning to go. I step off the porch, one foot on the walkway, the other still suspended in a kind of limbo, when she speaks again.

"Look, come with me today," she says.

I freeze, trying to figure out if I heard what I thought I did.

"You can see for yourself. You may want to change your shoes, though."

CHAPTER

SEVENTEEN

We make it downtown just as the sun begins casting those long, cinematic shadows, like everything is being slowly erased from the ground up. The storefronts are already glowing, signs humming, a few people milling around with that late-afternoon daze that always makes a place feel suspended in time. The five o'clock rush has come and gone, and now it's like the city is exhaling. Stevie says it is called the "Golden Hour."

My shoes tap against the sidewalk—sharp, deliberate.

"I actually like those...like, a lot. Where'd you get them?" Stevie nods toward my feet when I climb in the passenger seat of her Altima.

"Thanks! I bought them at a secondhand shop online." What I don't tell her is that the black and white saddle shoes are now the only things I own that have a drop of black in them. Well, almost. I guess Stevie's side-slit dress counts too. It's an acquired taste, but gazing at them now, the color is growing on me.

We wander without a map, using Stevie's eye as a compass,

following the light and whatever catches her attention. She shoots a peeling mural of Elvis Presley, which looms behind a crumbling laundromat wall. His once vibrant skin and jeweled suit blur into the chipped brick, as if even the King himself is trying to slip away unnoticed. There's something beautiful in the decay, like a shrine to what fame forgot—how people, even legends, fade, flake by flake, until only ghosts of applause remain.

And to think I've lived here my entire life and didn't even know it was there. Artists really do see the world differently. Or maybe they simply see the world while the rest of us walk around with blinders on.

I take a photo of an abandoned baby stroller tipped sideways, like it had been forgotten mid-chaos. This was at Stevie's urging to "Just point and shoot" when I asked how she found her subjects. It's hardly as poetic as the mural. It's more likely that the thing fell off some bumpkin's truck.

Neither of us talks for a while, but surprisingly, it isn't awkward. It's the kind of comfortable silence you have to earn. I won't poke at your scars if you don't poke at mine.

A group of teenagers skate past, laughing like the world is a game they've already won. Stevie watches them with this look on her face, half fond and half something else. Something a little... bruised?

"You okay?" I ask.

She gives me a crooked smile. "Yeah. Just remembering a version of myself that used to be like that."

"You were a skater girl?"

"I hate that word. It's very reminiscent of Avril in her 'Rock Chick' phase." She smiles. "But yes, briefly. One summer, I broke my wrist. I did not feel very tough for the next six months. I cried like a bitch."

I laugh before I can help it. "You? Cry?"

"Insufferably. I made it my entire personality."

"Do you have any cool scars?"

Stevie holds out her wrist to me. There's a raised line of skin running along the side I somehow missed before. "They had to put a steel bar to replace the crushed bone. I can't bend my wrist at all."

"That's awful."

"Nah. It's fine. I can throw a mean punch now. Don't feel anything."

"Because, *of course*, you've practiced."

"You won't catch me in these streets unprepared." She winks at me.

"I wish I'd known you then," I say after a moment, thinking of my own life at that age.

To be fair, I don't believe I was someone Stevie would have been friends with back then, but the thought is nice, that this cool, edgy skater girl could see the real me and want to hang out. I wonder if she would have been friends with Emma instead.

I don't like that thought as much, so I push it out of my head as quickly as it slithered in.

She glances up at me like she might say something back. Something real. But then she turns and lifts her camera again. I follow her gaze.

A man sits slumped against a brick wall, lighting a cigarette with trembling fingers. Beside him is a German Shepherd, upright, alert, proud in a way the man isn't. The man has something hanging around his neck.

Dog tags, I realize after closer inspection.

"That," Stevie says softly, lowering her camera. "That's a story."

She moves like she's approaching a wild animal, slow and reverent. Then she hesitates and turns to me, nodding toward my own camera.

"Me?"

"Yeah. Come on. Just—Here."

She steps in close behind me, too close, one hand curling gently around my wrist to guide it. Her fingers are warm. Her breath brushes along my ear. The scent of her shampoo settles in my senses like a drug.

I am supposed to be focusing on the shot. On the man and his dog. The way their loneliness matches yet contrasts in the most beautiful way. But all I can think about is the way she feels. Her body right behind me. Her fingers brushing across mine like a secret.

"Not too wide," she whispers. "See how his hand is resting on the leash? That's the connection. Frame that."

I click. Twice. The camera shutters and vibrates under my fingers. She steps back, and I can breathe again. She doesn't say anything when I turn to face her. Stevie is still staring at the man and his dog with this strange look in her eye. Before I can stop myself, I raise the camera once more and click.

The sound of the shutter brings her eyes to me, back to reality.

"I don't like being photographed," she says, her voice sharp.

"I'm sorry. You just looked so—"

"I don't care what I look like."

"I'm sorry." I lower my head.

Her eyes flutter, and she turns around.

"You talk about stories," I say. "About how you try to capture them in your photos. Well, you've got one too."

She pivots back to me, her expression unreadable. "Maybe not everyone's." Her eyes flick away, finding a crack in the sidewalk to study.

It isn't the kind of thing you say with a laugh or a smirk or even a wink. It lands like a dropped coin on concrete—hard and echoing in the growing chasm between us. It's insane how quickly the bridge collapses. I don't push, just put the camera strap back over my shoulder.

"You hungry?" she asks after a beat.

Subject changed.

"Starving." It's true. It is a couple of hours past my dinner time.

She grins, and just like that, whatever wall crept up between us has evaporated. "Come on. I know a place that'll blow your little health-nut mind."

We walk in step, the air turning cooler. The sun finishes sinking behind the aged buildings. A kid plays drums on upside-down buckets in front of a pawn shop. A man in a velvet suit shouts poetry at passing cars. It's all weird and beautiful and slightly broken. Just like everything I grow to love.

I should really get out more.

Stevie talks about the diner she is taking me to. About how Bodhi loves their fries and the jukebox and the fact the owner calls everyone "Sugar," like it's their actual name. Bodhi knows she does it to everyone, but it tickles him to death when she does it anyway.

But I'm not really listening. I'm watching her eyes.

There is something in them now I didn't notice before. Something I've only ever recognized in the mirror. It isn't just sadness.

Sadness is easy to spot in others. It cries. It clings. This is much quieter. This is grief in disguise. A sort of melancholy that drips from your bones no matter how many jokes you tell or how many beautiful photos you take. The kind that comes from a great loss.

It isn't just about Simon. It *can't* be. Affairs are practically currency these days. Everyone's had one. Everyone's lied about one. It doesn't sit behind your eyes like that unless it's something darker. Something sharp-edged and buried.

Stevie has a story, all right. And it's bad enough that she's buried it deep down inside of her.

If I'm going to dig it out, I'm going to have to try harder than I thought.

CHAPTER

EIGHTEEN

Our waiter resembles Simon. Or what I imagine Simon must have looked like before the cigarettes and whatever quiet rebellion he keeps bottled up inside. This boy is dressed entirely in black, tall but not imposing, a head full of brown curls which spring happily on his head when he walks.

He doesn't speak right away, just gestures to our table in the alleyway—yes, an *actual* alleyway—and lets us seat ourselves. The place is called Vozelli's, which sounds like a word you'd shout in a dream or right before falling out of one. The kitchen door is literally a slab cut into the brick wall, and the only thing separating the chefs from the town rats is a swinging screen door smacking shut every few minutes, like a lazy heartbeat.

The tables are mismatched. The string lights above them flicker just enough to make the place feel intimate or haunted—I can't tell which. There's a jukebox humming something slow and brassy. Old jazz. The kind that makes you feel like you're walking in slow motion through someone else's memory. It's not Joey Quinones and Thee Sinseers, but it's not bad.

"I have to pee," Stevie says, already turning away. "Order me a strawberry daiquiri, will you?"

"But aren't you driving?" I try to ask.

She's already too far away to hear me, toward a hallway that looks like it leads to nowhere. When she disappears, I set my camera on the table, careful not to allow the lens cap to roll. A voice breaks through the ambiance of the music.

"You a photographer?"

I turn in the direction of the voice, and there he is again, curly hair, black shirt, the lingering suggestion of something dangerous made safe by youth. This boy hasn't even had his first heartbreak. Looking at him now, I realize he reminds me more of Bodhi than Simon. He's closer, studying the camera with the same curiosity Bodhi has.

"I am, actually."

"That's cool. Would I have seen any of your work?"

"Maybe. I typically do black and white candid shots, but I just follow the art, you know?"

He nods, thoughtful. "Dope. I want to be a photographer too. I'm saving up my tips to get a nice camera."

"You can start earning that tip by getting me an unsweetened tea with lemon." I surprise myself with how parched I feel. "And a strawberry daiquiri for my friend. She'll be back in a moment."

"Yes, ma'am." He crouches beside me until we're eye level.

It's too intimate. I flinch inwardly.

"Unsweet tea. Lemon. Strawberry daiquiri. Do you need a moment to look over the menu?"

I do, but before I can answer, Stevie reappears.

"Well, what are you having?" She takes the seat opposite me and opens her menu.

I snort, flipping the menu around for her. "Penne for Your Thoughts? Hot and Bothered Alfredo? Ravioli Me Softly?"

Her laugh is quick and sharp. "Fifty Shades of Linguini. It's great, right?"

"The Slippery When Wet Noodles do sound delicious."

"Bold choice." Stevie nods up at our waiter, arching a brow. "And the Ooh La Lasagna for me."

"Coming right up, ladies." He winks, taking both of our menus with him.

We're still snickering when a woman approaches the table. She's tall, blond, and bronzed, like she belongs on a beach somewhere instead of some dimly lit alleyway. Her waves fall softly across her shoulders. A geometric tattoo wraps around her neck and down onto her collarbone.

For one breathless second, I think she might be her. The girl in the photograph. But this woman's older. Her hair less aggressive. Her eyes less lost.

"This seat taken?" the woman chimes, placing a hand on the empty chair between us.

"Oh my God!" Stevie stands, smiling wide, and they embrace for longer than necessary. "When did you get in town?"

I don't catch the name or the rest of the high-pitched exchange. An uncomfortable pinch of jealousy bursts in my chest, spreading and tightening while it bleeds into my veins.

Of course, she has other friends. Cool friends from the city, with tattoos and late-night schedules, just like them. It was stupid of me to think otherwise. I bet this friend is still allowed inside Stevie's home. But I wouldn't invite her over, that's for sure. Stevie's beautiful, but this girl could give her a run for her money if she wanted. I wonder if Simon has ever asked her to undress for him.

I think about the messages Simon sent me last night.

You are so sexy.

I read it twice. Three times. Let it root in me like a dare. That thread of power pulling tight.

???

Where did you go?

Open the damn curtain.

Tease.

You can't leave me like this. Just a peek.

There's something about abandoning him, reeling, that thrills me still.

"—and this is Karla," Stevie says, pulling me from my spiral.

They're both looking at me. Expectantly. I've missed something. "Sorry, what?"

Stevie smiles a little too wide. "Karla. This is Nikki, my friend from Arizona."

Friend. I stand more confidently. "Nice to meet you." I reach out my hand to shake hers.

Nikki seems startled by the formality but obliges me anyway. She nods, brushing a loose curl behind her ear. "Nice to meet you too. I'm only in town for a couple of weeks, so I have to run, but I'll still see you tomorrow?" She returns her attention to Stevie.

Stevie's mouth twitches at that. "Yeah. Come by."

While Nikki disappears into the crowd, I lean in. "What's tomorrow?"

Stevie hesitates. "Simon and his band are playing at O'Keefe's."

"That sounds fun." I say it lightly, leaving the silence wide enough for an invitation to land.

She finally breaks. "Do you...want to come?"

I pretend to think. "I don't even know if I have anything to wear to a rock show."

"I'm sure you'll figure it out."

Then something shifts. Stevie is no longer looking at me. She's gazing through me...or over my shoulder, rather. Her eyes darken.

And then I hear them too.

"Is that Stevie? I just can't believe she's here," a voice behind me hisses. "You'd think after what she did to Heather that bitch wouldn't show her smug face around here anymore."

I freeze.

Two young women sit at a table a few spaces from ours. The blond is trembling. Shoulders stiff, fingers fussing with her bun, her other hand picking at a cuticle, like she's peeling back a memory she doesn't want.

Her friend leans in. "You have every right to say something. She shouldn't be here. This is where Heather worked, for Christ's sake."

"I should." Her voice breaks. She's crying now. "It's just not fair. She's out here living her life while my sister is just...I just hate her so much." Her shoulders shake.

Her friend rushes around the table to embrace her. "Come with me. Let's get you cleaned up."

They vanish into the bathroom hallway. The string lights flicker again. While they pass, Stevie keeps her eyes forward, staring at the centerpiece on the table, her face sickly pale.

"Do you know them?" I ask.

She doesn't answer. Just says, "We have to go."

"But...our food—"

"I have to go, *damn it*. With or without you." Her voice slices through me.

With the most subtle of glances toward the table with the girls, she turns and walks away. I start to follow but then stop. If I leave, who's going to pay? I can't just dine and dash. Especially since I haven't even dined yet.

Our waiter returns with our drinks, looking confused. "Is everything okay?"

"Looks like it'll just be me, after all," I say, slightly embarrassed, but I don't know why. He nods and begins to return to the kitchen with Stevie's daiquiri, but I reach my hand out. "No. Leave that."

The waiter smiles and places the second drink in front of me. I take a sip, and the icy sweetness washes down my throat. Not bad. He turns to walk away, but again, I stop him.

"Can I ask you a question?"

"Sure."

"Do you know a girl who used to work here? Heather...something?"

"Heather Crosp. Yeah. I knew of her. She was gone before I started."

"Where did she go?"

"No one knows. She disappeared."

"Disappeared?"

"Yeah. Just vanished apparently. There was a missing person report and everything."

"And no one knows what happened?"

"Nope. But people have theories." He crouches again.

I lean back. "What kind of theories?"

"I think it's mostly small-town stuff, but one of the cooks said she was seeing someone. Really secretive. No pics, no name. But she said he was married, so..."

"And the police?"

"They questioned someone. Some public figure. Never released their name." He squints at me. "Why are you asking this anyway?"

"Just a morbid curiosity." I glance at his tag. "Thank you, Gabriel. Good luck with the camera."

I hand him a twenty and pull out my phone the moment he walks away, typing "Heather Crosp" into my search bar. Headlines flood my screen, some dating back as far as six months ago.

Local Girl Missing

Search For Missing Blair County Girl Intensifies

Have You Seen Me?

One photo in particular makes me gasp.

Ruby lips. Wild blond curls in a scrunchie. Striking blue eyes which pierce right through the screen.

It's her. From the darkroom photos. From the painting.

And Bodhi's sketchbook?

Gabriel is right. None of the articles I find list who the person of interest was.

As with all things, when there is a gap in information, we begin to tell our own. Could it be Simon? He and Stevie aren't married, though. Simon was married once before, to the Mom Blogger, but how long did Stevie say they had been together? Did she ever mention it? I click out of the articles and arrange for a taxi to come and get me.

Something inside my brain is screaming to leave this alone. I try my best to push it from my mind the entire ride home. After all, I should be furious with Stevie for leaving me to fend for myself like that. Women should never abandon their friends at night. There are dangerous people out there.

Even as I eagerly but carefully pull my first photographs from the developer and hang them on the string above my station, just like hers, I can't shake the growing suspicion that something is wrong. I stare at the portrait I took of Stevie, her face becoming clearer by the moment.

She's hiding something. I can see it in her eyes, but I'm not a detective or a private investigator. If anything, I'm just a nosy neighbor. But there's something else whispering...

Look a little closer. Get a better angle.

If anyone knows what it's like to keep secrets in the dark, it's me.

I kept my mother's secret for years. Detectives don't know what to look for when it comes to certain people. It's like they're blinded by beauty and privilege. They see a pretty face, a nice neighborhood, or a beautiful house, and they get sloppy. But I know what kind of evil can be hidden behind those doors.

In the end, it's the whisper that is the loudest.

CHAPTER

NINETEEN

I give myself another once-over in the mirror.

"I can feel your judgment all the way from in here, Mother." I apply another layer of mascara to my not completely unsuccessful attempt at a smoky eye. "It's a night out. This is how people dress for a night out."

But I'm not sure if that's correct. I've never been good at this kind of thing. You're supposed to "sex up" any outfit worn after nine o'clock, and I have very few things that can be sexed up in any way. I'm not dressed like a common streetwalker or anything, but I did manage to take in the hem of one of my favorite red dresses, a vintage number I found while thrifting a few years ago. It resembles the blue dress Marilyn Monroe wore in *Gentlemen Prefer Blondes*.

I figure if Marilyn can wear something like it and look like a goddess, then I have a shot at doing the same, even if I don't show an awful lot of skin. Then again, we all can aspire to look as dazzling as Marilyn, and we all will inevitably fall short.

Still, the dress doesn't look half bad like this. Now if I can only quit tugging at the hem.

My mother never approved of the fabric being so tight around the bustline, but she can just get over it. I'm not a child anymore, and I can wear whatever I want.

The red dress is paired with black platform Mary Janes.

I peek in at Mother while I pass her room. She is sleeping soundly. I close the door with a gentle click and leave her to rest.

O'Keefe's is nothing like it was the last time I was here. It's packed, and the stench of alcohol, sweaty people, and burgers lingers like a cloud over the crowd of patrons. The sound of their laughter and the sharp clink of glass rise above the muffled thrum of the juke-box, their volume only to be rivaled by the incessant cheering of a crowd gathered around the bar in front of three televisions featuring various sports.

While I'm not the biggest fan of crowds, I admit it's easy to hide in them, at least until I can figure out what my next move is.

I take a seat at one of the far-end stools along the bar. Only a few people are in this area—the TV is almost impossible to see from this corner. I place my clutch on the counter.

A familiar face appears from the back.

"Ash!" I say as she passes.

She's carrying two towers of draft glasses but stops at the sound of her name. Her face falls when she sees me.

"Hey. It's Karla, from the other day. Stevie's friend." I can't tell by her expression if she remembers me or not, but the look isn't welcoming at all.

"Yeah..." she responds, drawling out the word longer than necessary. "Stevie's *neighbor*. I remember. I'm going to just..." She gestures to the glass towers in her arms and begins placing them underneath the bar.

"Of course." I smile. "So, how have you been?"

"Peachy."

But I don't think she's really been peachy. Gen Z doesn't use that term unironically. There's an edge in her tone that I can't place, but it sounds a lot like annoyance.

"Is Stevie around?"

'Uh huh." She doesn't look at me.

Astrada takes three of the draft glasses, places them on the bar, and begins filling them with various liquids. She slides them into the crowd, and I'm surprised when a set of hands grabs them. Astrada immediately begins filling three more. She doesn't look toward me again. After all, she's being pulled in every direction, so I don't blame her for being busy.

"You came," someone yells in my ear.

With the rest of the noise in the bar, the volume is necessary, but still. I turn and find Simon standing there, looking like a rock star. His black hair is disheveled, but it suits him. He's wearing a plain white T-shirt and a leather jacket. The most surprising part is there aren't any holes in it.

"Stevie mentioned she told you about tonight."

"She did."

"You look...nice." His eyes gaze up and down. They may as well be a blowtorch on my skin. He hasn't messaged me any more since that night.

To be honest, I hadn't really prepared to see him. The last thing I need tonight is an awkward encounter with Simon. It's going to be weird enough seeing Stevie after she stormed off yesterday.

"Thanks."

"Let me get you a drink." Our arms brush against each other when he turns to Astrada. "Hey, Ash...Can I get a drink for my friend? Whatever the lady wants."

Her eyes dart between Simon and me, her eyebrows raised slightly, and I feel a hint of something satisfying in my gut. *Friend*.

"A Manhattan," I call out to her, then smile, tilting my head to one side.

"Coming right up." She pops her lips on the last word. Astrada begins mixing my drink, but she is watching us.

"Thank you for the drink."

"It's no problem." He leans in a little closer. "I know the manager."

As if being summoned, Stevie enters the bar area from the kitchen and immediately catches sight of the two of us. She appears taken aback for a moment, and I'm not sure if it's because I'm here or because Simon is standing so close.

"Karla..." she says.

Ash crosses between us, placing my drink in front of me.

"What the lady wants, the lady gets," she says, cocking an eyebrow at Simon before returning to the particularly rambunctious group of men yelling for beer.

Simon doesn't seem to notice the gesture, or if he did, he doesn't seem to care.

"My set's about to start. Gotta go." He leans over the bar and kisses Stevie's cheek.

She smiles, but it's noncommittal. He winks before disappearing into the crowd.

In spite of the noise in the bar, it seems eerily quiet being left with Stevie. I'm not sure what I wanted out of coming here, but it wasn't awkward silence. After all, *she* invited *me*.

"You're here?" she says finally, with the inflection of a question, getting right to the point.

It throws me off base so much I don't know how to respond. Is she serious right now?

"You invited me." I tilt my head as if it's the strangest thing she has ever said because it is. How do you invite someone to an event and then get upset when they show up?

"I did. But after—I didn't think you'd show up."

"Why wouldn't I? If anything, I'm just confused. I was hoping maybe you and I could talk about what happened." I take a sip of my drink, attempting to keep my tone casual, and it's glorious.

Astrada really knows how to make a Manhattan.

"I'm not sure we have anything to talk about." She crosses her arms.

"Really, Stevie? Those girls—"

"What girls?"

Being gaslit by men is expected. Being gaslit by my mother is a typical Tuesday. But there's something particularly burning about being gaslit by Stevie.

"Right. Well...I guess I'm a little crazier than I thought." And crazy attracts crazy, Stevie. Maybe you already know that.

An electrical sound rips through the crowd, silencing everyone and releasing me from the tension in Stevie's stare. We all collectively look toward the stage, where the sound originated.

Simon is standing there, instrument in hand. He grins with a million-dollar smile before strumming the guitar, sending an eruption of cheers and whistles from the crowd. The band behind him follows his lead, and the crowd eats it up. A shoulder slams into me when the sports crowd scrambles to join the stage floor all at once.

I down the rest of my drink to keep from spilling it. A shot glass is put in its place. I look up. Stevie is throwing hers back already. I don't even bother to say anything. She wouldn't hear me anyway. Instead, I toss the burning liquid into my throat and do my best not to vomit.

Stevie blows a kiss to Simon, who pretends to reach up and catch it. I blush when he takes his hand over the crotch of his pants in a lewd gesture before continuing the set.

The song isn't familiar to me, but everyone else in the bar seems to be familiar with it. When I look back at Stevie to see her reaction, she is at the other end of the bar, handing out shots to a group of girls who seem to be celebrating an engagement, if the veil on the woman in front is to be considered context.

Another shot has been placed in front of me. She's just trying to get me drunk. That doesn't stop me from swallowing it. This time, I actually almost do puke, so this will be my last.

She crosses back over and hands me a third. I only pretend to shoot it. When Stevie isn't looking, I pour it on the floor beneath the bar. It's not like anyone will notice in this crowd.

Simon's band performs two more songs, each one louder than the other, before handing it over to the next performer. The crowd dissipates, but only slightly.

That's when I spot her.

I haven't seen her in years, but I would recognize her anywhere. The moon-shaped scar framing the left side of her face is like a flashing neon sign, reminding me of who she is and how it got there.

How *I* got here.

Emma Davies.

CHAPTER

TWENTY

She saw me. I *know* she saw me.

She's with another woman, smiling brightly. They make their way to my location at the bar.

I turn a little too quickly, completely oblivious to another shot glass that has been placed in front of me. The glass tips, sending the feral liquid everywhere. A couple sitting a little too close to me jump up from their seats, cursing. The alcohol spills over onto their clothing.

"What the fuck is your problem!" a burly man in a now soaked jersey shouts.

The woman he's with is wearing way too much makeup and scrambles to grab her bag from the bar, but it's too late. The alcohol drips onto the floor in front of her, and she glares at me beneath thick black eyelashes.

There's so much commotion in the bar it's hard to believe this little scene was enough to attract as many eyes to me as it did. But when I glance around, several people are watching, including Stevie,

Astrada, and Emma. We lock eyes, and I know she recognizes me. She's giving me that look...

Such a pretty thing. It's such a shame about her. She's crazy. Crazy. Crazy. Crazy.

I thumb the scar on my hand until it burns. Their faces swim and distort, and my breath catches in my lungs. I remove myself from the bar stool. My legs are like jelly, so I use the stool to brace myself. The taunting continues.

"Are you all right?" Stevie's voice. She is standing right in front of me, but she may as well be underwater.

"I'm fine," I respond, more to myself than to her. "Where's your bathroom?"

She points toward the back of the building, where a flashing neon sign says "Restrooms," with an arrow pointing down a hallway. I don't look toward Emma again, but I can feel her eyes on me, more than anyone else in the room.

Once in the bathroom, away from most of the chaos, I begin to catch my breath again. I take a seat on a sticker toilet and gather myself. The bathroom is small, barely enough room for one person, the toilet, and a sink. The narrow walls made of plywood are painted black and layered in thick, multicolored graffiti, gum, and other questionable fluids. It's not an ideal place to recenter, but it'll have to do.

Despite my aversion to the grotesque aspects of this place, I don't find it *completely* unbearable. In fact, it's a little intriguing, a stark contrast from my clean-cut aquarium of a neighborhood. This is exactly the kind of place I've always been told to avoid, yet here I am, recovering from a panic attack while sitting on a sticker toilet.

Of all the places to run into Emma again after all these years, this was never what I expected. Seeing someone you used to love is like having the scab ripped from a wound which has only partially healed. It's not until then that you realize how delicate conviction is and how quickly it can be undone.

With a few deep breaths and a splash of water on my face, the room is finally stationary. The alcohol buzzes in my bloodstream, but it isn't enough to warrant whatever that was. That was all Emma.

It's exactly what happened last time. I need to get out of here. If there's one thing the previous incident taught me, it's that there is never a room big enough for us both to be in. Emma means trouble, and if she's here, I can't be anymore.

When I finally emerge from the bathroom, the crowd has dispersed, but only slightly. There's no sign of Emma anywhere. Stevie is leaning her elbows on the bar, and Simon is in front of her, closely listening to something she's saying. Whatever it is, it's serious. He furrows his brows and nods in agreement.

Just when I'm about to be in earshot, they stop talking and look up at me.

"I was about to come in there and see if you were still alive." Stevie and Simon share a look.

It's quick, unreadable. I wonder if I'm what they were talking about so intently.

"I'm good," I say, drawing out the last word. I stumble a little, landing heavily on the barstool. "I think I may have just been a bit... over-served."

I lean into Simon and point my clutch at Stevie. My body shifts, and the stool teeters a little. I make a show of struggling to brace myself on Simon's shoulder. He immediately catches me, his arm resting around my hip.

"It's your girlfriend's fault."

"Whoa there, lightweight." We both laugh, and he steadies me back on the barstool.

My stomach hurts from giggling so much, but if I want this to work, I have to sell it.

"Have a shot with me!" I say, patting the bar in front of me.

Stevie snaps a knowing look at Simon before responding. "I think you've had enough. Are you going to be able to get home?"

"I made it here, didn't I?"

"You can't drive, Karla."

"I'm fine." I draw out the last word again. "Just one more shot with me, and then you can cut me off."

"Or I can cut you off right now and get you a ride home." Stevie is already pulling out her phone. "Shit."

"What is it?"

"The Uber can't be here for another hour. I'm going to be another two hours at least, and I already sent Ash home."

"You don't have to worry about me! Seriously, I'll be oka—" I move to stand and catch my foot on the side of my heel, sending me sideways.

Again, Simon catches me.

"I'll take you home." He helps me back to my feet.

"Are you sure?" Stevie asks, but I notice the relief on her face.

"Yeah. I was heading that way anyway. Plus, we can't exactly put her in the car with a stranger like this."

"Unless *you're* the stranger and *I'm* the drunk girl, huh?" she says, cocking an eyebrow at him.

"I was a perfect gentleman." Simon places his hand on his heart.

"If that's you being a gentleman, then I need you to be the opposite of that." Stevie crosses her arms.

"Yes, ma'am." He chuckles, standing from his stool.

"I'm serious, Simon. Take her home. That's *it*."

"What else am I going to do, Stevie?"

She doesn't answer. The silence resting between them like a fog is answer enough.

"All right, lightweight. Let's get you home."

What We Do in Secret

CHAPTER

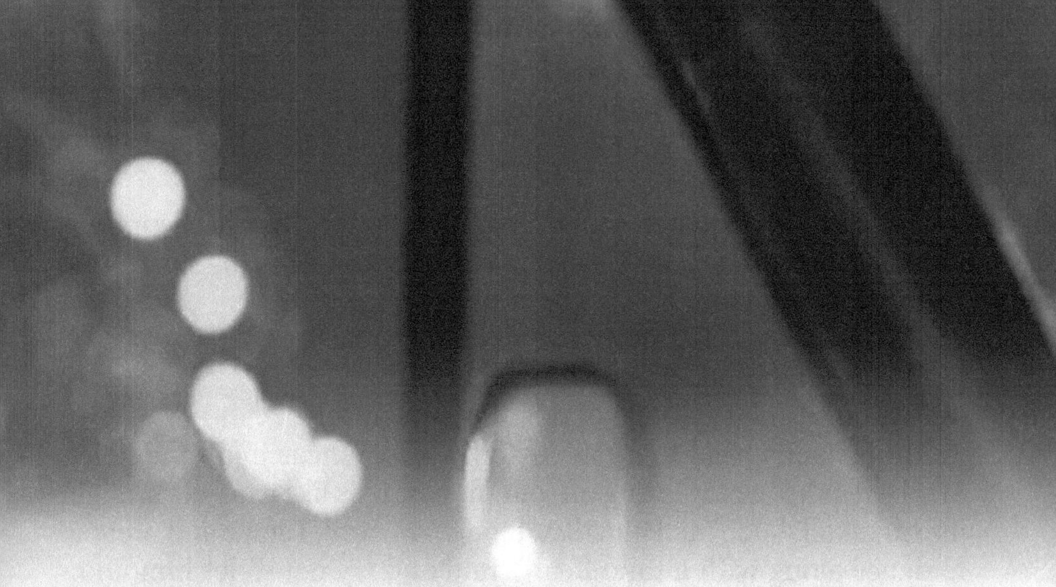

TWENTY-ONE

The inside of Simon's clunky black van smells faintly of beer, cologne, and rubber. It should repulse me, but instead, I inhale it into my lungs until I can't anymore. He has to move several items from the passenger side for me to sit down on the torn leather seat beside him. Simon apologizes and tells me he normally doesn't have passengers.

My chest is still tight from my little breakdown at O'Keefe's. I hate that Stevie saw me like that. I hate that *anyone* saw me like that.

Control your impulses, Karla. It's the only way you will ever be free. Dr. McCoy's voice echoes in my head.

I haven't been doing the best job of that lately, but then again, I'm sure Dr. McCoy didn't bet on me running into Emma Davies in the most unlikely of places.

Another thought sparks in my head. Surely, that isn't considered a violation of the restraining order? I had no idea she'd be there. How *could* I have known?

I need a distraction.

"Stevie doesn't ever ride with you?"

"Yeah. Sometimes, but she hates The Beast."

"Don't tell me you named your van 'Beast.'"

"*The* Beast. Don't call her out of her name. She's sensitive." He runs a hand gently along the steering wheel.

Simon turns the keys, and the engine roars to life in a cacophony of noises. It sounds a lot like people screaming while being ground up in a metal torture box made of nails.

"What is this?" I attempt to yell over the racket.

"Metal. It's good. Just give it a chance."

"It sounds like a bunch of demons screaming."

He bobs his head to a melody only he can hear in all the noise. Maybe it's the buzz wearing off, but the sound is like a needle straight into my skull. I don't tell him that, though. Instead, I smile and pretend to dance along with a tune I can't find and try not to let him know I've caught on to the stolen glances he keeps giving my thigh.

My stupid hem rides up when I move, and I make no attempt to fix it. In a strange way I don't quite understand right now, I like him looking. His eyes may as well be his tongue licking the skin where he's watching me.

When we pull into my driveway, I lean back in the seat and face him. He kills the van, silencing the godawful music, if you can call it that, and we are immediately surrounded in silence. Simon throws the keys in the cup holder and looks over at me.

"Safe and sound, as promised." He smiles.

"And such a gentleman," I say, mirroring their conversation from earlier.

The corners of his lips pull up in a grin, but he doesn't respond.

"I had fun tonight." I sigh, partially to pierce the silence in the van. "I'm glad Stevie invited me."

"To be honest, she didn't think you'd really come."

"Are you glad I did?"

"Of course," he says, but it's not convincing. Maybe he feels guilty for what happened between us.

I should get out now, should get out so he can go back to the bar or home or wherever it is he wants to go. But something is holding me here, anchored to this seat.

I want to ask him about Heather, want to tell him about the girls at the restaurant. If I asked him if he was questioned in her disappearance, would he tell me the truth? Do I really want to ask him something like that at all while I'm so alone with him?

What I really want to ask him about are the sketches in Bodhi's notebook, but something tells me that those are dead-end subjects. All of them. The kind that makes people shut down like a fortress rather than open up.

So, I don't ask him about her. I don't ask him anything that will make him want to leave. I don't want him to go yet...*can't* let him go yet. He is my only way back into Stevie's life. My only way back into Bodhi's life.

Bodhi...

"So, where's Bodhi tonight?"

"He's with his mom. He'll be back on Tuesday."

"Is he your only child?"

"The one and only." Simon finally turns his head toward me. "You seem surprised."

"No, not surprised. It's just..."

"Just what?"

"I don't know. I'm an only child too. It wasn't bad, just kind of lonely. You never considered having another one with your ex...or Stevie?"

"Stevie? No!" He practically laughs. "She doesn't want kids of her own. Bodhi is already too much of a challenge for...Anyway. My ex wanted more, but after Bodhi was born, things changed with her."

"What kind of things?"

"I don't know. She was fun before. Laid-back. After the kid, things got...serious."

"Kids can certainly change people. Not always for the better." I wonder if my mother would have been different if she hadn't had me. Would she have lost her mind as quickly, or was her unraveling inevitable and I had the misfortune of being a witness?

"We went from just enjoying each other to everything being by the book. I couldn't change the diaper right. I wasn't dressing him right. I wasn't swaddling him right. Then she started a blog, and suddenly everything in my life was monochromatic. Had to move all of my shit to one room to keep it out of the background of her pictures. I basically had a uniform for everything. Pictures, outings, birthdays... She started laying out my outfits like she was my fucking mother."

"That sounds...suffocating." I don't have to imagine what it was like. I know.

"It was. I didn't feel like me anymore. It didn't even feel like her, you know? I didn't even know who she was. So, hell no, I wasn't about to have another kid with her. I left. If I could have, I would have taken Bodhi with me. At least he has some semblance of normal now. He gets to eat pizza and wear the clothes he wants to when he's with me. He can just be a normal kid."

"I think it's beautiful that you gave him that. Sometimes, I wish when..." Sometimes, I wish when my dad left he would have taken me with him too. I try to say the words, but I stop just short. Rule #11: Never reveal anything. But he's finally talking to me. *Really* talking to me. Simon has even shifted his body to face me.

"What were you going to say?"

"I just know how you feel. I know how Bodhi must feel. I still wear my uniform." I gesture to the dress.

"That's why you always dress like a pin-up? Don't get me wrong. I think it's sexy as hell, but still."

Sexy?

"My mother had her own aesthetic. It just kind of...stuck."

"You could change it anytime you wanted, you know. She's gone. You're grown."

I don't want to talk about this anymore. But I also don't want him to leave yet.

"Do you want to come in for a nightcap?"

"I think you've had enough to drink for both of us tonight." Simon leans his head back on his seat.

My eyes sweep across the length of his neck, his lips. God, he really is beautiful, in a tragic sort of way. Against my better judgment, I can see why Stevie likes him. But it's more than that now. There's a wound we share that only someone with a similar hurt can sense. We both know what it's like to be made invisible by someone who is supposed to love you.

"I have a confession to make."

He seems momentarily taken aback. I am as well, by what I'm about to do. But I blame the liquid courage that Stevie has been forcing down my throat all night. I'm glad I stopped when I did. If I didn't, I might have been too inebriated by now to enjoy this.

"Oh?" He arches a brow.

"I'm not really that drunk. A little tipsy, maybe, but not drunk. I was faking it."

"You certainly seem to be fine now." Simon runs his hands along his jeans. He appears uncomfortable.

"I'm *more* than fine." I lean into him. His body stiffens when I run a finger along his arm, tracing the lines of ink in his skin.

"Why would you fake being drunk?"

"So I could get you alone." I keep my voice low.

"Now, why would you want to do that?" He grins and tilts his head toward me again.

I hover my mouth over his for a moment. He doesn't stop me or move away. Simon wants this. He's half smiling, almost daring me. I close my mouth over his, gently, and the contact erupts in my chest like a nuclear bomb.

His tongue fills my mouth then. He wraps his hands around my neck, holding me in place while he kisses me deeper. Deeper. Deeper. It's not enough. My body aches with the need to get him as close as I can.

As if reading my mind, he undoes his belt. I don't hesitate.

He pulls me onto his lap with one hand, and the other dips between my legs, moving my panties to the side. His mouth never leaves my skin. He's everywhere all at once. My neck, my shoulders, my breast...

I don't even realize he has pulled the top of my dress down until I feel his breath on my nipple. He pushes into me, and for a moment, I remember what Stevie's fingers felt like when she helped me adjust my camera.

We both let out a moan. I brace myself, one hand on the top of the van, and roll my hips into him in a way that makes us both cry out in euphoria.

Stevie's arms embracing me that first night we met, the way her skin still smelled of alcohol and her soap...Focus.

There's a fire between our legs, snaking its way through my veins and erupting from my skin in tiny, loud explosions.

I didn't know sex could be like this. Even the orderlies I played with at the hospital were quick, emotionless. Mainly on stairwells and in bathrooms. Somewhere we could be in and out without being seen.

It had been mechanical with them. No more passionate than a handshake. It was a business arrangement, after all. They got to sink their dick in me for twenty seconds, and I would get privileges in exchange. It was a win-win. But *this*...this is different.

Is this the way he fucks her? Is this why she stays when he's so easily tempted by other women? Are there other women? I have no proof of that, of course, but it seems someone who will randomly hook up with a neighbor in the middle of her driveway does it pretty often.

Stevie, you are so much better than this.

Each time he lets out a moan or sinks his teeth into my skin, my body reignites, but it's not with lust—not entirely anyway. At least some of it is anger. How can he cheat on someone as amazing as Stevie? How can he do that to her?

I grab him by the throat while he thrusts. With just a little bit of pressure, I could...

My skin is practically pulsing with anger and want and more rage. Beads of sweat form on us, and our skin becomes sticky and slick. We glide against each other. All of this is building up to something, and we don't dare stop until we get there.

If Stevie herself walked up to that window, I don't think we would have stopped.

Well, maybe for a moment.

"Karla..." He moans into my breast.

The sound of my name on his lips is like a trigger pulling me deeper. Stevie! What about Stevie? What about your girlfriend? Whore.

"Don't stop." I throw my head back and arch away from him, allowing Simon a full view of me.

He moves faster, his fingertips sinking into my hips, keeping up with my rhythm perfectly.

I feel dizzy. Can you pass out from sex? Has anyone ever died from this?

He grips my hips so tightly I am sure there will be bruises there in the morning, but I don't care. I am so high on this...this moment... that I would be happy to die with him inside me.

Simon moans my name one final, agonizing time and releases into me. The sound of his surrender is almost too much. Whatever had been building in me, it explodes between my legs, rippling through my body in shockwaves, and I cry out. Our bodies fall limp together, a tangle of sweat and skin.

"Fuck." He laughs quietly into my neck.

"We just did," I whisper in his ear before running my tongue along the rim.

"You really are crazy, you know that?"

"Then I guess you get hard for crazy." I wiggle my hips to prove a point.

"Oh, you have no idea." He kisses me before I can respond, growing hard again beneath me. "Now, get in the back."

CHAPTER

TWENTY-TWO

It's been four days. Even the worst two-timers text after three, right? At least, that's what they do in the movies. They call it the three-day rule. Doesn't that mean it's a rule?

If it is, maybe Simon is as passive with it as I've been with mine lately.

Stevie isn't texting me back either, but that's nothing new.

Ever since we exchanged numbers that first night, I've been having a one-sided conversation with myself, with the occasional "LOL" or smiley face emoji tossed in to keep me coming back. At first, I thought it was just because she was busy or sleeping, or she misplaced her phone again. But now I'm starting to think it's because she's avoiding me.

My last message to her, a generic TikTok encouraging people to share it with a friend they want to show appreciation for—a desperate grab for a response—is still showing unread. In fact, Stevie hasn't even looked at any of my messages in the last week. At this point, I would accept a lone reaction, but I'm not banking on it.

That's when the paranoia takes over. Does she know?

My texts with Simon are a bit newer. We didn't exchange numbers until the night we had sex in his van, to arrange to get my car—and to meet up again if we wanted a round two. I was trying to coordinate a time when we could potentially fulfill both those needs, but on Saturday morning, I woke up and it was in my driveway with the keys in it.

I texted to thank him for bringing it back, careful not to let my disappointment bleed into the words, and was met with a simple thumbs-up in response. He hasn't been ignoring me as hard as Stevie, but as the days have progressed, his single-word responses have dwindled from every message to every fifth one or so. Now I'm lucky to get the thumbs-up.

I'm irritated at their lack of consideration, and I'm frustrated that I have become so absorbed in them that I'm forgetting why I wanted to get closer to them in the first place.

Heather Crosp.

Like all people, most of her information was a simple Google search away. Heather was only seventeen years old, a kid. She had her entire life ahead of her. Heather was a dancer, a model, a sister.

If she didn't run away, if someone else is responsible for her disappearance, the most obvious answer would be her married boyfriend. The means imply the motive. It's always the love interest. *Always*.

Then again, they could have just run off together. A wife would certainly get in the way of a girlfriend. But that wouldn't explain why those girls at the restaurant were so angry about Stevie being there. Do they think her married boyfriend was Simon? With him and Stevie not being married, that part gets confusing. Yet I assumed they were when we met, so it can easily be an assumption others have made.

It would certainly explain why Stevie was questioned in relation to Heather's disappearance. But wouldn't Simon have been questioned as well? I didn't see anything about him being brought in, but I suppose police departments control what information gets revealed to the press. Why would they hide something like that?

I just don't think it's that simple this time.

Anyway, Heather was a kid! Simon wouldn't be involved with a minor. He may have his flaws and may not be the most loyal person, but he's a dad himself. I've watched him with Bodhi.

My stomach twists at the very thought. It's simply not true. He wouldn't be interested in someone that young, let alone hurt them or cause them to disappear into thin air. To be fair, I have a hard time picturing Stevie hurting one either, but I can understand why she would, if Simon had been messing around with her. More so than I can understand the opposite.

Stevie gave up *everything* to be with Simon. She lost her career, her reputation, her life in the city...everything. Just for some seventeen-year-old model to swoop in and take him away.

Every woman has a breaking point. Every woman will crack under the right amount of pressure. I'm not saying it's right. Just that I understand. Could Heather have been Stevie's breaking point?

I send Stevie a quick text.

Long overdue for a catch-up sesh. Let me know when you have a night off so we can arrange?

I hit send. While I don't have anything new going on—nothing I can tell her anyway—I'm sure Stevie has a ton she needs to get off her chest. The invitation is out there. Now to wait. It will give me another opportunity to ask her about Heather, if she seems open to it.

Was looking for your van in the drive earlier and didn't see it. I guess you're busy. Can't wait for next time X

That one is to Simon. He usually responds to the messages containing sexual innuendos a little quicker, but even those have been ignored today. I wonder what is going on over there. My heart sinks into my gut when I think of the only obvious explanation.

She found out. Stevie found out, and now they are both icing me out. Or maybe they realize I know about Heather, and that's why they aren't talking.

I open the curtains to look if their vehicles are in the drive. The Beast is still gone. Come to think about it, I haven't seen it in a couple of days. Maybe she discovered our secret and kicked him out. Wouldn't that mean he had even more opportunity to message me back? Stevie's Altima is in its usual place, which means she's probably sleeping.

Then I see him.

Bodhi is sitting beside his backpack on their front porch, his head resting on his fists. He looks absolutely miserable. The bus usually drops him off around 4:15, if it drops him off at all. The kid barely has any structure, but I assume his biological mother wants him as much as she can get him. Still, the door is usually unlocked for him by then.

I can tell he has just come from his mom's because he is wearing a white polo shirt with tan khakis and brown boots—Melissa Van Lowe's signature colors. It's nearly five now. Surely, Stevie and Simon didn't forget their own child. The poor thing is probably starving.

That's when I get an idea.

I open the door and head across the street.

What We Do in Secret

CHAPTER

TWENTY-THREE

"**I**'m sure they didn't forget you. They're probably just busy and lost track of time."

"Yeah, maybe," Bodhi says in an unconvincing tone.

He is sitting at the end of my kitchen table, patiently awaiting his dinner like a perfect gentleman, and has been telling me that his dad is usually the one who lets him in the house. Since he's out of town, Stevie may have forgotten Bodhi was coming today.

It explains why Simon's van has been gone for so long, but it doesn't explain how an innocent child can just be forgotten. If Stevie is ever going to be a good mother, she's going to have to start prioritizing Bodhi. I wonder where Simon went anyway.

"Why didn't you message your mother? Maybe she'll want to come and get you?" I ask, secretly hoping he hasn't called her because he doesn't *want* her to come and get him.

"Are you kidding me? With the way they fight already? No way."

"You're talking about your mom fighting with Stevie?"

"And Dad too. Sometimes, I hear them yelling on the phone."

"What do they fight about?" I ask as passively as possible while pulling the meatloaf from the oven.

The mouthwatering aroma fills the room, and Bodhi perks up. I place the pan on the wood block on the table and return to the kitchen to get the sides: butternut squash and vegetables covered in gravy and herbs, mashed potatoes, and every kid's favorite, macaroni and cheese.

"Mostly me. But they fight about other stuff too."

"What kind of other stuff?"

He shrugs his shoulders, done with the conversation.

"It's okay, buddy. If it makes you feel any better, all parents fight over one thing or another."

"Did your parents fight too?"

"Oh, yes. My parents fought so much that they couldn't bear to stay together. Both of them had a terrible temper. They were like fire and gasoline when they were together. Especially when they were drinking. In fact, they fought so bad the night my father left that he didn't even say goodbye."

I get lost in the memory of the last time I saw him.

"I was upstairs, and I could hear them yelling at each other. That was nothing new. But then, I heard a crash, and everything went silent. I was afraid, so I hid under the covers until I fell asleep. When I woke up, my mother was cooking breakfast. Pancakes and bacon. As she poured orange juice into my glass, she told me that my father had left us and wouldn't be returning. It wasn't until—"

Bodhi's expression tears me away from the memory.

"But that's nothing for a boy of your age to worry about. My father was a weak man who couldn't handle family life. Your dad loves you. He moved into that new house just to be closer to you, right?"

Bodhi nods.

"There you go. They'll find their way eventually. Right now, it's probably just hard to see eye to eye. Even though they're adults, that doesn't mean there isn't growing up to do."

"I guess."

"Enough of that. It's time to dig in." I place the last of the sides on the table and spoon a little bit of everything onto Bodhi's plate.

He picks up his fork eagerly.

After dinner, I talk Bodhi into listening to music with me.

"You don't have a TV?"

"I do, but we haven't used that thing in ages. I'd be surprised if it still works. I prefer to listen to music while I read. It relaxes me."

He seems to consider this before responding. "Do you mind if I draw?"

"Only if you let me watch."

He sits on the couch and pulls out a pencil box and a familiar sketchbook from his backpack. I place the needle of the record player on the disk, trying not to appear too eager, and adjust the volume. Just loud enough to hear, but not loud enough to be distracting.

"What is this?" Bodhi asks.

"Only one of my favorite songs in the whole wide world."

"This?" He sounds like he can't quite believe it.

"I wanna do everything...What a beautiful feeling." I sing and dance along with the lyrics. "Led me to a wonderland." I take a seat next to him. "Tommy James and The Shondells?" I may as well be speaking Mandarin with the way he's looking at me. "It may be a bit before your day. Mine too. I just love old music."

"Old clothes too."

Bodhi means it as more of an observation than an insult, but my cheeks flame. Children have always had a unique ability to be cruel in the most innocent ways.

"I suppose I like old things the way you like space things."

He nods as if he completely understands the comparison.

"What year did it come out?" Bodhi turns back to his sketchbook. The drawing he's working on is a planet I actually recognize: Saturn, complete with six of its seven rings.

"I'm not sure. The sixties, I think."

"Did you know that humans went to space in the sixties?"

"Who doesn't? Neil Armstrong in 1969, right?"

"Right, but there were a lot of milestones that led up to that. Alan Shepard was actually the first American to travel into space on the Freedom 7. That was in 1961! And in 1965, Ed White did the first spacewalk!"

"Is there anything you *don't* know about space?"

"Tons! But one day, I'll know everything. Like, did you know that Saturn is so light for its size that it could float in water?"

"No, I didn't."

"Yeah. So if you had a bathtub that Saturn could sit inside, it would bounce around like a beach ball."

"Like the ocean."

"Actually, the ocean isn't nearly enough. You'd need, like, over two hundred sextillion gallons of water to make it float! The ocean would be too small."

"I didn't realize that Saturn was so big."

"It's almost ten times larger than Earth. We are like a puddle in the sky compared to it."

A bundle of drawings falls out of the sketchbook onto the couch, and I pick them up.

"May I?" I ask.

He shrugs and continues drawing out one of Saturn's rings. I sift through the depictions of various space rocks, planets, and satellites until I finally reach what I'm looking for—the image of the bent woman in the puddle of red marker. After pulling the drawing out, I quietly tuck it in the couch beside me.

Bodhi is still focused on the Saturn rings and is none the wiser.

"Can I use the bathroom?" he asks, jumping to his feet.

"Sure. Down the hall and to the right."

He disappears down the long hallway, and I pick up his sketchbook, thumbing through the pages with a little more fervor. Something catches my eye, and I flip back to the page in question.

It's another drawing, similar to the other in a lot of ways. Heavy lines, gestures, and hurried shapes. This time, the crumpled figure is surrounded by something black instead of red. The circle is heavy, its thick, waxy lines pressed so deeply into the paper that there is a faint impression on the page behind it.

If I didn't know any better, I'd say it looked as if the figure was in a hole...or a grave.

Bodhi's footsteps lumber back down the hallway. I rip the drawing from the sketchbook, shove it beneath the cushion with the other one, and close the book. Bodhi comes in the room, his face washed in blue and red, then blue again.

It takes me a moment to register where the color is coming from.

They are coming from outside.

My heart sinks when I look out the window.

Two police cars are sitting on the street in front of my house, and one of the officers is making their way to my front door.

What We Do in Secret

CHAPTER

TWENTY-FOUR

There are three heavy knocks at my door. My eyes dart to Bodhi, who doesn't seem alarmed in the least. He has taken a seat on the couch and has continued drawing, like nothing at all is going on. Children are oblivious in that way. They don't realize the gravity of a situation the same way adults do. And my situation just got heavy fast.

"Miss Cooper. Blair County Sheriff's Department," the deputy calls out.

I smooth my dress and fluff my hair a bit. The deputy is just about to knock again when I open the door, catching his fist in mid-air. He's an older man with a slight frame. Maybe close to retirement. His mustache is ash white, and there's a hint of some kind of tattoo peeking out from beneath his uniform sleeve. The name on his plate says "R. Young."

"Can I help you, deputy?" I smile.

He takes me in for a moment, a look I'm used to from men, as fleeting as it is, before speaking.

"Sorry to bother you, but we've got a bit of a situation across the street."

"What kind of situation?" I ask.

That's when I spot Stevie talking to one of the other deputies. She has a phone up to her ear and is twisting her head around, flailing her free arm in the air, barely able to focus on whatever the deputy is telling her. Stevie seems terrified.

I understand what has happened.

Stay calm.

"Your neighbor's little boy is missing. Do you recall if he got off the bus today?"

"Oh goodness! Bodhi isn't missing. He's right here." I open the door, revealing the little boy sitting on my couch, doodling happily in his sketchbook.

Bodhi looks up at the sound of his name.

"Well, that solves *one* mystery." The deputy takes a step inside the door. "Hey, buddy. Your mom's been looking for you."

"Stevie's not my mom. And she forgot to open the door for me." Bodhi picks up his backpack and meets the two of us at the door.

The deputy and I share a look.

"I saw the poor thing sitting over there on the porch, all alone. I thought it was a bit odd, considering someone usually lets him in, so I invited him over for dinner." I gesture toward the table, where our empty plates are still resting exactly where we left them.

"Karla made meatloaf, and then she let me draw while I listened to her old music. It's actually not bad. What was it called again?"

"'Crimson and Clover.'" I smile, placing a hand on his shoulder.

"A classic." Deputy Young gives me another look. He's no longer talking about music.

"Does that settle up the confusion, deputy?" I ask, with both hands on Bodhi's shoulders.

"Afraid not, miss. If you don't mind, I'll have to ask you to come with me to take the boy back."

"Well, if you think that's necessary." I grab a robin's-egg-blue cardigan from the hat rack and pull it over my shoulders.

Deputy Young extends his hand, helping me down the stairs.

"Chivalry isn't dead after all," I declare, in my best Southern accent.

Bodhi leaps down the double stairs from my front door in one swift bounce and takes off toward the cop cars at full speed.

"Don't run into the road, Bodhi." I yell.

At the sound of his name, Stevie snaps her head in our direction. I watch her eyes dart from me to Bodhi to the deputy, then back to Bodhi. Recognition rises in her expression.

"Bodhi!" She opens her arms to him. He slows but accepts her embrace. "I was so worried about you, kid. God, you scared the shit out of me!"

When she looks up, Deputy Young and I are joining the pair and the other three deputies in the front yard. Stevie glares at me over Bodhi's head. Heat pools in my ears.

"It appears your son was at your neighbor's house." Officer Young places himself between Stevie and me.

"What the fuck, Karla?" she spits.

"Is that language really necessary?" I ask, putting a hand on my chest.

"You can text me all day about bullshit, but you can't mention when you've got my goddamn kid?"

"I'm sorry. I was busy making him dinner after you failed to let him in the house." Honestly, the nerve. "I didn't mean to scare you, but the poor thing was sitting out here, all alone. Anyone could have come along and snatched him up."

This silences her.

"I apologize for any inconvenience this has caused, fellas. I was just trying to be neighborly." I direct this statement at the other three deputies and then return to Stevie.

"No inconvenience at all," Deputy Young says quickly. "We're just happy it all worked out."

"What if I want to press charges?" Stevie practically yells.

"Press charges? You can't be serious," I say, losing a little bit of my composure. I swallow—an attempt to regain some of it.

"You took my child without consent!"

"What was I supposed to do? Leave him out here?"

Stevie looks at me like she would rather slit my throat and throw me in a hole than let me walk away from this without getting some kind of revenge.

"You were *supposed* to let me know."

"She didn't take me! I went with her. I didn't want to wait on the porch for you to wake up," Bodhi says.

Stevie flinches at his words. He pulls himself away from her arms and disappears into the house.

"Ladies, this feels like it's more of a misunderstanding than anything. I don't see any reason why we need to escalate the situation further. Let's just be thankful that the boy was found somewhere safe," Officer Young says, attempting to ease the tension tightening around us like a vise.

Stevie's lip quivers, and her eyes glaze over. She looks away, a weak attempt to hide the tears threatening to fall.

"You're right. I'm just...Thank you, Karla." She sniffles, refusing to look me in the eye.

"It's no trouble." I nod.

"If there's anything else you ladies need, don't hesitate to call."

"Thank you again, deputies. I'm sorry you had to come all this way." Once the officers are out of sight, I turn to Stevie. "I'm sorry again for all this. I didn't realize it would be such a ordeal."

"You didn't think taking someone else's kid without their knowledge would be a big deal?"

"That really is reaching. I was *trying* to help. In fact, if it'll help you get some more sleep, I'm happy to keep Bodhi after school while Simon's away."

"You're incredible." She scoffs. Stevie doesn't mean it as a compliment.

"It's no trouble at all."

"We don't need your help, Karla." She turns to head back to her door.

"Stevie, I—" I reach for her hand, but she jerks away before I can.

"Stop. Just...just leave me alone." Once inside, she slams the door shut behind her.

A small audience has gathered on our quiet street. There are blinds parted and curtains pulled back at just about every house within view of the scene. I dig my nails into the soft tissue of the scar on my hand.

It's such a shame about her.

She's such a pretty girl.

Such a shame.

Such a shame.

Such a shame she's crazy.

Crazy like her mother.

The voices carry this time, dancing through the trees, over the pavement from their windows, until they surround me on the lonely street.

What We Do in Secret

I'm at O'Keefe's with Emma all over again, only this time she doesn't look away. Her eyes bore into me, through me, straight into the girl I was the last time I saw her. Or is it Stevie whose eyes are boring into me now?

Stevie. Emma. Stevie. Emma. Mother.

I turn on my heels and sprint back to my own house, their judgment like soldering irons on my skin until the moment I close the door.

CHAPTER

TWENTY-FIVE

The doorbell rings, and my stomach flips. She's here!

My mother appears in the doorway of my bedroom. "Karla, your friend is at the door. Go let her in, please. Is that what you're wearing?"

"Yes, ma'am. I just thought that since you were letting us have a formal tea party that I should look nice."

"A woman should always look nice, regardless of the occasion. But this..." She gestures to my outfit, a canary-yellow A-line bouffant gown. "Overdressing is just as bad as underdressing. Worse, even. Honestly, Karla...You don't want to come across as desperate, do you? Put on a cardigan, at least."

She closes the door without waiting for a response. I leave the Harlequin romance I'm reading on the bed and grab a white cardigan from my closet.

Mother's right. This is the first time a girl from my school has actually wanted to come to my house for anything. Let alone someone as cool as Emma Davies. Last year, someone like Emma wouldn't have spoken two words to me unless they were teasing me about one thing or another. Teenage girls always find a wound to pick, especially if they are as visible as mine.

Which is why, when Emma approached me in the lunchroom two weeks ago, I immediately put my guard up. Even when she complimented my poodle skirt, I didn't fully trust her. It wasn't until she invited me to sit with her that I realized she was genuinely trying to get to know me. She even reprimanded Mallory Roberts, one of her little puppets, when Mallory made a sly remark about my choice of footwear—a black and white pair of Sadie Oxfords and bobby socks.

After that, we have been inseparable.

We walk with each other at school. I wait by her locker after each class to accompany her to the next one. She introduced me to the cheer coach and has been helping me practice for tryouts. Emma gave me a makeover once. She straightened my shoulder-length red hair and let me borrow one of her dress shirts and jeans. It wasn't really my taste, but it did invoke several compliments that I found flattering.

She even introduced me to her boyfriend, Desmond Jacobson.

I wasn't sure I liked him at first. He had a knack for pulling her attention away from me. I thought he was jealous of our friendship for a while, but when I confronted him about it, he shocked me. Desmond said he was actually jealous of me.

He told me he didn't want us being friends because he didn't want there to be any reason for me to turn him down when he asked me to the school formal instead of Emma. Desmond was planning on breaking up with her over spring break.

As much as it flatters me that a boy who had someone like Emma Davies on his arm could also be interested in me, Emma is my friend, and I am not about to risk that for some guy. She is perfect.

So, this afternoon has to be perfect as well. And if anyone knows perfect, it's my mother.

Even now, in her dressed-down state, she looks like Miss America. Her hair is cut short, perfectly styled into an elegant bouffant. She's wearing a sleek sheath dress with matching pumps. A simple string of saltwater pearls hangs around her neck, with one white pearl on each ear to match. She looks like Jackie Kennedy.

It's effortless for her. Me? Not so much. I always manage to mess something up. Sometimes, I wonder if she would be happier with a daughter who looks like Emma.

I slip the cardigan on and give myself a once-over in the mirror. My dress is freshly pressed, my lace top socks sit perfectly just below my knee, and my hair is pulled back with a yellow ribbon. The small table in my room is set, complete with the tea set Mother gifted me for my birthday. I even have separate bowls for the honey and the sugar cubes, just like she taught me.

Downstairs, Emma and my mother are standing in the entryway. The first thing I notice is how sloppy Emma looks compared to what I expected. It takes me by surprise, but a sense of pride blooms in my chest. Here I was, thinking Mama would much prefer a daughter like Emma, but Mother would rather kill me with her bare hands than have me show up to a formal tea party looking like that.

Emma is one of the most popular girls in school. Her family isn't rich or anything, but her father owns his own business. It's not like they don't have any money, yet she's wearing a simple mini-skirt and polo top. Her hair falls in messy, ashen waves down her back. Her striking blue eyes bore into me the moment I come into view.

I have to admit, in spite of her lack of effort, she's still prettier than half the girls at school. When you're that beautiful, you can get away with having the occasional fashion faux pas.

"Emma!" I exclaim, allowing my excitement to shine through.

Mother always says the key to making people like you is to speak with enthusiasm. If you seem genuinely thrilled to see them, they'll reflect that energy—even if they don't mean to.

Always make them feel like they're the best part of your day. Everyone wants to feel important; it validates what they already think of themselves. That's how you get them to trust you.

I didn't challenge her on it then, but I wonder if it only applies to strangers. My mother rarely seems excited to see me anymore— not since Dad left, at least. Maybe it's because family is supposed to love each other, so you don't really have to like them. Or maybe she doesn't feel like she needs to pretend with me anymore. Maybe she's just too tired for pageantry at home these days.

Whatever the reason is, the mother I have in private isn't the mother standing in the entryway with Emma in this moment.

"Well, it's about time," Mother says. "I was about to start entertaining our guest myself."

"Sorry, Mama," I reply, not so discreetly adjusting the hem of my cardigan. "Hi, Emma. You look lovely."

"Thanks. I just came from tennis practice, or I would have cleaned up some."

"Oh, that's silly. You're as lovely as a spring day. Is your mother in the car?" My mother turns to look out the window.

"No. My dad dropped me off. Mom's at a meeting. PTA." Emma shifts on her heel.

"Oh, I wasn't aware there was a PTA meeting this evening. Maybe I should head over there and—"

"It's not an official meeting. Once a week, my mom invites everyone over, and they drink wine and pretend to do business."

"I see." Everyone except me. I can almost hear it in the quiet way Mother responds.

The crack is so subtle I'm not surprised Emma doesn't notice it. But I do.

The fleeting falter in my mother's practiced smile, the twitch in her left hand, the way her spine stiffens like a cord pulled too tight. She reminds me of an old vinyl record on the turntable in the living room, interrupted when my book bag jostles it—a jarring skip that breaks the rhythm, leaving the melody momentarily fractured.

Some people break quickly. With others, it's more drawn out, their porcelain facades chipping away with each hit of harsh reality. It's only a matter of time before the cracks spread and they shatter entirely.

I know exactly how my mother feels. Whether she wants to admit it or not, we are the same in this hurt. She hasn't done anything wrong. Mother has just committed the cardinal sin of wanting too much.

She wanted to be involved in my education, so she joined the PTA, and they've shut her out. She wanted the perfect husband and to live in a nice house in a nice neighborhood they could build a family in, and then he left, leaving her with the stigma of being a single mother. Then she wanted a perfect daughter, and she got me.

I, too, understand how much it hurts to want things you'll never have.

Then she smiles.

"Well, you girls better head upstairs. I'll get tea."

The needle is once again positioned properly, music playing as if it was never interrupted to start with.

CHAPTER

TWENTY-SIX

Once inside my room, I shut the door behind Emma. She saunters past me, her eyes exploring with passive intrigue. I follow her gaze, wishing I had straightened the bed again before I went downstairs.

My room isn't much, but it's nice. There's an old record player sitting on a table in the corner. A shelf sits next to it, lined with books and records I love and a snow globe my father gave me from when he went on a business trip to New York City. It's a scene of the Empire State Building sitting atop an ocean of clouds. When you shake it, snow appears to fall.

My queen-size bed is against the wall, a bright blue canopy draped over the top. On the wall beside my bed, there is a massive collage of musicians I like: Paul Anka, the Shangri-Las, and Elvis.

"So, do you want to have a seat?" I offer her a chair at the tea table I agonized over setting.

"No." Emma fingers through my records. "Why don't you just listen to music on your phone?"

"I don't have a phone," I confess. "The sound is better on vinyl, though. Everyone says so."

"Who's *everyone*?" She laughs.

I don't know who everyone is. That's just what I've always heard.

"We can put something on if you want. See for yourself."

"Do you have any Taylor Swift or Ed Sheeran?" Emma asks, apparently not finding anything suitable in my collection. "These are all old."

"I don't. But I have Shelley Fabares." I remove the bright blue album from the mix and hold it out to her. "You'll love 'Johnny Angel.'"

"No thanks." She barely even gives it a look before waving it off.

I replace the album on the shelf. Something isn't right. She's acting strange. Emma has moved onto my bed, and she's looking at the various photos pinned there.

"Who are all these people?" She pulls out her phone, then snaps a few pictures of the collage.

My chest tightens with each shutter click, and there's a sick feeling bubbling like tar in the pit of my stomach.

"Just some musicians I like. What...what are you doing?"

"I'm taking pictures." She scoffs, like it should be the most obvious thing in the world.

"Yeah, but...May I ask why?" I cross the room to stand in front of her.

"*May* you? Do you hear yourself? God, how old are you? Like, forty?" Emma giggles and takes a photo of me.

The flash is momentarily blinding.

"Why are you taking pictures of my room, Emma?"

"Because if I don't, no one will believe me." She giggles and snaps a photo of my tea set.

"Believe what?"

"You're kidding, right? Look at this place! Look at your mom!" Emma laughs, gesturing toward me. "Look at *you*!"

My hands instinctively fidget with the edge of my cardigan. "What about me?"

"I suspected as much, honestly. There were rumors, but no one had any proof." She snaps another photo. "Until now. This place is like stepping into a 1950s sitcom. You guys are so weird." Emma studies my face for a moment, and her eyes soften. "You really don't realize, do you?"

"Realize what?" Tears are beginning to well in my eyes.

She closes the distance between us until she's so close I can smell her mint ChapStick. "That you and your crazy mother are *freaks*. Everyone says so."

Emma smiles and tilts her head to the side, bringing the phone to my face. She snaps a photo just as a crisp tear slides down my cheek. To my surprise, she raises her hand and wipes the wetness with her thumb.

"It really is a shame. You're such a pretty girl. It's too bad you're crazy."

"I'm not crazy," I almost whisper.

"Sure, you are. It's no wonder your dad got the hell out while he still could. Or...did your crazy old mom kill him, like everyone thinks?" Emma smiles at me over her shoulder, taunting. "You can tell me. We're best friends, remember?"

She giggles, tossing her hair around while she turns away from me. Her golden strands whip across my face.

Like a hammer against porcelain, something in me breaks. I reach up and catch a tuft of it in my fist, then yank as hard as I can. Her head snaps back, and a scream erupts from her lips. When she turns to me, her eyes are on fire...but she also seems mildly amused.

"Crazy bitch," she says, one hand holding the back of her head. "Look at what you did, you freak!"

I follow her gaze to my own hand, where a considerable lock of golden hair is still clenched tightly in my fist.

"Let's see if Des likes you after *this*!" As if reading my expression, she continues. "Did you think I wouldn't find out? He told me you hit on him and he turned you down! Did you really think he'd leave me for you? The only reason why he even talks to you is because of me. I'm the only reason why *anyone* talks to you. At first, I thought it was cute, the following me around and trying to do everything I do. You're even starting to dress like me."

Her eyes dart to the black bracelet around my wrist. One I bought with my allowance because it matched hers. I gave her the other one because I thought that's what best friends did. Share friendship bracelets.

"But coming after Des? Really, Karla? It's pathetic. You'll never be me. You'll always be a watered-down version of you."

She storms past me toward the door. When she's within arm's reach, my fingers find the edge of one of the tea plates. Before I can even register that I have picked it up, I swing the plate with all my strength, right at her perfect little face. The smooth ceramic splits on impact, and the jagged edge slices her skin in one clean rip.

Emma falls to the floor, holding her face. Red liquid escapes between her fingers. A deep red pool begins to form on the pale carpet beneath her. She pulls her hands away and screams at the sight of her blood-soaked palms.

I stand, stoic, watching her. She's even more beautiful than she was before. Even after all the nasty things she said. It isn't fair for someone to be so ugly on the inside and be so pretty on the outside. I raise the half of the plate still in my hand, ready to swing down on her again, when my mother bursts through the door, tea kettle in hand.

I freeze. Emma screams. My mother frantically surveys the room, trying to make sense of what she's seeing.

"Karla, what on earth are you doing?" she asks through short, staggering breaths.

I drop the broken plate, the spell broken, and follow her gaze to my hand. Emma isn't the only one ruining the carpet.

My palm is filleted open in a clean half-moon shape. My entire hand is drenched in bright red blood. It drips from my fingertips and onto the pale carpet beneath us. It's only then that time slows down enough for me to recognize the stabbing pain I should have felt all along, if not for the adrenaline pumping through my veins.

I scream, but it sounds deep and reverberated. My mother is yelling something at me, her face pinched with a mix of anguish and rage. Emma is still shrieking...or maybe she's laughing. I can't tell anymore. Time has slowed to a broken record speed, distorting everything around me.

My mother's hand smacks across my face like a hot iron, searing the skin. I bring my bloody hand to my cheek. The metallic liquid drips into my mouth.

Time resumes, but it's twice as fast as it should be. Two men in white barrel through my bedroom door. Before I can register what's happening, they take my hands, pinning them behind my back, and parade me out of the room and into the street.

Police cars surround the house, their flashing blue and red lights washing over our faces. Hot. Cold. My mother is standing at the door; one hand is holding her heart while the other brings a small handkerchief to her left eye.

Emma, now with a bandaged face, is pulled into an embrace by her mother. She shoots me a look that may as well be a bullet while I am escorted past them toward the open door of a white van. It has some kind of familiar blue branding along the side, but in my foggy state, I can't read it.

The neighbors, usually too proud to allow their snooping to be known, are now boldly lingering on their lawns, taking in the scene.

Mrs. Lowe watches from her wheelchair, every bit as dead as the last time I saw her. Stevie stands behind the woman. She leans down and whispers something in her ear before erupting in laughter. Mrs. Lowe giggles as well—at least, I think she's trying to. Her mouth opens, revealing a gum-lined void, and the entire action wrinkles her face in a way that appears more sinister than amused.

There's a swift nudge to my shoulder, forcing my attention away from the onlookers.

I'm forced into the darkness of the van by the men in white. They release me, and I barely find my footing, not inside the back of a van but at the top of a staircase.

At first, I think it's the stairs which lead down to Stevie's photo room. It only takes me a moment to realize they aren't. This staircase is the one in my own house.

I feel unsteady, my stomach lurching, threatening to expel whatever contents are marinating in there. The bottom of the stairs is so dark, and the descent feels endless. But I know there is a bottom, just beyond the shadow. It pulls me toward it, though I don't understand how.

Someone stands behind me. I turn slightly to see who it is, expecting one of the men in white. It's neither of them.

My blood ices over in my veins at the familiar face. Or *two* familiar faces, rather.

Emma stands there, wrapped in bloody gauze, staring at me through the one eye that's undamaged by my outburst. Heather is beside her, her eyes sunken and lifeless. Her once vibrant hair is caked in mud and hangs loosely, framing her pale face. She looks practically skeletal.

I would scream if every fear response I had wasn't catching in my throat. But I can't even defend myself when she reaches her hands up and pushes me into the dark.

CHAPTER

TWENTY-SEVEN

A shot of pain pierces my bottom lip, followed by the metallic taste of blood on my tongue. I rise from the table. My fork falls against the plate with a sharp *clink*. Both of Bodhi's drawings sit next to my partially eaten toast. I reach for the napkins, and a drop of blood drips onto the paper, right where the girl's squiggly line hair meets her circle head.

Once I have a napkin firmly pressed on my lip, I try to blot up the blood, but it's too late. Maroon stains the paper, making the image appear even more sinister than it did before.

How could I have let myself fall asleep at the table like that?

I gather the drawings and slip down the basement stairs, into what used to feel like a grave. Since I started developing film down here, it has shifted—less tomb, more laboratory. I slide the drawings into one of the deeper drawers, the one where I keep backup gear, and shut it with a wooden thump that echoes up the pipes.

That's when I hear the ringing.

What time is it? Mother must be starving.

The needle in my head stings with each step I take up the stairs.

Once in the kitchen, with the basement door secured and locked behind me, I whip up something fast, a fruit smoothie, and pour it into one of the glass jars.

If Mother notices that I'm in the same clothes as last night, she says nothing. Hunger overrides her self-righteousness at the moment, and I'm grateful. Before I can stop it, the thought forms in my head—maybe I should starve her more often.

I toss it away before it has a chance to flesh out. Thoughts like that, they become far too real too quickly to cling to them for even a moment. They're dangerous.

When we're done, I leave the glass sitting on her nightstand and return to my bedroom. I throw on a clean T-shirt, some simple pearls, and a fresh skirt. While I'm running a brush through my bird's nest of a head, a blur of black flashes in my periphery.

Simon is back.

His clunky van is sitting in its usual spot next to Stevie's car. The sight of it twists my stomach. I pull out my phone and check. To no surprise, I don't have a single message despite my many efforts to get him to respond. I even apologized for my boldness when I figured his absence was because he was feeling guilty about what we had done.

To be fair, I felt somewhat guilty too. Well, guilty adjacent. No matter what feelings Simon triggered in me or what kind of person I suspected Stevie of being, even if I didn't have the proof yet, women shouldn't do that to each other.

"It's not ladylike!" I can practically hear my mother screech from the next room.

Even though I know she can no longer talk, I hold my breath and listen for the bell. I'm tempted to look in on her again, but if she's finally drifted off to sleep, I don't want to risk her waking up. That would mean a lot of cleanup I don't have the energy for right now. Fruit smoothies run right through her. Besides, there's something I have to do.

I make my way downstairs toward the front door, swiping a small package from the entryway table as I do. Stealing someone else's mail is a felony, but I don't think that applies when it's wrongfully delivered to your house in the first place. I was just waiting for the right opportunity to return it. It's neighborly, not criminal.

I sprint across the street, my heels clicking against the pavement, and make my way up the walkway to Stevie and Simon's front door.

The house looks the same as it always does. All the homes on this street are beautiful but in a forced, curated way. Like a showroom no one really lives in. The only thing different about Stevie's is she hasn't bothered to clean up the clay shards of the broken pots from the other day. I like it. It's like one real thing among the falsities.

Of course, she hasn't cleaned it. Sometimes, I think Stevie is the only real person within a twenty-mile radius of me. Maybe that's why I'm drawn to her so much. When you live your life surrounded by fake houses, fake lawns, and fake people, finding someone real is like discovering a beacon of light in the dark. You gravitate toward it, cling to it like a moth to a flame. You crave the certainty they have in themselves. You want it too, even if it kills you.

I knock once, then again, softer this time, and call out just loud enough to carry through the door.

"Hey, Stevie. It's Karla. The funniest thing happened. One of your packages got delivered to my house by accident."

I hear movement. Footsteps. The shifting creak of wood floorboards under someone's weight. My heart kicks against my ribs, like it needs to escape. I take a few calming breaths and manage what I hope is a dazzling smile when the door opens. But it isn't Stevie standing there.

It's the blond from the restaurant. The one with sun-kissed skin and tattoos climbing up her neck like a noose. Her tan is even more pronounced in the daylight, a rich gold, and her bleached hair is gathered in a lazy bun, making her look expensive and effortless all at once.

"Oh, sorry...I didn't see a car. I didn't realize Stevie had company." I stumble, shocked and grasping for my words.

"Simon picked me up from my hotel. I'm staying with Stevie for a while before heading back to Arizona." She smiles brilliantly. "Karla, right? From Vozelli's."

"Right. And you're Vikki?" I say, with more uncertainty than I feel. I know her name is Nikki. But for some reason, I don't want her to know I remember anything about her.

"Nikki, actually." She doesn't seem offended at all.

It's annoying.

"Is Stevie here?" I tilt my head, smiling like this is just a neighborly duty and not a calculated maneuver. "I've got something for her."

"She's in the shower," Nikki says easily. "Simon's in his office. I can make sure she gets it."

She reaches out for the package, all painted nails and casual entitlement. But I don't let go.

"With all due respect," I say, voice smooth as syrup, "I'd feel more comfortable giving it to her myself."

Nikki's expression flickers—surprise, then something cooler. She nods once, tight. "Fair enough."

She starts to pull the door shut, but I step forward, catching it with my foot. Nikki's eyes sweep back up to my face.

"If you could just get Simon...I'd be happy to give it to him. You know...save me another trip over here during your visit."

A smile cracks across her face, like porcelain. She's studying me. There's something almost impressed in her gaze, but mostly, she seems amused.

"Simon's working on a pretty large piece for a tattoo. He asked not to be disturbed unless it's an emergency."

I raise my eyebrows, grin still in place, almost disbelieving. "You don't think a breakdown in the United States Postal Service counts as an emergency?"

"If you really believed that"—Nikki's voice is suddenly syrupy in a very different way—"you'd leave it with me...wouldn't you?"

I say nothing.

She shifts her weight, the air thick between us.

"Well," she says after a pause. "I'll be sure to let Stevie know you came by...and that you didn't feel comfortable leaving the package with me.

She closes the door, slow and deliberate, until I'm staring at wood grain and paint and the warped reflection of my faded smile in the brass handle.

Then the unmistakable sound of a lock sliding into place, as final as a coffin lid.

What We Do in Secret

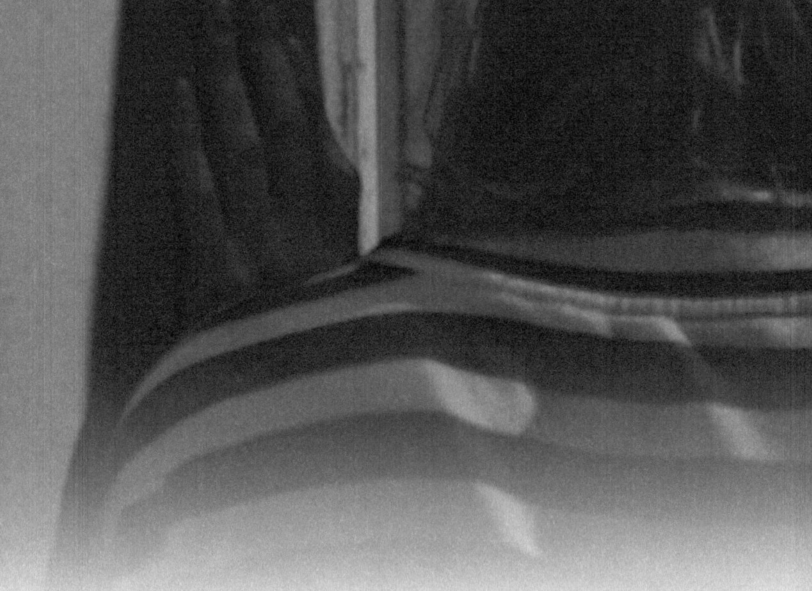

CHAPTER

TWENTY-EIGHT

Who does she think she is? She didn't even blink when she shut me out. Just stood there with that Botox smirk, like *I'm* the joke. She's visiting, for God's sake. Sleeping in someone else's guest sheets and acting like she owns the place. That smug look when she said Stevie was busy. Too busy to come to the door? Like I couldn't see right through it.

She's not even part of their lives. *I* am. I've had dinner with them. I'm the one who understands their child more than they do. Gone on photoshoots with Stevie. I'm—I'm the one sleeping with Simon. *She's* the outsider.

I bite the inside of my cheek and walk faster, fists clenched around the stupid package. The stray shards on the walkway crunch under my shoes like bones. I'm seething, sure, but more than that, I'm confused. Stevie didn't answer her phone this morning, and now Nikki's guarding the door like her own personal little watchdog.

Unless...

Unless she wouldn't get Simon because she couldn't. Because she wasn't alone in there.

What if Nikki and Simon—

God. No. That's insane. Isn't it?

But it's too late. The image has already taken root in my head in painful detail. Her fingers trailing over his arm while Stevie sleeps. Her face leaving makeup trails on Stevie's bed. The way he looks at Stevie...or me...Could he look at Nikki like that too? If it's even a possibility, I can't let them do that to Stevie. I can't allow them to have an affair right under her nose.

At the end of the walkway, I stop, my breath clouding the air. I still have the package in my hand. The reason I came over here in the first place. Well, partially. It's just an excuse, but it is a reason and a good one.

I get an idea. It's a little sloppy, so before I can talk myself out of it, I dare a glance at the window to make sure I'm not being watched. I cut through the side yard until I'm concealed beneath the shadows of the magnolia tree, where Simon and I met that first night.

My heart beats louder than my footsteps while I keep low, ducking beneath the window frames, sliding along the edge of the house like a shadow. I'm not being watched—I think. The curtains...well, the tapestries are mostly drawn. But I still don't breathe until I round the corner and see it.

The sunroom. Or as Stevie called it once in passing, Simon's "Sad Boy Bunker."

It is glass on three sides, messy with light and shadow. And inside—there he is. Crouched over a desk. He doesn't notice me at first, too caught up in whatever he's drawing. His back curves like a question mark, and for a second, I just watch him. Quiet. Curious. Then my stupid foot hits a clay pot, knocking it over with a sharp crack.

Simon jerks his head up.

Shoot.

He sees me.

Before I can stammer out a word, the side door to the sunroom creaks open. His face is tight with suspicion. "What the hell are you doing out here?"

I force a nervous laugh. "I—um..." My eyes dart down to the package still in my hand. My saving grace. "I was just bringing you this. It got dropped off at my place. I knocked, but your friend said to just bring it around."

His eyes narrow. I can't tell if he believes me, so I try to add a layer of harmlessness.

"I guess I'm not wearing the right shoes for walking through mud and mulch."

Something in him softens. Maybe I really do sound harmless, or perhaps it's the fact that I am lifting my skirt to avoid getting it dirty. Whatever the reason, I'm grateful he isn't looking at me like I'm an intruder anymore. He steps down and offers his hand.

"Come on."

The inside of the sunroom is even more chaotic up close. A beautiful kind of organized chaos, though. It seems in disarray, but it's not like Stevie's mess. Everything seems to have its place. It's calm in a strange way.

Music sheets scattered like fallen leaves, splattered with coffee stains. A keyboard in one corner. Canvases in the other. There's a guitar with a snapped string. There's even a bed shoved near the back, half-covered with a flannel blanket and a sketchpad.

It smells like paint and cologne and something sharp underneath. Like sweat. Like stress. I hand him the package. He doesn't even look at it. Just tosses it onto a table next to a stack of what appears to be art books.

"I missed you," I say quietly, daring a step closer.

His eyes meet mine, and he kisses me, but it's brief. Quick. Like he's afraid of it.

"Not now," he murmurs. "Not with Nikki lurking around. She never liked me, and she's like Stevie's little detective. Always watching me."

"Why?"

He shrugs. "Why do women do anything that they do?"

I change the subject at the sound of misogyny. "This place is... cool. Really. I've never seen anything like it."

That makes him smile a little.

"Thanks. It's not much, but it's my space. My head's too loud in the house."

"I get that," I say, thinking of the boxes that are probably still unpacked in the house. I wouldn't be able to concentrate in there either. "Nikki said you were working on something big. A tattoo design?"

"Sort of," he replies. Simon pulls out a folder and opens it for me.

Sketches spill out—intricate, strange, dark. Animals curled into symbols. People half-dissolved into vines. It's all a little unsettling but somehow beautiful.

"I'm really just working on some flash, but they leave me alone for a while if I tell them it's some big design."

"How long have you been doing tattoos?"

"Too long."

"You don't like it? It sounds like it would be an interesting job."

"I do. Well, I did at first. It's not what I want to do, though. Now I just do it because it pays and I can make my own schedule."

"You'd rather make music?"

"I like music too. The band is something fun to do on the weekends. What I really wanted to do is make art. Real art. Not butterflies and arrows and boyfriends' names."

"Do a lot of boyfriends' names?" I giggle a little, still sifting through the drawings. They are shockingly good. Some look like they belong in a museum instead of tucked away in a folder.

"The fastest cover-up I've had was from a pair of lesbians. Twenty-four hours. She got her girlfriend's name tattooed on her..." He raises an eyebrow and sweeps his eyes down my body to my skirt.

"On her...?" I ask with raised eyebrows.

He nods, enjoying my discomfort a little too much. My blush is exacerbated when I find the portraits.

The first one is obviously of Stevie. Bare shoulders. Lips parted. Her hair a waterfall around her. It's intimate and raw and looks an awful lot like the painting which ended up in the trash. He remains seated on the side of the bed, studying me, while I sift through them.

The next one is of a girl I don't recognize. Younger. Her eyes half-lowered. This one features a very revealing angle from the back. He left nothing to the imagination.

"Ex-girlfriend?" I half choke, passing the portrait to him.

He smirks. "Ex *something*. Not exactly a girlfriend."

There are more. One after another. Women in soft poses. Private moments. I feel like I'm seeing something I shouldn't. Yeah, he painted them, and he's letting me look at them, but would these women be okay with me observing them in such vulnerable poses? I sure wouldn't.

But I can't look away. The movement in the strokes, the depth of the color...They are beautiful. Then one portrait turns my blood to ice.

It's not finished. Just brush strokes and shadows and the beginning of a mouth. But I know that face. I've been staring at it nonstop since I heard her name.

Heather Crosp.

It's *her*.

My voice comes out slow. "Who is this?"

Simon freezes. His fingers twitch while he takes it from me. "That one...wasn't supposed to be in there."

"Another not-quite girlfriend?"

He flinches. "She was someone I used to know. A model. She let me paint her a couple of times."

I stare at the lines. At the way the light dances across her cheekbones. It's too intimate. Too knowing.

"Why didn't you finish it? When was this?"

"I don't know. Eight months ago, or something." His eyes are still on the paper. "She just stopped coming around."

"Eight months ago," I repeat, doing the math. "When you were still with Melissa?"

"It wasn't like that. Melissa and I were over long before I left."

Something sharp twists in my gut. Something wrong.

I swallow it down, but it's rising anyway. "She just...stopped coming?"

Simon nods, but it's stiff. Robotic. "Yeah. Why are you so worried about it? You jealous?"

"Jealous?" I scoff, smoothing my skirt. The room feels colder now. "I should go," I say quickly.

"What's wrong? You look like you've seen a ghost or something."

But I'm already backing up. I don't want to hear any more. Don't want to look at that bed again. Don't want to imagine what kind of "model" Heather was to him.

A bark slices through the tension. That dumb dog, Ollie. And Stevie's voice calling his name.

Shoot. Shoot. Shoot.

"I *have* to go," I say, barely breathing.

And before Simon can stop me, I'm gone. Around the corner. Past the tree. Heart pounding. Mind racing.

I suspected, but I never actually let myself believe that Simon would have had any kind of relationship with Heather. She was a kid. Seventeen years old?

And he didn't finish the picture because she stopped coming around, all right. Because she *disappeared*. And a person of interest was questioned. Could it have been him?

When I reach the front of the house, I can still hear their voices, Stevie and Simon, muffled but sharp, like glass on the verge of breaking.

And for the first time since I met them, I wonder if I ever *really* knew who I was dealing with.

There was something else in the drawing of Heather that caught my attention. Something I've seen before...on Stevie.

She was wearing a necklace in the portrait. A necklace with an origami bird pendant.

What We Do in Secret

CHAPTER

TWENTY-NINE

Melissa Van Lowe is even more flawless in person than she looks in her perfectly curated blog. I had half expected to be underwhelmed. People never resemble their social media in real life, but Melissa looks even better.

I watch while she walks up to the entrance of the chic little hair salon on Briarcliff, her blond curls bouncing happily, like a beige Miss America in her nude heels, tan wrap top over a pair of black leather pants. The same colors donned by her entire social media presence. She really does take her color palette seriously.

Melissa smiles and waves at someone out of my range of vision before disappearing inside.

It was easy enough figuring out a way to get in the same room with Melissa. She, unlike Stevie, has a very structured routine. Melissa only raves about this salon every single time she gets her salt-colored hair retouched, which is every two weeks on the dot. It was getting the appointment that was a challenge. Melissa put this place on the map, so naturally, the mommy crowd keeps them booked for months in advance.

"Salon13, how can I help you today?" the chipper voice on the other end of the line answered when I called.

"Hello, sweetie." I let the words drawl in that slow way Melissa used a million times. After watching video after video, I had perfected the pitch. "This is Melissa Van Lowe."

"Mrs. Van Lowe." Her voice perked. "So nice to hear from you. How can I help you?"

"Honey, I am just losing my mind over here. I'm trying to verify my next appointment. Bodhi has a doctor's visit on Thursday, and I need to make sure they don't overlap."

"Absolutely. Let me get that pulled up for ya," the woman said on the other line, followed by the click-clicking of manicured nails on a keyboard. A short pause later, she spoke again. "It looks like we have you down for one o'clock on Thursday for your usual touch-up and a trim."

"Wonderful. I'll see y'all then. Thanks, doll."

"You're welcome, Mrs. Van Lowe. You have a good rest of your day, and we will see you Thursday."

"Bye-bye now," I said, releasing the call.

That had been the easy part.

I waited a day before calling back to schedule my own appointment. It would be suspicious, two back-to-back conversations about the same timeframe. But when I called, I was told they were booked until December.

"We'll give you a call if we get any cancellations," she said, followed by the click.

Only the Melissa Van Lowes of the world received the embellished farewells.

Mitzi Robbins had one of those times lots. I knew this because she had commented on Melissa's post, telling her she couldn't wait for their next "catch-up session" at the salon. She's a granola mom who lives in Clover Park, one town over, in a modernized Victorian with her Golden Retriever husband and their perfect little poppet three-year-old, Jasper.

I watched him swinging happily on a tire swing suspended from a massive live oak. Mitzi lounged on the front porch in oversized sunglasses, sipping an iced tea as if she hadn't a care in the world. That probably wasn't far from the truth.

I kept my distance to remain unseen, tucked away in the little cove just north of her property. People like her don't notice much beyond themselves most of the time anyway, but still. It was better to be safe than sorry.

When Mitzie disappeared inside to take a phone call, probably the salon confirming her appointment in a few hours, I exited my vehicle and walked casually over to the yard. I got Jasper back in the car just as Mitzie was returning to her spot on the couch.

It wasn't hard. Most kids respond well to a nicely dressed lady with a picnic basket full of treats. Society never teaches children to fear women who look like me. If anything, I'm the one they run to.

Ten minutes later, she still hadn't noticed him missing. I backed out of my little cove and drove the opposite way out of the neighborhood.

Karla, the dognapper *and* kidnapper. I've evolved. But I'm a little more apprehensive about this one.

Jasper is on his third muffin when we arrive at the park, where I promised to take him to get him to come with me in the first place. I canvassed this park closely.

No security cameras and it was empty for the most part this time of day. When we pulled up and there were no cars in the parking lot to speak of, I was relieved.

I got Jasper secured in one of the swings so he couldn't wander off, then told him his mom would be there to pick him up shortly. He smiled up at me when I ran a hand through his thick brown hair. Jasper was so precious, with his face covered in chocolate muffin.

I handed him a sippy cup of water and another muffin and told him I had to run back to the car. He waved bye and said something in his little baby talk that melted my heart. Jasper was still swinging in my rearview when I pulled away.

I was a little sad to leave him like that, but this is a good neighborhood. Nothing bad ever happens to anyone here. Not really. Some mom or the police would come across him eventually. He was so sweet, though. Didn't talk my ear off...

Come to think of it, verbally, I assumed he would be further along than he is. Probably because Mitzie spends more time on her phone than talking to her son and helping to develop his language skills. Part of me wants to go back, scoop him up, and just take him home with me. But I have more pressing matters to deal with.

Before I even arrived home, my phone rang. I smiled when I read the name on the screen.

"Hello. I'm trying to reach a Ms. Corinne Cooper."

"This is she?" I said, cringing at the use of my middle name. But I used it to stay safe.

"Good news! We've had a cancellation for a 1:30 time slot. I know it's short notice, but if you are still interested, the spot is—"

"I'm interested," I replied, probably a little too quickly.

"Wonderful. The previous spot was for a cut and color. What were you hoping to get done today?"

"A cut and color is fine." I hadn't even thought of that. To be honest, I hadn't had my hair done at a proper salon in years. I would have to come up with something soon.

"Great. I'll write you in. We will see you then," she said.

When I enter the salon, I am instantly hit with the aroma of hair products—expensive ones by the scent of them. It smells delicious in here. The space is airy, with high-vaulted ceilings and mirrors in every direction. A narcissist's dream. A stylist in a black T-shirt greets me at the door, and by her upbeat demeanor, I can tell this is the one I spoke with both times.

"Hi. Welcome to Salon 13. What's your name?"

"Cooper. I have an appointment."

While she looks down at her tablet, I take in the rest of the room. The openness of the space means that every single stylist and client is visible to all the rest. Melissa is sitting in one of the far chairs, getting her roots foiled and talking in an animated Southern drawl to three other women who have huddled around her.

"Yes, girl. They found him at the park on Bristol! Can you imagine that baby walking all that way by himself! It's a miracle he didn't get—"

"Ma'am?" the woman says to me, again pulling my attention away from Melissa. "I said we have you down for a cut and color. You'll be with Audrina today."

A brunette approaches me wearing a matching black T-shirt. Her hair falls down her back, all the way to her waist, in loose waves.

"Nice to meet you. Right this way." She leads me to a small salon chair on the complete opposite end of the building.

I can barely see Melissa from over here. Let alone talk to her. Once seated, she drapes a cloth around me, snapping it behind my neck. She turns me away from the room, away from Melissa, and toward the mirror.

Such a shame. Such a shame. Such a shame.

I swivel back around, and her eyes widen.

"Um, do you mind if I face the room while you work? I'd like the ending to be a surprise," I lie.

"It's no problem. I do like a grand reveal," she says. Audrina fans my hair over my shoulders. "You have beautiful hair. I have clients that pay a lot of money to get this color red. Are you sure you want to dye it?"

"I am. It's time for a change." I look in Melissa's direction.

In more ways than one.

CHAPTER

THIRTY

There's something about the way a salon smells, with all the chemicals, that reminds me of a hospital. Sterile. Controlled. Like a crime scene after the cleanup.

I pretend not to notice Melissa at first, even though I have spent the last thirty-five minutes watching her through the wall mirror, catching quick reflections of her blond head tilted back in the basin, foil folded like origami across her roots. And I've nodded along to Audrina's small talk—her new kitten, her ex, the bachelorette party she is afraid he'll show up to.

"Some people just don't know how to let go," I offer, and she nods in agreement. But my focus has been across the salon the entire time. I came here for *her*.

But to what? See her? Talk to her? To look in her eyes and gauge the depth of what she knows about the couple across the street? And up until now, I've had nothing but distance and a bad magazine to keep me company. When Melissa finally steps outside, with her foil-wrapped head and a glossy copy of *Southern Moms* tucked under her arm, I count to ten, then excuse myself, like I suddenly remembered I left my phone in the car.

I find her on the brick side of the building, hidden from the main parking lot, leaning against the wall, a big green dumpster in the background. With a lit cigarette in hand and a halo of smoke curling around her, she's so unlike her pure, beige aesthetic online. Melissa seems...real. And, to my annoyance, even prettier up close, like a former pageant queen.

Who am I kidding? She could still win any beauty contest she entered and put all the other contestants to shame.

Ugh.

"Mind if I bum one?" I ask casually, like I've heard them do in the movies.

She smiles through the smoke, already digging through her beige Birkin. "Sure, but don't tell anyone." That Southern lilt wraps around her words like sugar on the tongue.

"I won't if you won't."

She hands me one of the Virginia Slims, and I fake it well, hold it between my fingers like I've done it a thousand times. Inhale just enough to fill my mouth, but I never let the nasty stuff into my lungs, then release into the air. It causes a little tickle in my throat, but nothing I can't handle. She's eyeing me up and down, a soft smirk playing at her lips.

"That outfit is adorable. Vintage, right?"

"Thank you." I beam. "It's new. Got it from a little boutique online called Timeless Madam." I don't mention it's the first thing I've purchased in black. A halter with a flared hem and sheer white blouse for warmth in the fall weather. I wanted to dress to impress today, and it seems I have. "I'm Corinne, by the way."

She exhales. "Melissa."

"I know." I let the words hang just long enough to catch her attention. "I read your blog."

She preens just a little, and I can't tell if this surprises her or if she gets recognized all the time. I guess it would depend on the place.

"Oh? Friend or foe?" she asks with a playful tone.

"I love it. Honestly. It's real. And fun. And you have such a way of making people feel like they aren't alone."

She stubs out her cigarette and leans in a little. "Well, look at you, making my day. So, how old are your kids?"

"I—I actually don't have any?"

"Not my typical audience, if you know what I mean."

"I lost my baby a few years ago. Miscarriage." I shrug.

"Oh, honey." Sympathy blooms across her face, just like I hoped it would. She touches my arm, her voice dipped in velvet. "That's awful. I'm so sorry."

"It was a rough time. My boyfriend helped me through it, though. He has a son. So, in a way, I still get to be a mom."

Her face softens again. "Mine too. Seven going on twenty-seven, girl. They're wild at that age."

"I can't get a word in edgewise," I say with a mock sigh. "But he's smart. Really smart, actually. So, I guess we're doing something right."

"You must be." She smiles back at me.

For a split second, I wonder what it would be like to be her friend. Like this, in this environment, with her cigarettes she doesn't want anyone to know she smokes and the gentle way she touched me when she found out about my miscarriage I didn't really have. She seems so genuine.

Does it really matter if an online persona is fake if the real flesh-and-bone people in your life get to see the real you? Why would Stevie have this friendship and then throw it away?

The door creaks open, breaking my concentration. One of the stylists pokes her head out, eyes darting to Melissa.

"Sorry to interrupt, ladies, but if we don't rinse you soon, you're gonna end up bald."

Melissa laughs, tossing her cigarette to the ground. "That's my cue."

Inside, the lighting's too bright again. Too artificial. Melissa is already at one of the basins, head tilted back like she's offering her throat to the salon gods. I'm about to return to my faraway seat when her voice rings out across the room.

"Hey, Audrina? Can we move my new friend a little closer? She reads my blog." Melissa says the last part like it's all the reason she needs. And maybe it is. Maybe it's a name stamp on a command meant to say, *Do you know who I am? Give me what I want.*

No matter the reason, my stomach does a little flip, and I don't have to act surprised.

Audrina grins at me through clenched teeth. She quickly softens them so I won't notice. "Sure thing, Mrs. Van Lowe."

"And bring this woman a champagne, for Christ's sake. She's been sitting in that chair for thirty minutes, and no one's offered her a proper drink."

"Champagne flutes are usually reserved for gold members."

"For goodness' sake, just put it on my tab, then. All these rules and regulations, like we all aren't already being overcharged."

Within minutes, I receive a glass of bubbly champagne, and my chair is right across from Melissa's. Our reflections blur into each other in the mirror. Melissa is halfway through her fourth glass of champagne when she starts in on a reality show she has been watching.

"I mean, the woman bought a peacock. As an emotional support animal. A full-grown, emotionally unavailable peacock. Thing died like two weeks in. Can you imagine?"

She howls and I manage a chuckle, but the scenario seems more sad to me than funny. The banter feels easy with her at least. She's sharper than she lets on. Not book smart, but she knows how to read a room. Or women. And that's something. At least she did before she was four glasses deep in alcohol.

Sharp edges tend to dull when you introduce alcohol. So does discretion. I take the opportunity to push while I can.

"So...how's co-parenting going? I know you write a little about it, but...really?"

Her face clouds like someone pulled the blinds.

"A nightmare, girl." Melissa leans closer, conspiratorial. "He moved right up the street. Not even a mile. Which is *fine*, I guess. But then he moved *that woman* in with him."

"You mean Stevie Cole?" I'm careful to say both her first and last names. Only people who know someone call celebrities by their first name.

Melissa makes a face like she tastes something sour. "God, yes. Although my lawyers say I shouldn't say her name out loud anymore. But that bitch deserves a little backlash after what she did."

I nod in agreement. Taking someone's husband is bad by any standard and worthy of some karmic kickback. But then she says something else. Something which turns the floor under my feet to water.

"She was *my* friend. Practically my assistant. I gave her everything. But she was mine first, and then he just—he just *took* her. Or she took *him*. Whatever."

Wait. *Friends?*

Stevie told me she didn't even know they were together. Said it was a total surprise. But if she was friends with Melissa—close friends—she *had* to know. Why would she lie?

Melissa's words are starting to slur now, the champagne pooling behind her lips, making everything spill.

"Oh, the stuff I could tell you about her. Taking your best friend's man is just the *tip*, honey. The tip of the iceberg with that one. I tell ya. She's a bad seed. Always has been."

My heart is pounding, but I try to keep my face calm. "What do you mean?"

She blinks slowly, looks at me like she's trying to decide if I'm real.

"All I'm gonna say is...that one's got skeletons in her closet. Or...somewhere." She bursts out laughing at a joke I've apparently missed, spewing drops of champagne everywhere. Someone really needs to cut her off. Then she does this grand zipping motion across her lips, like a child keeping a pinky promise.

Before I can press again, Audrina swoops in with a towel and a grin.

"All done! Ready to see?"

She swivels the chair toward the mirror.

And for a second, I forget where I am. *Who* I am. I wait for my mother's voice to intrude. For all the voices telling me how much of a shame I am, but they don't come this time.

The reflection staring at me is haunting...and not mine.

The cut is choppy, just below the shoulder. The exact shade of blood-red simmering beneath jet-black strands. It looks familiar. *Too* familiar.

I look like her. *Just* like *her*.

I tense, paranoid Melissa will notice and accuse me of something I can't explain. And I can't explain.

But Melissa just sips her champagne and says, "Damn. You look badass. Very rockabilly with that outfit." She hiccups, laughs, and leans in like we're old friends. "We should do this again soon."

She's still talking, but I've tuned her out. Her voice becomes a low hum, vibrating under the surface but never actually reaching me.

If Stevie could steal her best friend's husband, someone she claimed to care about, and then destroy her family and lie about it...lie to me...What *wouldn't* someone like that do?

I don't want to believe it. I don't want to believe Melissa. After all, I just met her. I don't know this woman at all, and it seems she's made a career out of masking for an audience.

That's not it, though. As many reasons as I have to not trust her, I have just as many reasons to *believe* her.

Maybe I just don't want to believe that I have been looking at the wrong monster the entire time.

CHAPTER

THIRTY-ONE

She's still there. *Still*. There.

I should've stopped watching days ago. Should've closed the curtains, turned off the notifications, shut the obsession down cold. But I can't stop watching the house across the street like it's the only channel left on Earth. I can't let go of the fact that Nikki is still there, like a ghost haunting the halls, haunting *me*.

A week now, maybe more, and she has become a permanent fixture. Even when Stevie and Simon are gone, she's still there, making herself at home with them. I even saw her walking Bodhi to the sidewalk one morning in her bare feet and one of Simon's sweatshirts, sleeves hanging off her wrists with an ill-fitted intimacy. The sight of it twisted something in my gut until I had to look away. Why does Stevie trust her so much?

Simon barely answers my texts anymore. Stevie doesn't answer at all. Understandable, I suppose. She's still angry about Bodhi. The rare responses I do get from Simon are so dry I can practically hear them crackle. No emojis. No veiled flirtation. Just the cold, clipped kind of replies someone sends when they know someone's watching.

I wonder if Stevie checks his phone. If she's the reason he's gone quiet. I can see it. Her scrolling his messages while he's in the shower. That's why he doesn't dare send anything that could even remotely hint at something damning between us. I could understand that far better than just going radio silent after what was otherwise a fun night. He seemed to enjoy it, at least.

I tried messaging him from my ghost Instagram account. He hasn't so much as looked at it.

But I'm running out of time. Opportunities. Patience. Ever since my chat with Melissa, I haven't stopped thinking about what else might be inside that house. I missed something. And now, while I sit behind my bedroom window, with the blinds tilted just enough, I watch Stevie stretching at the edge of their driveway.

I'm about to get the best chance I'm going to have to find out. Her earbuds are in, her legs long and lean in reflective running tights. She twists at the waist and tosses her hair back like she's warming up for something bigger than a jog.

Stevie pauses, just for a second, and looks across the street. *At* me. I swear she stares right through the slats of the blinds and into my eyes.

I drop like a brick.

My pulse skips up my throat, hot and furious in my ears. But when I peek again, she's gone, already sprinting up the block in her perfect, rhythmic stride. Simon's van pulled out an hour ago. He usually doesn't get back until late into the night.

Bodhi's still home. Which means Nikki is too.

I won't be able to get inside the main house, not with her lording over it like a hot gargoyle. But Simon's studio, his office, should be clear. Nikki's supposed to be babysitting their kid, right? So, she should be in the main house. Not poking around in his office. That's *my* job.

I don't waste another second.

Within five minutes, I'm dressed in my newly Amazon-purchased stealth uniform: black hoodie, black leggings, black cap. Cliché but functional. Forgettable. I'm just a night jogger, like Stevie. Except I'm not jogging. I'm hunting.

In a crouch, I cross the road, my heart thumping so hard it echoes in my ears. One glance down the street. Another behind me.

All clear. I vanish beneath the magnolia tree like a shadow, taking the same route I took before.

The side of the house is quiet. When I round the final corner, I find the studio dark except for one small table lamp left glowing, casting an amber haze over an otherwise empty room. I inch closer and lightly pull at the sunroom door.

Locked because, of course, it is.

I don't give up just yet. A thought scratches at my memory. A whisper of something from before. The key! There was a key back here somewhere, wasn't there? I check all the usual suspects. Run my hands along the doorframe. Nothing. Beneath the flowerpots. Nothing again. Then I see it: a brick, just slightly off in color. It's subtle, but not to me.

I grip it. To my relief, it gives. And there it is. A key, tucked inside like a secret.

I slip it into the lock, twist. The click is as subtle as a stab in the dark.

Inside the studio, I move quietly. It's familiar. Everything is the same as last time I was here yet completely different. It's funny how knowledge and perspective can change the way you see a thing. Or someone.

I sift through the portfolio where Heather's portrait had been tucked. They are all still there, except Heather's. Hers is gone. It was here—*I saw it*. I rush to the stack of canvases leaning against the wall and thumb through them like a madwoman, my fingers trembling.

Gone.

I pivot to the desk, yanking open drawers. Binders, folders, receipts. A few labeled in that sharp, deliberate handwriting I know too well. I pull out a leather case. Inside, I don't find Heather's drawing, but I do find a box of condoms, opened with a few missing. He never used these with me.

Something curls in my stomach. Does he use them with Stevie? Or Nikki? The thought makes me sick.

I keep digging. Something clatters. A paperweight falls off the desk and hits the hardwood floor with a heavy, solid thump. So much for being careful.

I freeze. Waiting.

Inside the house, Ollie growls, a low, annoyed snarl, but he doesn't bark.

No footsteps. No door creaks. No voices.

Still safe.

I bend to pick up the paperweight, and that's when I see it. A glint of silver. A flash or a reflection, I'm not sure, but it's coming from under his bed.

I crawl forward, heart pounding in my ears. It's a fireproof lockbox, black and compact. My fingers grip the handle and slide the box from beneath the bed. I twist the key that's already in the lock and lift the lid.

The contents are unimpressive at first. The treasures of a grown man are not that different from those of a teenage boy. There are loose guitar picks—one signed by someone named Jim Morrison. There's a wristband from a long-ago festival. A folded set list on crumpled paper. A tiny metal tin filled with needles and ink cartridges—tattoo stuff. A burner phone, maybe. I don't know.

A letter. Handwritten. The paper is creased and soft, folded like it's been read again and again.

S,

I need to see you in person. It's important!

Love, H.

There's no date. Just those few words, and they feel like a scream in a silent room. I shove it into my pocket and rise to my feet.

A sound ricochets in my ears like a stone.

Footsteps.

They are soft and muffled at first but growing louder by the second. Closer. The inner door, the one leading into the main house. The knob begins to turn.

I bolt for the exterior door. My fingers fumble at the knob. Panic rushes through me like ice water.

I'm almost there, almost out.

But I'm not fast enough.

The door behind me creaks open.

And someone steps inside.

What We Do in Secret

CHAPTER

THIRTY-TWO

I spin around so fast I nearly trip over my own feet, already rehearsing a dozen different lies in my head. Something wild. Like the truth. Or at least a half-truth. Simon and I have been sleeping together. She'll at least feel like she holds some power. People always do when they have a secret, but it won't be anything compared to what I have.

But it's not Nikki's voice I hear. It's Simon's.

"Karla? What the fuck are you doing in here?"

It isn't quite relief that washes over me because I would prefer not to have been caught by anyone, even Simon, but it's certainly something relief-adjacent. My shoulders drop. My heart, not so much. Simon, I can handle.

At least, I think I can.

Simon stands in the doorway, and his presence feels shockingly intimidating. Anger has a way of filling a space. My mother's was the same. His black leather jacket hugs his frame, a white T-shirt snug across his chest, black jeans slung low on his hips. His hair is tousled, like he has been running his hands through it or has just gotten out of a car with the windows down. He looks good. Annoyingly so.

I blink, feigning surprise, then a coy smile.

"There you are. I was starting to think you weren't going to be back on time."

He doesn't answer, just stares at me like he's trying to read something in my face. Or my hands. My pockets.

I scramble for a story, something believable, simple. Something which won't give away that I was hoping to find a thread, a trace, a leftover clue about Heather. About Stevie. About whoever the hell Simon is when no one's looking.

Instead, I tilt my head and say the thing I know will work. It does feel a bit like I'm grabbing the low-hanging fruit, though.

"I missed you," I purr, stepping close enough to touch. "I saw Stevie leave, and I was hoping maybe I could catch you and we could..." My fingers slide along the zipper of his jacket.

He smirks despite himself. The edge softens. He shuts the sunroom door behind him. The latch clicks with a sound that feels more like a trap than a seal.

"You're crazy," he says, even while he steps closer. "Nikki and Bodhi are upstairs."

"I know," I murmur. "It was a dumb idea. I should go."

"Wait," he says. His tone drops low enough to land right in the pit of my stomach. His fingers are wrapped around my wrist. "You changed your hair." He pulls the cap off my head, freeing it to fall down my back.

There's heat now, thick and familiar. It rises between us like steam. One hand finds my waist, and the other runs through my curls. He smells like whiskey. The scent reminds me of the burn.

"I missed your crazy ass too."

Simon leans in, and I almost pull away. *Almost.* But instead, I let it happen. His mouth meets mine, hungry and rushed. My mind splits. Half of me is here, going through the motions. The other half is focused on the letter in my pocket, like it's oxygen.

"What are you doing?" I ask, half breathless.

"We have to be quick." He's already unzipping his pants.

My sweats are down around my knees before I can think twice. I pause only to ask—

"Do you have a condom?" I just want to see.

He laughs, low and amused. "Since when do you care?"

I don't answer. He lifts me like it's nothing and lays me back on the small bed in the corner of the studio. The rest happens so fast that it's almost too easy to detach from. When it's over, I can't help but notice how much the room smells like sweat and cigarettes.

He lights one lazily, like we've got all the time in the world, even though we both know we don't.

"You really should go now." He blows smoke toward the ceiling. "If Stevie sees you leaving—"

"She'll kill me?" I finish for him. I don't know why I said it.

He turns to me and smiles. "She'll kill us both."

I'm already pulling my clothes back on, careful—*so* careful—not to let the corner of the folded letter slip out of my pocket. Not that he would notice. Simon doesn't look at me again, even when I turn to say goodbye to him while I slip out the sunroom door.

I move low and fast, like a prey animal. My legs feel shaky, my chest tighter than before. But I did it. I got the letter. It's not everything, but it's something.

I'm halfway down the driveway when I feel it, that pull, that tight coil at the base of my neck. Like I'm being watched.

I glance down the street. No Stevie.

But I don't linger.

I round the corner of the fence and dart across the lawn, heading for my house like it's the only safe place left on the planet. Ironic, how things change.

The letter is still in my pocket. My fingers twitch to read it again, but not yet. Not here.

A sound, low and familiar, perks my ears. It's so subtle I think it was manifested from my paranoia. But it wasn't.

It wasn't a branch snapping or a rock cracking beneath my shoes.

It was deliberate.

Like the click of a camera shutter.

I freeze. Just for a second. My eyes flick behind me, but the darkness is still. *Too* still.

I don't check. I won't.

I shove my key in my door and disappear inside, locking it behind me.

But the uneasy feeling lingers, scratching at the edges of my mind, keeping me from getting any sleep.

I haven't been sleeping even an hour when my eyes shoot open, sudden panic gripping my chest into a vise. Slowly and all at once, I realize what the sound had been.

The subtle click of a door shutting, quietly, like they didn't want me to know it had been open.

Someone saw me.

And I have a feeling I know who it is.

THIRTY-THREE

I watch from between the blinds while Simon's van pulls off our street around four o'clock. My heart thuds like I've been sprinting, even though all I have done is pace the bedroom for hours. My hand hovers on the doorknob. I have to get to Stevie's. Now.

Something isn't right. Maybe I'm just paranoid, but I believe paranoia has its own kind of instinct, and mine has never been louder.

And there's only one way to find out for sure.

I grab my house keys, but my phone rings. It's Dr. McCoy's office.

Shoot.

I almost let it go to voicemail. But not answering, again, would mean a house call, and the last thing I need right now is a mandated mental health visit on top of everything else. I swipe to answer.

"Hello. Karla Cooper," I say in the most cheerful tone I can muster.

"Ms. Cooper," a familiar voice replies, smoother than I expected. Not the receptionist. It's Dr. McCoy herself.

Of course, it is. This is not going to be good.

"I hope I'm not catching you at a bad time," she says.

"No, no," I lie. "I'm fine. Just...tired. It's been a long week."

"I'm sure," she continues. "I suppose that's why you've missed our last two appointments?"

"I'm really sorry. I've just been so busy. There's been a lot going on."

"Yes, I can tell. Unfortunately, your court agreement doesn't really care about busy, Karla. The consequence for missed appointments is a house call, tentative to further punishment. I'm actually halfway to your house now."

A cold flush washes over me. "Right now?"

"Yes. I was hoping we could talk in person."

Panic flares. "Now's...really not a good time."

"I'm terribly sorry to hear that." Dr. McCoy's voice drips with faux empathy. "But I'm not the one who missed her court-mandated sessions and silenced two follow-up calls."

I wince. She knows. Of course, she does. Dr. McCoy is sharp like that. I curse myself for not answering, but to be fair, once I was in the middle of taking care of Mother, and the other time I was learning photography with Stevie.

"I understand," I answer quickly, forcing calm into my voice. "Really, I do. It's just—I'm not home right now." I peek through the blinds again, like I expect her car to roll up right then and there.

"Oh? And when do you plan to be home?"

"Tomorrow," I say. "I'm babysitting for a friend. The parents won't be back until then. I can't leave the kid alone."

She sighs. "There's no way you can come home today?"

"I'm afraid not."

"Well," she continues after a pause, "I'll expect you in the office first thing tomorrow. And if I don't see you then, the next visit will be a house call. Without a heads-up."

"Yes. Yes, I understand. I'll be there."

When I finally end the call, I see my battery is at fifteen percent. Perfect. One more thing to worry about. But it gives me an idea.

If Dr. McCoy *does* swing by on a hunch—and I would, if I were her—I can't be here. That makes going to Stevie's house all the more urgent. Two birds. One stone. I would read the room and stay visible. And unavailable.

I lock the door behind me and tuck the key into my pocket. My fingers tremble slightly while I cross the street. Nikki answers the door with a smirk, like she's been waiting.

"Stevie! Your neighbor's here!" she calls into the house, already turning away like she can't be bothered.

Stevie appears, ponytail messy, shirt slightly stained. "Hey. What's—? You...changed your hair."

"I did." I try not to linger too much on how similar it is to her own. "I'm so sorry to bother you. It's the dumbest thing, but I locked myself out. My phone's almost dead, and I was hoping I could charge it while I wait on the locksmith?"

"I can probably get you back in. I've got a crowbar—"

"No!" I say too quickly. "No, it's fine. I'd rather leave it to the professionals. I'm thinking about selling soon, and I don't want to risk any latch damage."

Stevie narrows her eyes but nods. "Sure. Come in."

I step inside. The tension in the room hits me like humidity in July. Nikki is already seated at the dining room table, eyes glued to me, grinning from ear to ear.

"Android or—?" Stevie asks.

"IPhone."

She plugs the charger in on the bar, and I hand over my phone, trying not to glance in Nikki's direction.

"Nice hair. What was your inspiration?" she asks.

"I just wanted to go a little darker for fall. You know, something different." I wave her comment off.

First shots fired, I think.

"So, I see you got Simon his package." Nikki's tone is sugar-laced and bitter. She ignores my response to her hair jab entirely, wasting no time. Nikki knows. She *definitely* saw me.

Stevie blinks. "What package?"

"The one she dropped by the other day to give you," Nikki says with a bit of certainty in her tone, glancing at Stevie. "Didn't I tell you?"

Stevie turns to her. "No, you didn't."

I sense the slightest bit of hostility.

Nikki shrugs. "Guess I forgot. I was cleaning and saw it on his desk later. Figured she came back by." Her eyes bore into me, head cocked in mock innocence.

It's infuriating.

"I actually left it in the mailbox," I say. "He must've gotten it out."

"Mmhmm," Nikki hums.

"Next time, just leave it with me," Stevie says. "We don't need anyone swiping packages from the box."

"Of course. I tried, but Nikki said you were busy. And Simon couldn't be disturbed." The jab lands exactly where it's meant to.

Nikki's smile flickers slightly. Before she can strike back, Stevie's phone rings.

"Melissa," she stammers into the phone. A second later, yelling erupts from the other end. Stevie's entire demeanor changes. She appears smaller. "Okay...Stop yelling, Melissa. I can...barely hear you...Okay...I'm sorry...Yeah...I'm leaving now."

She hangs up.

"I forgot to pack Bodhi's inhaler, and he's having an attack. I've got to go. Let yourself out, okay?"

Before I can respond, she swipes something from a drawer in the kitchen and is out the door.

And then there were two.

Nikki doesn't move. I open my mouth to speak, but she cuts me off.

"Save it," she snaps. "It's just you and me now. I'm onto your bullshit."

I keep my expression neutral, trying to steady my voice. "I have no idea what you're talking about."

She smiles like a shark. "Oh, I get it, girl. You don't have to explain why you started sleeping with him to me. It's not like he never tried with me. It was pathetic, really. He'll fuck anything that moves. Going through with it, though? That's a whole other level of slutty."

I don't flinch. I won't give her the satisfaction.

"I'm going to tell Stevie. I'll go ahead and get *that* on the table." Like she just told me what the plans are for a fun night out. But the words drop between us like a grenade.

I swallow. "And you think she'll believe you?"

Nikki leans forward. "I *saw* you. Leaving his studio. I heard what was going on. And I've seen the way you look at him. Honestly? I'm shocked Stevie hasn't figured it out. But then again, that girl loses all sense when it comes to that boy. Plus, it helps that I have photos of you taking the run of shame."

Her tone is casual, but her smile has a scalpel's edge.

"And I'd like to thank you, honestly," she adds, surprising me.

"I beg your pardon?"

"For being the key to finally getting Stevie away from that waste of skin. I never liked him. From the beginning, he reeked of entitlement. He was married, you know. When Stevie met him. So, you?" She laughs softly. "You're a goddamn blessing. Better now than after a wedding. Or worse, a baby. You've been wonderfully sloppy. I never could catch him in the act before. So, I'm grateful, really."

My fists clench under the table. "Don't."

"Sweetheart," she says, standing, "you think I care what happens to you? You think this is about you? No. It's about saving Stevie from herself. You can let yourself out."

She turns toward the stairs, not the kitchen.

And that's when something inside me cracks.

Before I can even register what is going on, I grab the nearest object to me—a baseball bat from the bar, probably Bodhi's. I follow her up five or six stairs before she realizes I'm behind her.

It isn't something I remember deciding. Only doing.

The bat cracks against the back of her skull before she can react. To save herself.

Nikki stumbles, losing her footing, and goes down the stairs in a twisted, snapping tumble.

I press against the wall, the breath stolen from my lungs.

At the bottom of the stairs, her body crumples like a dropped doll, neck twisted and bent in ways that make my stomach feel like it needs to empty itself. Blood blooms beneath her head like a dark flower. It's strangely beautiful...and familiar.

I wait. Wait for her to move. To moan. To speak. But she doesn't.

I descend slowly, every step like glue underfoot. Her eyes are fixed but not seeing. Her limbs are all wrong. Her face slack.

She's dead. I don't even need to check her pulse.

I look away, squeezing the bat in my fists to simply have something to hold. To tether me to reality. Otherwise, I may float off.

When I turn back, her eyes are staring right through me, and my heart seizes. But it's just my nerves. She's gone.

Not Nikki. Not anymore.

Just a heap of broken parts.

It's insane how quickly you can reduce someone to almost nothing. I have to get out of here. But before I do, I swipe her cell phone from the table. I carry it over to where Nikki's body is lying at the base of the stairs and use her finger to unlock the screen.

It doesn't take long to find the photo. Or photos. Taken from the front door, it seems. That explains the sound I heard.

There I am. Guilty as sin, running in my stalker outfit from the side of the house. Then another under the magnolia tree, gazing up the street, a wild look in my eye. Me crossing the street.

I hit the delete button on them all, then go to her trash folder and empty it. After a quick swipe of the phone to make sure there's nothing else incriminating, I place it back on the table.

Then I open the side door leading out to the gated yard, where Ollie is playing. He won't come in while I'm here, but eventually, he will.

With the scene set, I leave, like I was never there.

What We Do in Secret

CHAPTER

THIRTY-FOUR

A sharp pain rips through my fingertip when I pull another sliver of nail from the quick. I wince but never allow my eyes to leave the blue and red lights flashing across the street.

Ever since I made it back home, I have been watching the house. A dozen times, I wanted to run back over, just to see. I didn't even check Nikki's pulse. How could I have just her there without checking?

If she wasn't dead and somehow survived, I'm done for.

What am I thinking? She looked more dead than alive, right? I think back to her lying at the bottom of the stairs. She was more a pretzel than a person. Nikki couldn't have been alive. I'm sure of it.

Still, I watched the front door, expecting her to walk out, her neck all crooked and terrifying, making her way into my house and dragging me to the basement stairs. It's because of this my eyes never left the door. Not even when Stevie arrived back home. I heard her scream from here.

Simon whipped into the driveway not long after that, spinning tires and dust. He pulled all the way up to the house, so close I thought he might crash into the garage. Simon left the front door open, and I caught glances of them while they moved in and out of the kitchen, Stevie on the phone with what I presume had been the emergency responders.

They arrived minutes later, their lights and sirens piercing the evening. A few of our neighbors peeked out of their own windows to observe the scene.

So nosy.

After a reasonable amount of time, I decide I need to go over there. After all, we were all friends not that long ago. And it looks more suspicious for me *not* to.

I pull on my white cardigan and hurry across the street in a half run. A deputy holds his arm out to stop me just as I am about to break the threshold.

"Ma'am, you aren't allowed in there."

"Oh my God, Stevie!" I yell through the door, hoping she'll hear me. I turn back to the deputy. "Is Bodhi okay? Did he get hurt?"

"I'm sorry, ma'am, but this is a secure scene."

"Just tell me if he's okay! Bodhi! Stevie! Simon! Are you okay?" I yell.

Tears are rolling down my face now. The deputy doesn't budge. I try to push past him, but he grabs my arms. It's at that moment that Simon rounds the corner to the door.

"Simon, thank God! Is Bodhi okay? Where's Stevie?"

"Bodhi's fine. Stevie's inside." He turns to the deputy blocking my path. "She's okay. She's a friend."

Hearing him call me that lights a fire in my chest. I almost smile but manage to hold back for now. Instead, I just let it warm my chest.

The deputy nods and drops his arm, allowing me to pass. Simon reaches out and places a hand behind my shoulder, guiding me inside. The chaos shifts to an uncomfortable silence once we enter the main room.

Simon's hand is now on the small of my back. He leads me into an area between the family room and the kitchen, where the stairs split the floor plan. My eyes go straight for the spot where Nikki was earlier, but the only thing remaining there is a pool of blood.

The paramedics are a few feet away, kneeling over a figure under a tarp.

She *is* dead. Thank God.

Relief fans the flame already ignited in my chest. And I was so afraid for nothing. It is then that one of the paramedics moves a few inches to the right.

Nikki is on the stretcher. The tarp covers almost her entire body, but it slips from her face.

For a moment, all I can see is her eyes, like darts staring right at me. I look away, putting my hand over my mouth. When I glance back, her head is hidden again. The paramedics lift the stretcher and begin to walk toward the door.

I watch her while they move past, and I fight the urge to lunge into it with all my power, to send it flying from their arms.

Stevie turns around then, her eyes bloodshot. I hadn't even noticed her standing there. When she sees me, she walks straight over, wraps her arms around me, and begins sobbing into my shoulder.

I glance at Simon, and he gives me a small smile. His eyes are swollen as well.

"It'll be okay," I say, embracing her.

"I don't know how this happened!" she sobs. "I don't know...She was fine when I left. When did you leave?"

"Minutes after you did. She was fine," I half lie.

"How could this have happened?"

"What did the police say? The paramedics?"

"They said she fell. When they got here, Ollie was going crazy, and they think he might have gotten underfoot while she was climbing the stairs. I just...I was just texting her and now—" She begins to gasp into my shoulder, and I cradle the back of her head in my hand.

"You talked to her?" A knot forms in my stomach.

"Right after I left. She said she had something to talk to me about and it was important."

"Do you know what it was about?"

"I don't know. She said she had to talk to me in person and to get home, but I was so busy with Bodhi and appeasing Melissa...I should have just come the fuck home!" She pulls away from me and grips her hair in both hands.

I grab her wrists to keep her from yanking it out in chunks.

"Stevie! Stevie! Look at me! It's not your fault. It's not your—"

"Yes, it is, Karla! It is! If I had just come home, then..."

"It was an accident. She just lost her balance! The police said so. There was nothing you could have done."

Simon places a hand on her shoulder and caresses it. Her breathing slows.

"I have to go down to the coroner's office. Oh God. I have to call her mom. She doesn't even know! I have to—Bodhi! Oh no! Bodhi! He's going to get off the bus and see all this and—"

"You go and do whatever you need to do. I'll stay here and wait for Bodhi," Simon says.

"I don't know if I can go by myself, babe. I just—can't. Melissa—"

"No. I'll need to talk to Melissa later. She'll ask me a million questions that I don't have the answers to yet, and it'll just lead to a fight. I'll just stay and wait for him, and then I'll be up there as soon as I can, okay?"

"Babe..." Stevie cries.

"I'll wait for Bodhi," I say.

They both look at me.

"Karla, I couldn't ask you to do that."

"Simon, you go too. She shouldn't be driving in this state. I'll wait for Bodhi. I'll clean this up, make dinner, and get him in bed. Take as long as you need." I give Stevie's shoulder a gentle squeeze. "Take as much time as you need."

She looks like she may start crying again, but to my surprise, she hugs me. Simon offers a small smile over her shoulder.

"Go! Give me a call later and let me know what's going on."

"Thank you, Karla. I-I'm sorry for how I've been treating you."

"Go!" I brush off her apology, as warranted as it may be.

She hugs me again and is out the door in a flash. Simon lingers behind her. I like the softness in his eyes while he considers me.

"Thank you," he says, and for a moment I think he may lean down and kiss me in front of all these people.

When he doesn't and briefly touches my shoulder instead, I am slightly relieved. It would be in bad taste right now, with everything going on.

"It's no problem. Seriously. You should be there for her right now."

He nods and walks out behind Stevie.

That's right, Stevie. Karla to the rescue.

This will show her how secure I am. How reliable. Sending her off while I stay at home with their kid and scrub up blood from her hardwood floors. If she didn't before, Stevie certainly sees me now. How capable I am of supporting her little family in all the ways they deserve. How capable I am of protecting them.

Once the medics drive off, Stevie and Simon follow in her car. The police and fire truck leave soon after.

I am alone and turn to the blood at the base of the steps. There is a flash of Nikki there, but only briefly. If that bitch had just kept her nose out of my business...

I need to get this cleaned up before Bodhi comes home.

CHAPTER

THIRTY-FIVE

The secret ingredient to removing blood is a thin layer of peroxide. Let it sit for about fifteen minutes, then go over it with cold water and baking soda. Wipe it away gently with a microfiber towel.

Even with this foolproof technique, it takes over an hour to clean it all up, and it still leaves a slight stain at the base of the stairs. My hands have a tint which refuses to wash off, no matter how hard I scrub them with a Brillo pad and bleach. By the time I finish, I'm not sure if the red on my skin is from the blood or if it was rubbed raw.

It doesn't matter. Dinner needs to be started soon if Bodhi is going to eat tonight.

I decide on something quick but nutritious.

Bodhi comes through the door, slinging parts of himself everywhere, while I'm taking the roasted chicken out of the oven. A backpack thrown here, a shoe there. Nothing together. He tosses himself over the back of the couch and pulls out his phone, clicking away at a game that sounds violent. His hair is a mess. One foot is stuck out over the back of the couch, and his dirty sock is halfway off his foot.

I shake my head.

"Bodhi," I call.

He peers over the back of the couch. Surprised.

"Hey, Ms. Coo—I mean, Karla. Where's Dad?"

"He and Stevie had to go and take care of some things. I made you dinner." I gesture for him to join me.

"I'm starving." He jumps to his feet and follows me into the kitchen. His eyes widen at the modest spread. "Is it a holiday?"

"A holiday? I don't think so. Why?" I ask, taking the apron off and hanging it on the hook on the wall.

"I only see food like this at Thanksgiving!" Bodhi takes his seat at the table, and I begin the process of spooning food onto his plate.

I already know the kinds of things he likes, so it isn't hard. He watches me enthusiastically. It is a little more than he is used to, but it is hardly Thanksgiving dinner. Roasted chicken and vegetables, wild rice, mashed potatoes, macaroni and cheese with bacon bits. And I made an apple crumble for dessert.

The poor thing needs more to eat than chicken nuggets and grilled cheese.

"Well, Thanksgiving shouldn't get all the fun," I say.

He nods in agreement, but his mouth is already full of mac and cheese. Bodhi resembles Simon so much. I have to force myself to look away from him and finish my own plate.

After dinner and telling me all the newest NASA-released information, Bodhi takes a shower and gets into his pajamas. We settle on the couch, and I read a novel I found in one of the boxes. A novel by someone named Tarryn Fisher. It feels a little kitschy.

Bodhi opts to doodle in his sketchbook. I didn't mind that we weren't talking; I like cuddling with him like this. If all goes as planned, very soon, we'll be doing this all the time.

I wake up to him asleep on my lap and run my fingers through his honey hair.

He could easily pass as mine on the street now. No one would know the difference.

After a while, I carry him up to his bedroom—Bodhi is a lot heavier than he looks—where I tuck him in and turn on his galaxy nightlight.

I check for a message from Stevie.

There are none.

Simon messaged me, though. Nikki's mom is flying in, and they are going to meet her at the hotel instead of at the house, for obvious reasons. Stevie is still understandably upset.

I message him back to tell him that our boy is fed, watered, and sound asleep. There's a plate in the oven, and I put the rest in Tupperware in the fridge. It should be a few days' worth, so they won't have to worry about cooking.

Simon: Why are you so wonderful?

To read those words a month ago would have warmed my entire body. Now, it's like snake venom. But I have to play the part if I'm going to be able to get Stevie and Bodhi away from him. Plus, it's a good thing they will be a while longer. That will give me time to do some digging for those skeletons Melissa was talking about.

Me: You just figuring this out? ;)

The doorbell rings at that exact moment, sending a tone throughout the entire house. The last thing I need is someone waking Bodhi up after I've just gotten him down. The tone is followed by several aggressive knocks.

I run to the door and open it, expecting the police or something. At the sight of the beige ensemble and salt-white hair, I immediately regret not at least checking to see who it was first.

CHAPTER

THIRTY-SIX

Melissa Van Lowe is standing in the doorway, and the expression on her face probably mirrors mine. Shock... Confusion. But then hers morphs into something else.

Anger.

No. *Rage.*

"Corinne? What the fuck are you doing here?" Her tone is sharp. She takes a few steps into the house, and I move back instinctively.

"I—"

"When I heard that one of Stevie's little bitch friends was keeping my son without my consent, without anyone telling me what the hell is going on, that was bad enough. But you? *You're* the friend!"

She takes another few steps toward me.

"I-I live next door. I'm just trying to help."

"No. No. See, don't lie. I knew something was off about you when I met you, but I couldn't put my finger on it."

"I'm not lying. I—"

"Stevie put you up to talking to me, didn't she? That bitch just doesn't know when to quit."

"Stevie doesn't know!"

"Oh, I'm sure." She scoffs, rolling her eyes. "So, you're just crazy, then? I honestly wouldn't be surprised. You are the company you keep, honey, and that 'friend' of yours is the queen of crazy. You know what? I don't give a shit about any of this. I'll handle it in court. Where's my son?"

"He's asleep. Please don't yell. I just got him down."

"I will do as I please with my own child. I'm taking him home with me. Now! His *real* home. Bodhi! Mommy's here. It's time to go. Pack your stuff!"

If she keeps this up, she'll wake the entire neighborhood.

"Melissa, please, just listen."

"I'm *done* listening. I've been more than accommodating to my ex-husband and his whore. Sending one of her groupies to stalk me, though, that takes the cake." Melissa pushes me out of the way and heads toward the stairs. "None of you will ever see me or my son again. I swear, Simon attracts some of the craziest—"

It happened so quickly, but it was only flashes.

The glass dish I baked the chicken in is on the bar, waiting to be washed. I slam it over the top of her head. But she doesn't fall. She just sort of...stops.

When Melissa turns toward me, a clean line of blood pours down her forehead and over her cheek. Her eyes are wide with shock, and she glares at me. She lifts her finger to her head.

The blood is down to her jawline, and she trembles as she moves.

She takes in the blood on the pads of her fingers, and her entire body begins to shake. Melissa looks back at me like a wild animal, about to pounce. Or maybe *I* am the wild animal in this scenario.

Her eyes move toward the stairs, just briefly, but enough for me to anticipate her next move. She darts up the stairs in a knee-jerk movement. It's impressive how quickly she can still move with that injury.

Her high heels make so much noise clipping against the hardwood of the stairs. I scale them two at a time and catch up with her easily enough. If she weren't so dazed from the head trauma, she may have been able to reach the top before me, but she can barely keep her feet steady. She slams into one wall and then the other, one hand seesawing between holding her bleeding head wound and steadying herself on the wall, leaving bloody handprints in her wake.

When she is within reach, I grab both her ankles at the same time and yank as hard as I can toward me.

She falls forward in a quick snapping motion, and her neck hits the top landing. The crack when it makes contact with the wood resonates. She doesn't move again.

I step over Melissa's body and make my way toward Bodhi's room. He is still sound asleep, sweet little face as serene as ever. I smile and ease the door closed.

Now to clean up this mess...again.

CHAPTER

THIRTY-SEVEN

Turns out, murder is nothing like burglary. There is no blueprint. No familiar rhythm. No adrenaline rush subsiding into cocky relief. And worst of all, no list of rules to make sure everything goes smoothly.

Burglary is clean. Calculated. You plan, you enter, you exit. If you're smart, no one even knows you were there until days later, maybe even weeks.

Murder? That's messy. In fact, it's the messiest thing I've ever experienced in my life. So...much...blood. And the worst part, I have no list of rules to keep everything from going awry.

Most of my burglary rules are transferable, I suppose, but I don't think there is anything which can prepare you for the after. Because *after*...there's always a body to consider. Luckily, Google is a generous teacher. Ask the right questions, and it'll give you answers. Detailed ones. Disturbingly so.

Seriously, it's concerning.

I'm not in a position to complain, though. Researching how to dispose of a body is about as easy as stalking someone's tax history. Public. Casual. Strangely normalized. And there are so many tried-and-true methods to choose from.

Burn it. Bury it. Weigh it down and drop it in a lake. Dissolve it in acid. Feed it to pigs.

But practice is where theory falls apart. Especially when time is of the essence.

I ultimately decide on the "No body, no crime" theory. It has a poetic kind of logic. If there is nothing left, there is nothing to accuse. People go missing all the time, and what's better, if you are an adult, you are allowed to disappear yourself anytime you want.

So, Melissa just took off. That's the story. Got tired of her personal life being so public and she just went dark. And if I do this right, that's all anyone will ever know.

I do feel a pinch of sadness for Bodhi, poor thing, since I murdered his mother, technically. It won't matter much to him that I didn't have a choice. I couldn't let her take him away from us, couldn't allow her to expose me to Stevie and Simon. I just couldn't.

Can you imagine having a "Momfluencer" as your only access to the world? The poor thing would never get to just be a kid. I know what it's like. My mother probably never even heard of a blog. I can't imagine how emboldened she would have been had she had an audience to encourage her. And anyway, it's not like every biological mother makes you whole. I'm living proof of that too.

All that matters now is that Bodhi has someone who loves him. Someone stable. Someone who will protect him. And for now, that person is me. Maybe Stevie, once I find out what she knows or doesn't know about Heather. But that has now become a problem for another day.

Tonight, I have a mess to clean up.

It wasn't as hard as I thought it would be.

The saw in Stevie's garage proves capable of getting the job done.

Don't get me wrong, I am certainly not built for manual labor. Carving through bone proves to be...a challenge. But there is something oddly serene about it once I get in a groove. I don't feel sick, and I don't cry. Just...did what needed to be done.

Hands. Arms. Legs. Torso. Head. In that order. Wrapped in layer upon layer of trash bags and sealed with duct tape.

I drag the parts out to the garden in the dark. The moon is bright enough to see by, but not so illuminating that I am nervous of being seen. The cinderblocks lining the garden floor have to be moved first. They are heavy bastards, and my manicure will never return from this. But underneath them, the soil is soft. Welcoming.

I am halfway through digging when my shovel hits something hard with a loud *clang*.

I pause. Wipe sweat from my brow with the back of my gloved hand. It could be a rock. Or an old pipe. Either way, I don't have time to find out, and I can't risk breaking something which may need a professional to come poking around about.

After moving six inches to the right, I start digging again. The earth gives more easily here.

When I'm done, I lower the bags one by one, covering them with a thick layer of dirt. I stomp the graveside down with my boots and replace the stones. It isn't perfect, but no one has any reason to look here. Not unless they are psychic or deeply unlucky.

A rustling from behind causes me to turn.

Ollie stares at me from the doghouse like he knows.

"What are you looking at, beast?" I snap.

He grumbles and lowers his head, but luckily, he remains quiet. Maybe he's not completely stupid after all. Or the smell of blood wafting from me has alerted him to who the real alpha is here, and he has finally learned his place.

The garage is worse. Blood in the grout. Smudges on the walls. A smear on the ceiling where something must have slipped from my grip. Thank goodness for the pressure washer in the corner.

It takes an hour, maybe two, to get everything clean. I scrub until my hands ache and the smell of bleach burns behind my eyes. Afterward, I take a glorious shower in Stevie's bathroom again, opting to borrow a large T-shirt and a pair of pajama pants.

Surely, she won't mind. It looks like I'm spending the night anyway.

Melissa's vehicle is another thing entirely. I don't have time to take it to the next town and abandon it like the internet suggests, so I park it in my garage for the time being. No one will come looking for it there, and when I get a moment, I'll take it and dump it at the Fulton Marina or the airport. Maybe they'll assume she drowned herself or caught a flight somewhere beautiful.

I'll decide in the car.

That's where I find Melissa's phone, tucked between the seat, still on the charger. I grab it and head back to Stevie's house before anyone can see me. I hadn't planned to go through Melissa's things, but when I realize it is unlocked...I can't resist.

Curiosity isn't even the right word. It's something darker.

I sink into the couch with a glass of wine and start by opening her gallery. It doesn't take me long to realize something about Melissa: She's completely obsessed with Stevie.

Photo after photo. Candid shots from years ago, when they were friends. Even photos of her sleeping? Weird, Melissa. Stolen images from Stevie's social media when she had one. Blurry zooms of Stevie working at O'Keefe's. Some of these appear recent. Some even seem like screenshots from surveillance footage. Others...I don't even know how she got them.

There are more photos of Stevie than there are of her own son.

And the notes app...Jesus. That's the smoking gun. They are nothing like her blog posts she curated so carefully. While those were damaging, these are straight vile. Uninhibited. Hate pours across the screen in frantic digital ink. She wrote about Stevie like she wanted to skin her alive. If Melissa weren't buried in Stevie's garden right now, I would be afraid for her life.

Bitch thinks I don't remember. I remember everything.

Does she think I won't tell?

She betrayed me. After everything. After what she did.

She knows the truth and still walks around like she's innocent.

What truth? What has she done? She can't have killed Heather. No, Stevie isn't a killer. She isn't...But...

I scroll faster, heart hammering.

Then I find it.

A photo.

I don't have to guess who the girl in the picture is. It's Heather Crosp. And the two people positioned on either side of her are none other than Melissa and Simon. Bodhi stands in front of Heather, and her hands rest gently on his shoulders, like she's familiar with him. He seems to be comfortable with her as well.

Melissa looks like Miss America, as always, and Simon is completely different. He's clean-cut, tattoos almost entirely covered with a white button-up. His hair is not in its usual state of disheveled and is instead slicked back, like a 1920s gangster. All four of them are beaming, completely oblivious to what will happen to Heather in just a few short weeks, considering the date of the photo.

I stare at the screen until my hands go cold. The room feels like it's closing in around me. And for the first time since all this started, I wonder if maybe I buried the right monster, after all.

CHAPTER

THIRTY-EIGHT

Covering my tracks with Melissa proves to be a whole lot easier when Nikki's parents decide to fly her body back to Arizona for her funeral. That means Stevie and Simon are out of the picture for at least forty-eight hours, enough time to make sure I left no breadcrumbs—wipe the prints, kill the trace, take out the trash.

Literally.

It is the only reason I turn down keeping Bodhi while they are away. Believe me, it isn't easy, especially after listening to Stevie vent about how Melissa ghosted them out of spite for not telling her what happened to Nikki.

That little boy has a way of grabbing your heart, like he was meant to live there. It is difficult to turn down quality time with him, but I have business to handle. *Quiet* business. The kind best done alone. So, when Stevie offers me their spare key instead and asks me to at least feed their beast of a dog, Ollie, I smile and nod like the trustworthy neighbor I am.

He'll eat. Eventually.

With the three of them gone, I finally have room to move.

Nobody notices when I pull out of my garage in Melissa's car and take it to the run-down side of town, a place I never would have ended up if I had not looked into Heather's family. When I saw where her sister lived, I figured two birds, one stone. I leave it running in an alley with no cameras, keys in the ignition. Windows down. It's practically begging someone to make it disappear.

I walk the last few blocks on foot. The soles of my shoes are sticky with heat and anticipation of where I'm going next. I stop in front of a gray brick apartment with a rusting screen door. Cigarette butts line the stoop.

Heather's family wasn't hard to find. It's almost disrespectful how easy it is to track people down. Apparently, after having a falling out with their mother, Heather moved in with her older sister, Shelby, the woman from the restaurant, who was little more than a kid herself. I can't imagine being twenty-two and responsible for a teenager. No wonder it ended like it did.

I knock once, and to my surprise, Shelby answers quickly. Too quickly. A girl like her should know better in a neighborhood like this. But grief doesn't leave much room for good judgment.

"Yes?"

Her eyes narrow, already suspicious. Hazel, hard. She looks like Heather, a version life weathered longer.

"I'm not selling anything," I say quickly. "I just wanted to ask a few questions about Heather."

Her mouth tightens. "Let me guess. Reporter?"

"No. God, no." I chuckle like it offends me. "I actually know Stevie."

That changes everything. Her face contorts like I've spit in her drink.

"Get out." She steps back to slam the door, but I press my hand gently to the frame.

"Wait. Just hear me out. I think Stevie might have had something to do with Heather's disappearance."

Her eyes flick to mine. There it was. The hook. Shelby's grip on the door loosens slightly.

"How do I know you're not just one of her spies?"

"You don't. I'm not asking you to believe me. Just let me ask you a couple of questions."

"And you're friends with her and thinking like this?" She almost laughs in disbelief.

"I'm *not* friends with them." My voice is lower now. "She moved in next door a few months ago, and…things haven't felt right. Especially with Bodhi. I'm really concerned about him."

Her posture softens like I've spoken a magic word. Shelby opens the door, and I step inside. The apartment is modest but cute. The bones are pretty rough, with exposed wiring and dingy carpet, but she's done her best to make it appear presentable. A place rug here and art hanging on the halls in a way that distracts from the erosion around it.

"Heather loved that little boy," she says. "She used to babysit him all the time when Simon and Melissa were still married. The family paid pretty well, and she was saving up for college. Heather wanted to be a child counselor." Her voice cracks at the last word. "She had such a good heart. I think she just got in too deep with that whole messed-up family."

"She babysat for Melissa, right?" I ask, even though I already know. "How did she know Stevie exactly?"

"She met Stevie through Melissa. She modeled for her sometimes." Shelby nods slowly, then pauses. Her jaw clenches. "And…"

"Simon?" I offer gently, but if anyone can confirm my suspicion, it's her.

She presses her lips into a line. "I don't have proof," Shelby says, whispering now. "But when she started modeling, everything changed. She got secretive. She'd leave after school, say she was doing a shoot, but she wouldn't come home until four in the morning. Who the hell takes photos that late? I begged her to drop me a pin. She never would. Then, one day, she just didn't come home at all."

My heartbeat ticks in my ears.

"So, the last place you *knew* her to be was with Stevie?"

Shelby nods. "She vanished. Just gone, off the face of the planet. The cops talked to Stevie, but I guess she had an alibi. She claimed they didn't even have a shoot that day, but I showed them the messages. She had powerful friends. Anyone could've lied for her."

Or Heather was the one who lied. This is the thread that needs to be pulled, but I don't. I'm sure Shelby has already entertained that thought.

"Did Heather have a room here?" I ask.

Shelby hesitates. "Yeah."

"Would it be okay if I…took a look? I know it's a lot to ask."

"I haven't touched anything," she says, her voice brittle. "Just in case she comes back."

Shelby leads me down a narrow hallway which smells of old cigarettes and Febreeze. Inside Heather's tiny room, the scent is no better, but there's also the stench of neglect. This room hasn't been opened in a long time.

It's cute, though. Soft pink bedding. Tea lights strung across the headboard. Band posters litter the wall. There are dozens of books stacked by the bed—psychology, mostly. *The Developing Mind*. *Trauma and the Body*. The kind of books someone reads when they are desperate to understand what's been done to them.

Shelby's phone rings in her pocket. She frowns. "I've gotta take this. I'll be right back."

I nod with wide eyes. "Take your time."

The second she's gone, I get to work.

Closet. Empty, aside from a hoodie which smells faintly of mold and vanilla musk perfume. There's nothing taped beneath the desk and nothing under the mattress but a few candy wrappers, a hair tie, and a Boba Tea receipt.

I am starting to think this is a waste of time when I notice the vent near the floor. It looks a little...off.

I kneel, tugging it open.

Bingo.

Tucked away inside the vent is a copy of Lolita. Of course. It's not a diary like I hoped, but this was obviously worth hiding. I just have to find out why. My fingers tremble while I flip it open. A caption has been scrawled on the inside front cover, in handwriting I'm all too familiar with.

My Sin. My Soul. —S

My stomach twists.

A photo falls from the pages. It's Simon and Heather. They are in a bed, but it isn't Stevie's. I'm familiar with her dark aesthetic, but this one is white. Too bright for Stevie's taste. I know whose taste it *does* match, though.

Melissa's.

He's shirtless, his arm around her waist, his lips against her cheek. She's young and in love. He looks like a predator.

There is something else tucked inside. I pull it out, and I can't breathe.

It's a sonogram. A sonogram with Heather's name typed at the top.

The date—a week before she vanished. My pulse is a thunderstorm in my chest.

Heather was pregnant. Heather was *pregnant.*

I barely have time to shove the book into my purse before Shelby's footsteps return. When they stop at the doorway, I stand quickly, brushing imaginary dust off my skirt. Heather's sister walks back into the room.

"I have to get to work," she says.

"Of course. You've been so generous with your time."

She looks me over, softer now but still cautious. "I hope this helps. But be careful with that woman. She's dangerous. All of them are. If Bodhi's still with them..."

"I know," I say, nodding.

I reach the door but pause with my hand on the knob.

"Would you mind...not telling anyone I came by?"

Shelby hesitates before finally agreeing. An understanding that if anyone knew I was here, I might be the next face on a cereal box.

I leave without looking back. The book weighs heavy in my purse, like a live grenade.

Heather was pregnant. She was seeing Simon. And those late-night "photoshoots"? I'm willing to bet everything I have she wasn't posing for Stevie at all. She was with Simon.

I didn't just have secrets in my purse.

I have a weapon. Maybe the very one that got rid of Heather.

Perhaps I can use it to smoke out her killer as well.

CHAPTER

THIRTY-NINE

So maybe my plan is a little risky. But this is a situation which requires a certain amount of risk. I'm not just dealing with a missing person now; I'm dealing with a potential murderer, and they live right across the street. And worse, because of me, he's the sole parent of a precious little boy who has no idea how much danger he's in.

So, the way I see it, I have two options. I can kill him. More mess. More cleanup. Back to the straightjacket I'll go. Or I can convince Stevie to leave him and take Bodhi with her. The latter feels like the more appealing option for me.

That's what leads me to sending a very provocative photo to Simon. One he can't ignore, leaving nothing to the imagination. Sure, I could have just snuck over there, like I did before, but I think maybe a part of me is preparing for Option One in case Option Two goes south. It will be much easier to manage in my own territory, where Stevie and Bodhi aren't piddling around.

He takes the bait pretty quickly. Men are simple like that.

A few tablets of Seroquel in his wineglass ensure he will

"accidentally" sleep over. Once I hear him snoring, it is difficult to find sleep myself. I don't dare take the pills; I need to be awake for the next part.

The sun is just beginning to filter through the sheer curtains, washing our skin in a hazy glow. I turn to Simon, who is still sleeping soundly, his chest rising and falling beneath my head, his heartbeat slow and rhythmic. My fingertips trace gently down the center of his chest, then his abdomen, the lines of ink on his skin, until my hand disappears beneath the blankets covering his waist.

Without opening his eyes, Simon smiles. "Good morning to you too," he says in a hushed, sleepy tone. He moves his hips into my hand while I continue to caress him.

"Good morning." I kiss his chest once, twice, three times.

God, he really is beautiful. I'll give him that. It should be illegal to be that attractive and that dangerous at the same time. Someone has to even the playing field.

"What are you trying to do to me, woman?" he murmurs.

"Keep you." I bite my lip.

He grins at this. Bodhi has that same smile.

The thought saddens my heart. Would Heather's child have resembled them? Will Bodhi inherit that boyish charm which seems to attract prey like honey?

God, I hope so. And I'll do everything in my power to make sure he isn't like his father in any other way.

"I'm right here, aren't I?" He turns to kiss me then.

I let out a sigh when he maneuvers his body over mine. We have sex twice before we sprawl in a tangle of sheets, fevered skin, and breathless bodies. He laughs, satisfied, and slowly pulls himself from the bed.

I fight the urge to lure him back. Back to this. Back to our little cocoon of just me and him before it all goes to poop. Because it is absolutely about to all go to shit. Part of me still wants to savor this version of us.

"Don't go," I whine.

He moves onto the bed again, propping one knee on the mattress.

Simon leans in to kiss me.

"As much as I'd love to stay here and ravish you all day, I have to return to the real world."

"Ugh, the real world is a thief of happiness," I groan.

"Maybe. Alas, responsibilities await." He grins again and continues to gather his clothes. His back is turned to me, every muscle perfectly contoured in the gentle light.

This is the money shot. I have to capture it. I reach for my camera on the nightstand and focus him in the lens. He hasn't noticed me yet. His head is slightly turned enough to make out the small dimple on his right cheek.

It is just like one of those candid shots I saw the first night I explored their house, only better. Better because the intimacy I have longed for since that first time I saw them embrace on the street is now mine. This beautiful man is half naked in my house, his hair tossed from my fingers running through it, his body still glistening from a night of making love to me in every way someone can imagine.

This is a moment that is mine, and I want to capture it because now I know that none of it was real. It wasn't real with them, and it isn't real now. Everything about him, about them, is an illusion.

I snap the photo, followed by the subtle shutter click. It's barely even a noise, but he heard it. Simon whips around, his eyes confused at first, but as they register the camera in my hand, they widen with something I don't comprehend at first. I've seen it before, sure, but it has never been directed at me.

"What are you doing?" he snaps.

"You looked so sexy standing there. I—"

"Delete it."

"Delete it? You're being stupid." I laugh.

The muscles in his jaw flex.

"Delete it, Karla. Please."

"It's just a picture. And besides, I need something to remember you by when you leave me for that other woman," I joke.

He doesn't laugh. "It's not *just* a picture. Give it to me. I'll delete it myself." With that, he crosses the room, hand outstretched.

I jump to my knees and maneuver the camera behind my back playfully.

"If you want it, come and get it," I tease. I yelp in surprise when he lunges for me, one hand gripping my shoulder and the other snatching the camera, almost too easily.

He practically pushes me away once he has what he came for. My shoulder hits the back of the headboard hard enough to sting.

Maybe I didn't think this one through. I've put myself alone in the bedroom with someone I suspect is a killer, and I have intentionally provoked him. Who do I think I am?

I'm someone with a knife hidden within arm's reach, that's who.

"What the fuck, Simon? That hurt."

He doesn't respond. Simon is looking down at the camera, his thumbs clicking at the controls.

"Hello? Did you hear me? You hurt me!"

When he is done deleting the photograph to his satisfaction, he tosses the camera onto the bed and glares at me.

"There. I'm leaving." He pulls his shirt on over his head.

"What did I do? It was just a fucking picture, Simon. I don't know why you're acting like this."

"That was careless, and you know it. We said we'd be careful, remember?"

"Careless? What do you mean? It's not like I was going to post it for all the world to see. It was just—"

"It existing is careless!" He's practically yelling now. "It's the quickest way to get caught. If it exists, then someone can and eventually will get their hands on it."

I squirm beneath his gaze. His anger practically fills the room. It's almost suffocating. I calculate how long it would take for me to grab the knife hidden beneath the nightstand and swipe it across his throat if I need to. This is something I consider before saying what I say next.

It doesn't land with the confidence I hoped it would but, instead, almost a whisper.

"Would that be the worst thing?"

"Excuse me?" he asks, taking a step toward me.

"I said would her finding out about us really be the worst thing?" Tears fill my eyes—a trick I learned to utilize a long time ago. Every girl needs to know how to cry on cue.

"You've got to be kidding me." His anger is replaced with something else.

Fear.

"I'm *not* kidding. I don't care if we get caught anymore. This sneaking around, stealing moments...It's stuff teenagers do. Not consenting adults. I—"

"What are you even saying right now?" Simon takes a few steps back toward the door, as if he may flee at any moment.

I try to soften my tone to control the shaking in my voice.

"You got with Stevie to get out of a bad marriage. I get it. But that doesn't mean you have to stay with her to prove anything."

"To prove—What are you even talking about? I love—" He shakes his head.

I chance a step toward him.

"No, you don't. You don't love her. If you did, you wouldn't be here, with me."

"This was just supposed to be sex." He sets his lips in a tight line. "I was fun. You were fun. That's what you wanted too, I thought!" He runs his fingers through his hair.

"I know, but things have changed." My voice cracks.

I close the distance between us, but he holds his hands up and catches me by the shoulders. Not in a violent way, but like how a parent comforts a child. He leans down and levels his eyes with mine. His words are gentle, but they cut like a knife.

"Nothing has changed, Karla."

"Everything has changed!" A half-truth. Everything *has* changed. Just not in the way he thinks. I almost laugh, tears still pouring from my eyes. Now for the kill shot. "I love you."

He releases my arms like I have burned him.

"I don't even know what to say to that."

"So, you are going to stand there and tell me that you don't feel anything for me?" I challenge. Heat rises to my throat. "You even said it. You said you loved me last night."

"Christ, Karla. We were fucking, and you asked me to! People say all kinds of shit when they fuck. It doesn't mean anything!"

The words feel like stones in my chest. Anything I wanted to say in response catches in my throat. I have a flash of Nikki at the bottom of the stairs, her body bent at all the wrong angles, but this time, it isn't her. It's Heather. Her neck and spine that jutted out, the skin white and taut around her skeleton, like some kind of flesh cling wrap.

"Is that what you said to Heather?" I'm not looking in his eyes when I say it like I planned, but I can sense the shift in him. I prepare myself to dive for the knife.

"What did you say?"

"I said, is that what you told Heather when she told you she was pregnant with your child? That it was just sex? It didn't mean anything?"

Simon's eyes narrow, his voice low. "I don't know what you're talking about."

I step to the dresser. My hand slips beneath the false bottom of the middle drawer, not to the battered copy of *Lolita*, not to the grainy sonogram, but to the photo. I know better than to keep all my secrets in one place.

I pull it out and hold it in the air so he can see. "You still don't know what I'm talking about?

He lunges for it, but I jerk my hand back so fast my elbow slams into the lamp, knocking it sideways.

"Don't," I snap. My voice is steady now. Strange how rage can become a kind of armor.

"Where did you get that?" he demands, his breathing quick, like a rat caught in a trap.

I smile, but it doesn't reach my eyes. "I have my ways. You're not nearly as clever at hiding things as you think."

Simon takes a slow step in my direction. I match it in reverse, inching toward the nightstand. My hand brushes the handle of the knife tucked underneath. Just in case.

"What are you trying to do right now?" he asks, his voice controlled but venomous.

"I'm just trying to figure out what happened to her."

"Why the hell do you care? You didn't even know her."

I ignore that. "Did you know that every single time she was supposed to have a 'photoshoot,' she texted her sister?"

Simon tilts his head slightly, like he's trying to follow the thread but can't see where it's going. "So, Stevie photographed her? That means I did something to her?"

"No," I say. "It doesn't. But her sister thought it was strange when Heather never followed up. Never said she made it. You know, it was always a weak cover. A photoshoot at four in the morning? Come on, Simon. That alibi is paper-thin. We both know she wasn't going to see Stevie the night she went missing."

Silence.

"You can't be serious," he says finally. "You think everyone else is hiding shit, but you're the one with all the secrets."

He snatches the photo from my hand so fast I barely have time to react. I reach for it, but he's already tearing it in half. Then into quarters. Then into confetti.

"No! Simon, stop!"

He doesn't. Simon throws the shredded pieces like ashes across the room and then turns on me. "What else are you hiding, huh?"

He rips through the top drawer. Then the second. Then the third. I try to block him, but he shoves past me like I'm weightless. His eyes are wild now, red and wet and blazing.

"Stop it!" I scream. Is he going to destroy my entire house?

I'm thankful in that moment that I moved the painting of Heather to the basement, where he wouldn't see it. There's no telling what he would do if he saw it. What he would think.

He storms to the closet and begins yanking hangers down in fits, flinging clothes over his shoulder with a force that is frightening. But then he freezes.

He takes one of the items of clothing and holds it up. I recognize it immediately.

The slit black dress. The one I took from Stevie's closet.

He pulls it free and holds it up in front of me. "Are you serious?" His laughter is cold.

My mouth opens. "I-I just...borrowed it."

Something softens in his gaze, and he half smiles. "You're so beautiful, Karla," he says. "It's too bad you're batshit crazy."

The words land like a backhand across the face.

Such a shame about her. Such a pretty girl.

My fist clenches. Just once. Reflex. But before I can move or speak, he tosses the dress on the floor like it's trash.

"Leave me and my family alone," he says at the doorway, without turning around. "Seriously. Don't let me catch you on my property again."

Something unravels in me. A last stitch snapping.

"I'll tell Stevie," I say, my voice raw. "About us. About everything."

Simon stops. Slowly turns. There's no anger in his expression now, but something worse—amusement.

"No, you won't," he states, calm and cruel. "Because if you do, you'll lose her too." A pause. Then a smile that feels like a knife to the gut. "Crazy bitch."

He leaves.

And I don't move. Not for a long time.

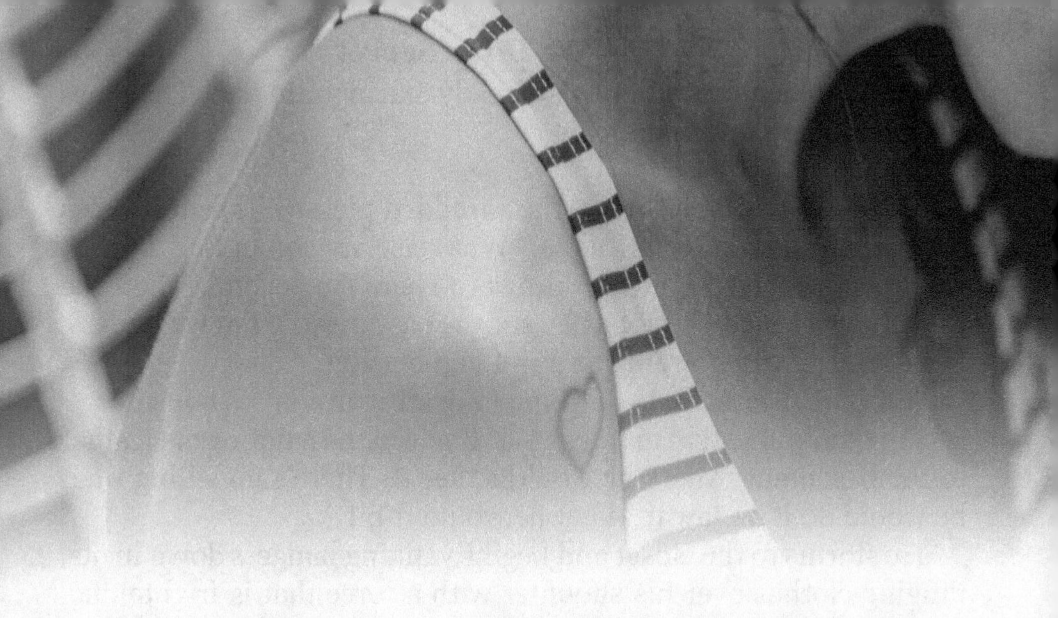

CHAPTER

FORTY

The air smells like old wood and bleach, not unlike the first time I visited Stevie here not that long ago. O'Keefe's hasn't opened yet. Five p.m. is still a little early for the bar crowd.

It's just Stevie and Astrada inside, clanking around in the half-light, prepping for the shift ahead. I watch them through the smeared glass of the front window.

Astrada is wiping down tables. Stevie is behind the bar, pouring something from one container, completely oblivious to the grenade I'm about to throw at both of our lives. And Bodhi—God, little Bodhi. He's sitting in one of the booths nearest the window, head down, sketching in his pad with that concentration only kids have.

His tongue pokes out the side of his mouth while he draws. My throat tightens. He's the only thing pure in this whole mess. If this goes wrong, I may never see him again. But I've made peace with that. If the price of saving his life is my absence from it, I'm willing to pay it.

I push the door open, and the bell jingles overhead. Astrada looks up, eyes flashing, and gives me a half-hearted roll before ducking into the kitchen, like she can't be bothered. She doesn't even try to hide her disdain for me anymore.

Fine. Let her run. Today isn't about her. There's only one goal.

Stevie looks up and smiles faintly. "Karla?"

Before she can finish, I slap the photo down on the bar between us. It's the one I took of Simon half-naked in my bedroom. He thought he deleted it, but technology is an amazing thing. Who knew you could back up photos as you take them with the download of a simple app?

The tattoo on his ribs is unmistakable. The curve of my camera's light leaks like a scar down the corner of the print—a signature. I don't say anything.

Her eyes track it, then flick up to me, hard.

Her lips are tight. "What is this?"

I hesitate. My voice catches in my throat.

"What is this, Karla?" Stevie says again, louder this time, slamming her hand down on the bar and pointing at the photo. It's loud enough to make Bodhi glance up.

I look at him too. He's watching us now, blinking slowly, sensing something is wrong but not knowing what. I smile at him in hopes this will settle his nerves and he'll return to drawing. He does.

"I slept with Simon." The words taste like rust. "More than once."

Stevie straightens. Shoulders squared. Her jaw works like she's chewing on glass.

"I didn't do it to hurt you," I say quickly. "I promise. I did it... Well, I did it because..."

I give up on explaining.

Reaching into my coat pocket, I slide the note out and place it beside the photo. It's creased, the paper brittle at the edges.

"I found this in a lockbox under Simon's bed in the studio. I think something bad happened to the girl who wrote it."

Stevie doesn't look at it yet. She's still staring at me like I'm a stranger who just slit her tires.

"So, you slept with my boyfriend because you found some letter in his room?" Her voice is calm.

Too calm.

"No." I can hear the desperation rising in my throat. "I slept with him so I could get the letter. You weren't talking to me, Stevie. You were icing me out. I had to find another way in. *He* was the way in."

That lands like a slap, but I keep going.

"Stevie, I know this doesn't make sense. Not yet. But trust me—something happened to that girl. She went missing. Heather? You knew her."

"I knew of her. Yes. We've both already talked to police about that. They cleared us both. And Simon—"

"Simon was the last person to see her alive. And he had motive."

She stares. "And how do you know all this?" Her hands are flat on the bar now. Steady. Ready for a fight.

"I talked to Heather's sister. I have proof. I'll explain everything to you, I promise, but right now, I'm scared for you. I'm scared for Bodhi." My voice breaks. "Don't go home today. Please. If I'm right—and I am—you're both in danger. Just come to my place. I'll explain everything there. We can go to the police together."

"The police?" Stevie echoes. She raises her eyebrows like I've suggested she join a cult.

"I know it's a lot. I know. But I need you to trust me right now. Just this once."

"Trust you!" She scoffs. "You just told me you've been sleeping with my boyfriend."

Stevie is right. She has no reason to trust me. None at all. But a flicker of hope ignites in me when she glances down at the note. Then the picture. Then back to me.

"So, let me get this straight." Her tone is sharp, mean in that way Stevie gets when she's trying not to cry. "You're telling me my boyfriend might be a murderer? That you've been sleeping with him to get evidence? That I shouldn't go home? That I should pack up my kid and run off to you instead?"

I nod. I can't say anything else. Anything more will ruin it.

"Even if all of this is true, Melissa would never allow that anyway." She rolls her eyes. "You think she's just going to let me take her kid off somewhere?"

"Melissa won't be an issue anymore," I say flatly.

Confusion flickers across her face. "What does that mean?"

"He's dangerous. Melissa will see that too." I reply too quickly. Damage control. I shouldn't have brought up Melissa.

My deflection seems to work.

She lets out a sound, a bitter laugh or maybe a choke. "If he's so dangerous, Karla, what does that make you? You're the one who's been crawling into bed with him, knowing what you think you know."

I wince.

I deserve that. Every word.

"Just come," I say. "Don't tell Simon I was here. He can't know. Not yet." I glance at Bodhi, who's now watching us wide-eyed, pencil still in hand. "I'm scared of what he'll do."

Stevie looks at her son. Then at me. I can't read her expression anymore. Something has calcified in her eyes. But there's something else there as well.

Doubt.

And that is all I really need right now.

The photo and the note remain on the bar. It's a risk leaving evidence here that I could otherwise turn in to the police, but she needs to see it.

When Stevie shows up—and she will—we'll leave together. We'll disappear. I'll get them somewhere safe.

And finally, the truth will be out.

What We Do in Secret

CHAPTER

FORTY-ONE

It's only while I place the meatloaf and vegetables on the table that I think I may have gone a bit overboard. There's barely any room remaining on the surface of the table for our plates.

I've made meatloaf and garlic and herb chicken bites roasted in a broth, with vegetables seasoned to perfection, baked potatoes, and croissants lightly drizzled in a butter sauce, which tastes pretty superior, if I do say so myself. A separate pan of spaghetti for Bodhi, extra seasoned meatballs, just like he likes it. There's a variety of desserts of about every kind of pie and pastry you can think of. It looks like a Thanksgiving meal for twenty people instead of a family of three.

So what if I did go a bit overboard? This is a special occasion.

After tonight, Stevie will know the truth about everything. She'll understand exactly the kind of man she is tethering her life to, and she will finally be able to walk away from him.

Stevie isn't returning any of my messages, but I suspect she's had plenty of time to think about what I said. I haven't gotten any angry texts from Simon, so perhaps Stevie has done what I asked and kept this between us.

I'm not so naive to assume this will be a clean cut. There's a lot involved here: a kid, careers, a house to divide, eventually a murder trial and testimony. My chest tightens at the thought of Bodhi having to testify in front of a courtroom full of people. Given that drawing, I don't see a way out of it for him, though. He clearly saw something. Something a child should never see.

But whatever challenges may come, we will work through them.

I peek out the window at the house across the street. It's still and dark, both of their vehicles absent from the driveway. It doesn't surprise me that Stevie would take her time returning home tonight, but Simon will surely be back at any moment for Bodhi. Except Stevie is going to be bringing him to me instead.

If it's up to me, Simon will never see that little boy again for as long as I live. Maybe Stevie will bypass his house altogether and pull straight into my garage, like she lives here already.

My face warms at the thought. A real family would live here for once, erasing all the bad things which happened. And maybe after we have a chance to discuss our future, we can move out of this neighborhood altogether.

I wouldn't mind living in a loft in the city. Sure, a suburb is better for Bodhi, but kids thrive in the city all the time. Stevie seems happier there. There's so much going on. She could take her photos straight from our bedroom window.

Stevie deserves a chance to be in her natural habitat.

I seat myself at the far end of the table after decorating our plates with the feast I've prepared. A bottle of wine has been placed beside Stevie's glass, and I filled Bodhi's cup with chocolate milk.

It won't be long now.

CHAPTER

FORTY-TWO

I can't sleep.

I can't eat.

The food on the table went cold several hours ago. Not a single headlight has broken the darkness of our cove since I last checked. Stevie isn't coming. She really isn't coming.

The words are hot coals in my chest cavity.

What self-respecting woman would stay after I told her what I did about Simon?

A dumb one. No sense. To be so smart, so creative, she's being incredibly stupid right now. I expected more from her. He'll never let her go.

The hot coal continues to flame, and the heat rises to my head. I pick up my plate and let out a scream, slamming it down onto the hardwood floor, sending shards exploding in all directions. With some of the anger released, it is being replaced with heaviness.

What if Simon found out she knew already? What if Stevie's not here by any decision of hers but his? What if he threatened her...or worse? What if something has happened to her? To Bodhi?

My breaths become short. Shallow. A sound I don't recognize escapes my lips. It's something between a cry and a laugh.

I run my hands through my hair, trying to gather myself. It is time to think. I need to figure out a way to find them. When I kneel to pick up the mess I've made, grabbing some of the bigger shards and stacking them on one another, one of the edges catches the side of my hand. A bite of pain shoots up my arm.

"Shoot!" I drop the glass back on the ground, grab a handkerchief from the table, and press it against the gash.

It saturates the cloth faster than I can make it to the sink, and my head begins to spin. I grip the edge of the sink, letting the water pour over my hand, unable to make myself look at the crimson pooling in the basin again.

You would think by now I would be used to copious amounts of blood, but it's different when it's your own.

At that moment, the doorbell rings, and my heart skips. She's here. Later than expected, but still. At least she's finally here. That's all that matters.

I wrap a clean towel around my fist and make my way over to the door.

"Stevie, I thought you were—" But my words catch in my throat when I open the door to two men standing on my porch.

They are certainly not Stevie. Not even close.

"Hello, ma'am. Sorry to bother you this late." One of the deputies glances behind me briefly.

The other deputy stands a few feet behind him, hands on his hips. I recognize them both from my last run-in with law enforcement.

"Deputy Young. Can I help you with something?" I ask, hating how my voice shakes.

"We're here to do a wellness check on a Ms. Karla Cooper." He glances at his partner, who whispers something in response.

"You're looking at her. What's this about?"

"We've been asked to check on you at the request of a Dr. Sarah McCoy. She'll be here shortly as well."

"Dr. McCoy is coming here?" My voice escapes in almost a whisper.

I've been here before. Police, medics, and the next thing you know, I'm being carted off to the asylum again.

"Ma'am, are you okay?"

At first, I don't understand what he's asking me, but then I notice the blood on the door where my hand was resting.

"Oh! It's just a cut." I remove the towel enough for them to observe the laceration but instantly regret it. My vision does a somersault. "I-I broke a dish and sliced myself pretty good."

I try to sound casual, but my expression must have given me away.

"May we come in? That's a pretty nasty cut. You may need stitches." Deputy Young doesn't wait for a response. He takes my injured hand in his and examines the ripped skin.

I have to look away.

"It's nothing really. I just get a little lightheaded at the sight of my own blood." My face flushes.

He walks me back over to my sink and goes to work cleaning it up. The other deputy, much older than the one aiding me, remains by the door, hands still at the ready.

"I don't think you'll need stitches, but you may be sore for a few days. I can get you a medic out here to check you out if you want?"

"No. No. That's too much trouble for a little cut."

"You have a first aid?"

My stomach sinks.

"In the bathroom." I point down the hall opposite the main living room.

"May I?"

"Of course." I watch him while he makes his way to the bathroom, hoping he or his partner will not notice my eyes dart quickly to the stairway leading to Mother's door.

"So, what happened here?" the old officer asks.

I didn't notice him close the distance between us. He looks up at me from the mess on the kitchen floor, nudging a few of the larger shards with the tip of his shoe.

"I'm just clumsy. I was trying to clear the table and knocked the plate when I turned around. I was trying to clean it up when this happened." I raise my hand a little.

"Clear the table? This is quite a spread. Doesn't look like it's been touched. Were you expecting company?" The older cop examines the various dishes on the table.

"I am. Well, I was...My date...They got...held up at work."

"He's missing out." His name tag, now in view, reads "T. Wilkes."

I nod in agreement.

The door to the bathroom hasn't opened again. I glance nervously toward the hall. Hopefully, Mother keeps that stupid bell quiet for five minutes.

"When is Dr. McCoy arriving?" I ask.

As if on cue, headlights wash across the living room window. A part of me hopes it's Stevie, but I'm beginning to settle into acceptance.

If she doesn't show, should I tell the officers what I know anyway? Maybe they can help me find her. It's a possibility, but first I have to handle Dr. McCoy.

As if summoned, the front door opens. Dr. McCoy enters briskly, her expression unreadable but clearly lacking warmth. She doesn't greet the older officer. Her eyes find mine and stay there.

"Karla," she says, voice tight. "You should know why I'm here."

I nod. "I do."

She steps in closer, eyes already flicking to my hand. "How did you injure yourself?"

"I told the officers. I dropped a plate while clearing the table. I was trying to clean it up, and I sliced my hand on a shard." I keep my tone even, steady. Practiced.

It is at this moment that Deputy Young returns with my first aid kit in hand. He gives the older cop a nod and returns to the sink.

"Thank you so much. I don't know if I'd be able to do this myself. I just can't stand the sight of it."

"Protect and serve," he offers with a smile.

I keep my head turned while he wraps my hand, trying to focus on what Dr. McCoy is asking instead.

She doesn't let up. "And what have you been up to that you haven't returned my calls? My emails?"

"I've just had a lot going on with my mother." I brush a loose strand of hair behind my ear, pretending to be calm.

"I'd love to meet her while I'm here. I have a couple of questions for her." Her tone is laced with meaning, and I catch it.

"I'm afraid that won't be possible. Actually…I took your advice. I moved her into an assisted living center this week."

She raises an eyebrow at that but says nothing. I press on.

"This past couple of weeks have just been too difficult. The whole process…interviews, paperwork, packing…It's been…taxing. One of the reasons I haven't been in. Or available."

Dr. McCoy gives a curt nod. "That could be a good thing, considering your current situation. What's the name of the facility? I'd like to follow up on that. It may be a factor in the board's decision on whether to re-admit you."

"Re-admit?" I echo, too loudly. "Dr. McCoy, you'd re-admit me for missing two appointments? Even after everything you know I have going on?"

Her voice doesn't rise, but the edge is unmistakable. "Karla, this is not my decision to make anymore. I'm here to evaluate you. To monitor your fitness to remain out of the hospital. But how am I supposed to monitor you if you keep skipping your appointments? These were court-ordered, due to the violent nature of your incident."

I inhale slowly, steadying the shake in my voice. "I understand. I do. But it feels...unfair."

"The name of the facility, please."

There's no softness in her eyes now.

"Safe Haven. Just a few miles north of Blair County." I keep my eyes steady.

She'll figure it out eventually, but I'll burn that bridge when I get to it.

Dr. McCoy scribbles it down without looking at me. "And your medication. Are you taking it?"

"Yes."

"How have the hallucinations been?"

"Less frequent," I say.

"How's the photography?"

I shrug. "In progress."

She doesn't believe a word of it. I can tell. This is a sad game of tug-of-war, and we are both losing.

Behind me, Deputy Young finishes winding the bandage around my palm. His partner leans forward and grabs a croissant off the untouched plate, chewing thoughtfully. I sneer at him. He doesn't notice.

Dr. McCoy watches me carefully, longer this time. Her gaze makes my skin itch. For a moment, I contemplate telling her about Simon. About Heather.

But there's something in her expression, too detached, too calculating. This isn't a safe place to talk about that. Maybe it never was. I wouldn't put it past her to call the ambulance herself, have me wrapped and hauled off back to the hospital tonight, if I so much as mention my sleuthing.

She closes her notebook. "I'll be in touch first thing in the morning with the board's decision."

Dr. McCoy pauses at the door. Turns.

"And Karla, answer your phone."

Then she's gone, leaving me with Andy and Barney Fife. I've got to get rid of them.

"I'm sorry both of you had to waste a trip out here. I know you must be busy. Care to take a plate for the road? I can wrap you up something."

"Ye—" Deputy Wilkes starts, but Young cuts him off.

"No, ma'am. We appreciate it, but we have to get going."

Deputy Wilkes appears defeated while he makes his way back to the door, with Deputy Young following behind. I close the door behind the two officers, and my shoulders relax, but only for a moment.

Those idiot cops had been easy to convince. They had devoured my story like puppies. But Dr. McCoy didn't believe a word I said. I can tell. And that can only mean one thing.

It is only a matter of time before she finds out there is no such facility as Safe Haven near Blair County. At least, not one that I know of. And on the off chance there is such a facility by that name, she won't find one with a Lanora Cooper living there.

It won't be long before they end up back here.

I have to move now if I want to stay ahead of them. There isn't any more time to be angry at Simon for destroying everyone's lives. I don't even have time to be angry or afraid for Stevie at this point. It is something I will have to deal with later. For now, I have one thing and one thing only I need to do.

The distant ringing of Mother's bell pierces the darkness. Only this time, the ringing isn't coming from her room.

It's coming from the basement.

What We Do in Secret

CHAPTER

FORTY-THREE

I pull into my driveway, the Altima humming to a stop just as two squad cars and a third unmarked vehicle begin to reverse out of Karla's. Red and blue flash across the rearview mirror, and for a second, my stomach drops.

"You've got to be kidding me," I mutter, cutting the engine. "That bitch actually called the cops."

Bodhi is in the passenger seat, kicking at the floor mat. "Did you know that the color of the stars can tell you how hot they are?"

"No, buddy, I didn't know that. Aren't they all white?"

"No! They can be all kinds of colors. Blue stars are the hottest, and they can get up to fifty thousand degrees!"

"Really? I would think red would be the hottest?" I say, only passively listening. I watch the first police officer leave.

To my relief, he goes the opposite way from my house.

"Not at all. Red is actually the coolest. Still super hot, though. They're about five thousand degrees! Blue is way hotter."

"Go ahead and go inside, bud," I grab my keys. "I'll be right there."

He doesn't ask questions, just yawns and slips out of the car, backpack bouncing against his shoulder blades.

I hurry across the road just as the second patrolman pulls to a stop. Before he can take the turn out of Karla's driveway, I wave him down.

"Hey! Excuse me!" I half run, half flail my arms, like I'm signaling a plane to land.

He rolls down the window, face neutral, professional.

"Everything okay over there?" I jerk my head toward Karla's house. "Because whatever she told you, Simon didn't do anything, all right?"

The officer gives a practiced smile. "I'm not sure who Simon is, but that's nothing to worry about, ma'am. Just a routine mental health check."

I blink. "A mental health check?"

He nods toward the third car, the unmarked one. A heavyset woman is impatiently waiting to be let out of the driveway. The logo on the side reads: "New Beginnings Behavioral & Wellness Services."

"Per her doctor," he adds, and then he's gone.

I head for the woman before she has a chance to pull up. "Hi. I'm sorry to hold you up like this. I'm Stevie Cole. I live across the street. I'm a...a friend of Karla's."

She turns, calm and unreadable. "Dr. McCoy," she says. "Neighbor?"

"Yes."

Dr. McCoy smiles. "You the photographer?"

"She told you that?"

She shrugs. "I can't discuss clients, but she did mention a new friend that took pictures. It's nice to meet you."

"Is she...okay?"

"Again, I'm sorry, but I can't discuss my clients with anyone who isn't next of kin. Now I—" she starts, but I cut her off.

"I don't think you understand. I really need to know if she's okay."

Dr. McCoy tilts her head. Her expression shifts in that calculating therapist way. "Is everything okay with you, Stevie?"

Touché.

I look around, aware we are still in Karla's driveway. My skin crawls.

"You want to come in for coffee?" I ask. "We can talk in my kitchen. It's quieter."

Inside, I hand her a mug full of freshly brewed coffee and try not to fidget. I'm not even sure why I invited her in. Maybe I'm hoping someone finally says what I've been too afraid to believe.

"I'm just…worried," I tell her. "At first, Karla and I were friends. I lost my dog. She helped me find him. We had a drink that night. But after that? Things got weird."

She nods, listening. Not writing. Just watching.

"We invited her to dinner," I continue. "I caught her snooping in my darkroom. Then one day she just…took Bodhi after school. Didn't tell me. Just brought him into her house."

I take a deep breath.

"She changed her hair to look like mine. She texts me all the time. Look."

I grab my phone and show her. Message after message. Karla talking to herself. Paragraphs, voice notes, question marks. I haven't answered in days.

"I know she's in a vulnerable place right now. She mentioned visiting her mom every Thursday, but—"

Dr. McCoy pauses. "She told you she goes to see her mother at the assisted living facility on Thursdays?"

I nod. "Ever since we met."

"And how long ago was that?"

"Couple of months, maybe?"

She presses her lips together, like she wants to say something but doesn't.

"Have you ever seen her act violently?" she asks. "Aggression, threats?"

"No." I shake my head. "Nothing like that."

But I hesitate, and it doesn't go unnoticed by Dr. McCoy.

"What is it?" she presses. "Even something small. It matters."

I chew the inside of my cheek. "My friend died. A while back. Nikki. It was an accident, they said. Fell down the stairs. But…" I lower my voice. "Karla was the last one to see her. Nikki didn't like her. Said she gave her bad vibes. And then…" I break off. "And then she's dead. It made no sense. She did gymnastics all through high school, and I'm supposed to believe she lost her balance walking up a flight of stairs?"

Dr. McCoy's face softens. "I'm so sorry."

"But that's not even the worst part." I swallow, my throat tight. "I just found out Karla's been sleeping with my boyfriend."

That catches her off guard. She lifts her brows. "Oh."

"Yeah. And in the same breath she told me that, she accused him of being involved in some missing girl's disappearance. Said she had evidence. I don't know what's going on with her, but I'm a little concerned."

I worry I've said too much. I do that sometimes when I'm nervous.

Dr. McCoy seems to mull this over. Then she pulls a card from her coat pocket and slides it across the counter.

"I'd really like you to come in later this week," she says. "Go on record. We might even be able to revisit your friend's case."

I nod. She leaves without saying much. I don't blame her, of course. She has been given a lot to think about.

Fuck. I've given *myself* a lot to think about.

It's one thing to have these thoughts and keep them to yourself. It's another entirely to speak them out loud to another person.

After she leaves, I just sit there, reeling.

Nikki. Heather. Karla. Nikkie. Heather. Karla. How does it all fit? Karla isn't dangerous. What am I even thinking? I'm just being paranoid because I'm angry.

My phone buzzes. It's another message from Simon. He's staying at the shop for a few days while I think about what I'm going to do concerning our situation. The man didn't even deny it when I asked about Karla.

I don't know what to do. Leaving feels like tearing Bodhi's world in half. Again. He has already had one family split. Now this? All because Simon can't keep it in his pants. Why should Bodhi keep suffering?

And where the hell is Melissa?

As much as I hate to admit it, I could really use her help right now. I haven't heard a word since the slew of angry texts the night Nikki died. Not a single spiteful call or comment. It's unlike her to be so...peaceful.

There have been a few Facebook posts, but that doesn't mean anything. She schedules those things six years in advance. Melissa isn't anything if not efficient.

I need to check Bodhi's phone. Surely, she would have talked to him by now at least.

I tiptoe quietly into his room. He's already sound asleep, curled up with the blanket kicked halfway off. I brush a loose curl behind his ear before taking the phone off the nightstand.

Back in the hallway, I scroll. No texts from Melissa. But a few from Bodhi to her with no replies.

That's weird.

I tap the location tracking app, the one Melissa insisted we download because "Little kids go missing all the time." It was just a way to keep up with us when we had him, but it wasn't worth the fight.

It loads slowly. A small dot appears, and my blood turns to ice.

This can't be right.

Her location is right across the street. Karla's house.

And she's been there...since the night Nikki died.

CHAPTER

FORTY-FOUR

I refresh the tracking app and verify Melissa's location dot on the screen again, just to be sure.

No. No, that can't be right.

Why is Melissa's phone pinning right on top of Karla's house?

I try calling her again.

Straight to voicemail.

My heart is already pounding when I glance back toward Bodhi's room. I crack the door open just enough to see him, tangled in his blankets, breathing slow and deep. Blissfully unaware.

I close the door quietly behind me and duck into my bedroom. My hands tremble while I tug on one of my black zip-up jackets, then grab one of Simon's baseball caps from the dresser.

This is stupid. Insane. What are you even doing, Stevie? But my body keeps moving until I'm standing in front of the house across the street.

The cops were just here. If Melissa was at Karla's, wouldn't they have found her? Wouldn't they have said something? I guess they don't have to tell me anything.

It still makes absolutely no sense why Melissa would be over there, though. They don't even know each other.

The porch is dark, lifeless. I skip the front door and creep around the side, boots crunching softly against gravel and damp leaves. Something tugs at me, like instinct or dread, guiding me toward the back entrance.

I pause, lift a finger, and tap gently on the door.

Nothing.

I hesitate. Then check the knob. It turns easily.

Why isn't it locked?

Inside, the kitchen is dim. Only a few lamps burn low, casting a tired glow on worn wood floors and still air.

No Karla. No Melissa.

I step inside, and the first thing I notice is the table, fully set with an insane amount of untouched food, like someone was expecting company and forgot. She told me to come over here after work, and I didn't. Was this...all for me?

A shattered plate lies like a wound on the ground, ceramic shards dusted in something thick and red.

That's blood. It has to be. Dried, smeared on the edge of the sink like someone reached out in a panic.

My fingers hover over it.

I move slowly through the space, hyperaware of every little creak and groan of the house. A red door near the kitchen catches my eye, slightly ajar. Something about it makes my stomach twist.

I reach toward it, resting my palm against the wood, but freeze when headlights flash across the window. The beams stretch long shadows across the hallway. I exhale when the lights continue down the road.

Leaving the creepy red door be for now, I move deeper into the house.

I take the stairs slowly, heart galloping. The steady thump in my ear has been the only consistent sound so far. Nothing is chasing me. But everything about this place feels off. Wrong.

At the top of the stairs is a bathroom on my right and two doors to my left. I press lightly against the first.

My heart seizes in my chest.

There's a figure in the bed.

I suck in a breath and almost choke on it—until I realize it's just a mound of pillows casting shadows in the moonlight. The room smells unused. Cold, like it's been empty for a very long time. I step back out.

The next room is different. Warmer. Alive. I recognize the wallpaper instantly. It's the same as the background in the photo Karla took of Simon. The bedding matches too.

I'm in her room. The thought of being in the same space as they were when they betrayed me gives me an uneasy feeling in my stomach.

I would probably linger on it until I hurt my own feelings if the room weren't in such chaos.

Some kind of paper is torn into confetti, littering every surface. The closet has been gutted. Something soft brushes against my ankle.

I kneel and lift the small lump of fabric to the light. It takes me a moment to accept what I'm looking at. It's...it's my dress. The black slit one I haven't seen since the week we moved in.

I drop it back down onto the floor. A cold sweat breaks across my back. How the hell is it here?

I think I know the answer, but I can't acknowledge it yet.

Something glints in the corner of my eye, and I turn my head toward the window facing the street. A camera is perched on the sill, lens pointed at my house. My bedroom window, Bodhi's room, even the front steps, clear and unobstructed.

My throat tightens, and I reach out to grab it, trembling. I'm about to click it on and go through the photos in the memory card when I hear a thump coming from somewhere in the house.

My hands fumble the camera, and it drops with a sickening crash to the floor.

Another clatter echoes from below, then silence.

I wait. Listen.

Did they hear me?

There are no footsteps. No creaking wood.

I tiptoe downstairs, heart hammering with every step. The kitchen appears exactly the same. The entire house remains just as frozen as it was when I got here.

Still no Karla. Still no Melissa.

But I heard *something*.

Maybe she left.

I can't be sure, of course. She might have been gone when I got here, for all I know, and now she's back and is going to catch me red-handed, doing exactly what she did during dinner.

I need to get out of here.

My way to the back door is clear. I'm about to go for the door handle when—

Thump.

Muffled. It's coming from somewhere below. Behind the red door.

I shouldn't. No. I should open the back door and leave this house. Go back home and figure out what I'm going to do with my own life instead of worrying about whatever weird shit is going on here.

I should...but I don't.

Instead, I pull open the red door, and a soft crimson glow filters through. I catch something out of the corner of my eye, but the red hue is too low to see it.

To light my way, I pull my phone from my jeans pocket and hold it up to the bottom of the door. It is covered in scratches. Claw marks. There are hundreds of them, deep and frantic, as if something tried to escape. Like an animal.

Like a dog.

A thought creeps into my mind, but before it can flesh out, I push it away. That's just my paranoia talking. To think that Karla would take Ollie is...insane.

My phone vibrates in my hand. Another text from Simon. I click on it, but I don't read his message.

I'm at Karla's. Come home now. We need to talk.

I hit *send* before I can stop myself. That will get his attention. He may not be my favorite person at the moment, but if there's anyone who has always been on my side, it's him. I need Simon here until I know what I'm dealing with.

I turn my attention to the stairs leading down to the basement.

Needles dance on my skin, and each hair on my body stands on end. Still, I head down the steps, one step at a time.

The air is different—wet and heavy. The wood creaks beneath me. My exhales reverberate too loudly in my ears. I consciously hold my breath against the stench of chemicals and mildew until I reach the bottom and am forced to either inhale or pass out.

I don't know what I expected to find down here, but the scene before is not it.

The entire basement is washed in red light. A table sits in the middle of the space, similar to my own. Basins, chemicals, focus finders, and tongs. I know immediately what I'm looking at. It's a darkroom. An impressive one at that.

But that's not what catches my attention. It's the photos. Dozens. No...*Hundreds.*

And they are all...me.

Well. Me and my family. There's a photo of me at the grocery store, picking out cereal for Bodhi. Several of them are of me doing yard work, checking the mail, and jogging. Even a few of me working at O'Keefe's. I didn't know she had been there some of those days.

Then I find one which causes me to almost lose my balance. My hand flies to my mouth to stifle the gasp. One is of Simon and me in bed together...sleeping.

What the actual fuck, Karla!

My mouth goes dry. I stumble backward, dizzy from I don't know what. The chemicals. The photos. All I know is I need to go.

The backs of my thighs hit something solid.

Cold.

I turn to find a deep freeze. Otherwise normal, if not for the strange something hanging out of the lid in the corner. Is that?

I run my fingers along the object, and it's soft. Stringy. Like... hair.

I grasp the lid to the thing, force it open, and nearly lose all the contents of my stomach.

The light in the deep freeze spotlights a face. A human face. And it's staring right at me, but any life behind the eyes is long gone. The skin is blue and pale and clings to the bones. Ice peppers her entire body, like frost in the early morning.

But even through all that, I can see she resembles Karla, just older. I remember the look on Dr. McCoy's face when I mentioned that Karla visited her mother at the living facility on Thursdays. Like she wanted to say something. Was that a lie? Could this be...

This woman has been here a long time.

I take a few clumsy steps backward and slap a hand over my mouth, fighting the scream rising in my throat.

Get out. Get out. *Get out!*

I bolt toward the stairs, blood thundering in my ears, and that's when everything goes black.

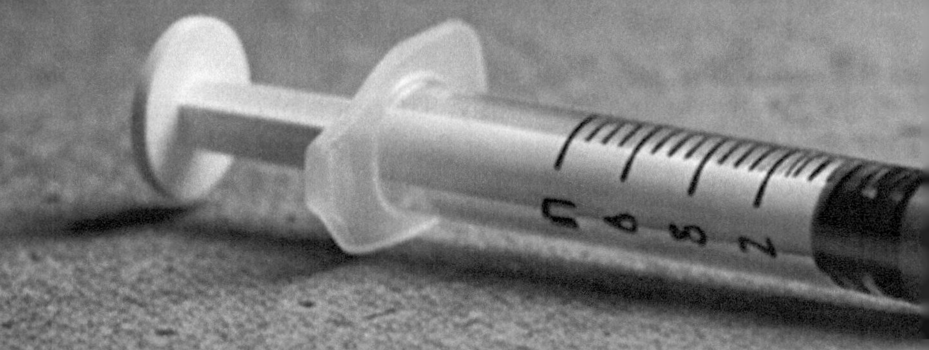

CHAPTER

FORTY-FIVE

The dark is soft at first. Like velvet. Like death. Then the light creeps in, red and dim and cruel. My eyes flutter, and the lids sting. There's pain behind them, pulsing like a drumbeat in the back of my skull. My mouth tastes like iron.

I try to swallow but choke on the dirt coating my lips. My tongue sticks to the roof of my mouth like glue. I suck in a breath and cough again, this time harder, my body convulsing in weak spasms.

Something sharp slices through my side. My ribs scream. My hair clings to my face in sweaty, sticky tentacles. I try to raise my hand to push it back, but nothing moves. My arms are...heavy.

No...bound.

What the hell?

A slow, electric panic begins to hum through me. I blink hard against the red light and try to will my brain into order, but it's like wandering through a fog. I shift, and the bindings on my wrists press against skin. My knees are screaming too, like I've been folded over for hours.

Maybe I have.

Then I see them.

The photographs. Clipped up. Taped to the wall. Hanging from strings, just like in my own darkroom. My face. Bodhi's face. And below them...the freezer.

Oh God.

The memory returns in rapid-fire snapshots. The hair sticking out of the deep freeze. The body inside, stiff under a thick layer of frost. The eyes...wild yet empty...frozen in their last moment.

I try to sit up and immediately regret it. White-hot pain ricochets through my skull. I moan through clenched teeth.

"I know what you're thinking," a voice says from somewhere just out of sight.

Even in my fog, I recognize that chirpy little tone.

Karla.

"I didn't mean to do it."

I turn my head and blink until the shape of her takes form in the red haze. A blur at first. Then color. Red on red. Her voice is drawn out, like a child confessing something they don't understand. It's high-pitched and close to breaking.

She steps into my field of vision. A cloth presses to my face, cold and wet. It's a shock but feels nice on the red-hot pain piercing through my head.

My brain functions slowly return, not nearly quick enough, but they return, nonetheless. I desperately try to make connections to what is happening. A smaller version of me is in my head, like that meme from *It's Always Sunny in Philadelphia*, with the red string on the wall. I don't understand how it all fits together, but at least I know there is a puzzle to solve.

Then, just like that, another piece snaps into place.

That person in the freezer, that woman, was her mother.

And why would she be in the freezer? Unless...Karla killed her.

"An accident," she says.

Well. Isn't that just the word of the day?

My limbs start to burn again. The ache has teeth. I try to move, but the tape bites back. That sharp pain in my head? Yeah. That was Karla too, no doubt. Knocked me out and dragged me down here, like a sack of flour.

Am I going to end up in the freezer next? Same blue, almost translucent skin covered in ice for God knows how long? My stomach lurches, and for a moment, I think I will vomit after all.

"Stevie, I would never..." she begs, voice shaking.

Strange, isn't it? The first instinct isn't always fear. Not exactly.

Fear isn't what I feel right now, even though I probably should. To be honest, I don't feel much at all. Emotion is more of an undercurrent. Maybe this is the animal brain everyone is always talking about.

On the surface, there is only a single thought. How can I get out of here alive? My mind forms a list of scenarios which don't seem to end well for me. Except maybe one.

One of the biggest mistakes people make when they're in danger is assuming that fight or flight are the only exits. But not all predators respond to resistance. Some you have to read carefully. For those, there is a third option. A third "fear" response.

"I know you wouldn't kill anyone, Karla." I say, even though the throb in my skull and the tape biting into my wrists tell a different story.

She's watching me, trying to decipher if I mean it. There's something soft behind her eyes. Almost childlike.

"Kill?" she says with a dry scoff. "She wasn't dead for quite a while. But she did get hurt. And I couldn't go back to that hospital. I just couldn't. So I...helped her pass on."

She *helped* her pass on.

And just like that, we've graduated from a lot creepy to completely unhinged.

I've seen this before, with criminals on interrogation tapes. Delusion is armor. Ruby Franke, when the game was up, just went cold. Shut down like someone unplugged her. I think Karla's the same breed. If I touch that illusion, challenge it even a little, she might freeze or worse. Explode. And I'm the only target in her sight right now.

"Do you mind loosening these bindings?" I ask, gently changing the subject. "They kind of hurt."

"No," she says flatly.

"Please, Karla. I won't run, I promise. I just want to be able to get some circulation in my fingers."

"I could care less about your fingers. You can lose the entire hand for all I care," she snaps, stepping closer. "You're going to tell me the truth about Heather, and it'll be a lot easier for me if you aren't able to fiddle around too much."

Not this again.

"Karla, please. Just let me go. I'll tell you whatever you want to know, but you have to untie me."

"I'm not an idiot. You're not walking out of here until I know exactly how Simon killed her. I was willing to give you the benefit of the doubt. I cooked for you. I was going to tell you everything. We could have gone somewhere. You. Me. Bodhi. Safe. But you didn't want that. You wanted him. For a moment, I even thought he might have hurt you…Then I see you sneaking around my house?"

By the end, her voice is practically shaking.

"Karla, you don't know what you're talking about. Simon didn't kill Heather."

That's when the knife flashes. A sudden sting tears through my arm, hot and wet. I scream before I can stop myself. If fear was an undercurrent before, it's on the surface now.

"Quit lying!" she shrieks.

"I'm not lying. Please. Simon didn't kill her—"

"Then who did!" Her voice cracks. She's unraveling. "I know something happened to her. I know! Don't play dumb."

"What is it exactly that you think you know?"

"She was pregnant," she spits. "And it was Simon's. That's the leading cause of death for women."

Silence.

I close my eyes. A deep, dangerous pause.

She's right. Sort of. Maybe a half-truth will buy me some time.

"You're right. She was pregnant," I say carefully. "And it was Simon's. But he didn't kill her."

Karla narrows her eyes.

"Then what happened to her?"

"I can't tell you that."

"Because he killed her!"

"Because it's not my business to tell!"

"You'd sit here and defend a murderer?" Karla says. "What kind of mother would you be to Bodhi? What kind of role model?"

She's losing it. Arms flailing, the knife flashing again. Her face is twisted into something that looks like grief and rage and betrayal, all sewn together into a single trembling mask.

"He didn't kill her!" I scream. "No one did! She's alive, Karla!"

Karla freezes mid-step.

I push forward, breath shaking. "Melissa caught them together. Heather wanted out. She wanted a future. Melissa gave her money to disappear. Simon just...drove her to the station."

"You're lying," Karla whispers. But she sounds unsure now.

Doubt is a powerful weapon when wielded properly.

"That girl's life was already falling apart. Then she got pregnant by Melissa Van Lowe's husband. That girl had two choices—humiliate herself in front of the entire world...or disappear. Do you really think Melissa would let *that* become a headline?"

"She didn't have a problem bashing you when he left her for you," Karla mutters.

"Yeah, because I was a grown woman. Heather was a child, Karla. Melissa is the queen of the mommy market. She knew the fallout. Trust me—Heather got off easy."

Karla goes quiet. Her mouth tightens. Her eyes. Unfocused. And then she kneels.

I don't recognize her face anymore. This version of Karla, this posture, this strange stillness...Maybe I'm meeting the real her for the first time.

"I don't believe you," she whispers.

Karla pulls something from her dress pocket. It's a small piece of paper. She unfolds it carefully and places it in front of me.

It's a drawing. A child's drawing, from the looks of it.

"What's this?" I ask, but I already know the answer.

The image is a gesture sketch mixed with crayon. Red, mostly. A bent, broken figure. Hairlike squiggles. A pool of red crayon bleeding across the page. As vague as this drawing is, there's no mistaking what it is.

"I found it in Bodhi's sketchbook." Her eyes never leave mine. "Bit of a departure from meteors and rockets, wouldn't you say?"

"This doesn't mean anything. He's a little boy."

"He's an *observant* little boy."

"And you think he 'observed' this?"

"I know he did. And if you're helping Simon hide what happened, you're just as much a monster as he is."

"I'm a monster?" I laugh. Just once. Because it's either that or sob. "Tell me—were you ever my friend? Or was it always about him?"

Karla rises, the knife held against her chest like a crucifix.

"I resent that," she says. "I tried to be your friend. Every single time, you pushed me out. I told you what I knew, and you still didn't show up. You chose him."

She turns, walks to the shadows, and returns with several shopping bags. Karla begins to remove various items from them. Trash bags. Prescriptions. Gasoline. Matches. There are several items I can't identify from this angle, but I get the gist.

"Can you believe I got all this for thirty-nine forty-nine?" she says with a smile.

I shift, heart pounding. My hand brushes the leg of the table. Something sharp scrapes across my wrist. A loose piece of metal, maybe? Or a nail. Whatever it is, it'll have to work. I press the duct tape on my wrists against it and begin to scrape. Slowly. Quietly.

"Don't worry," she hums. "I've had practice now. With you and Simon, it'll be much less messy. I prefer it that way. Blood is such a pain to get out." She giggles.

I scrape harder.

"My mother was diabetic," she tells me, like she's reciting the recipe to a pie. "Every month, I picked up her insulin. I didn't want to raise suspicion. But now? I've got enough to take down an elephant, I think."

She draws a needle, loads it, and gives it a squeeze. A perfect arc of clear fluid sprays from the tip. Karla smiles as if she's triumphant and steps toward me.

"I'm really sorry that we never got to be as close as I wanted. I tried. I really did." She sounds almost mournful. "And I can't bear the thought of you dying thinking Bodhi is going to be raised by some murderer. Everything I've done...I did for him. To keep him safe. If anything, I'm like...an anti-murderer." She grins from ear to ear like some fucked-up pinup commercial.

Karla moves the needle closer.

I scrape the tape vigorously against the nail, my intentions hidden only by my frantic breathing. I'm not free. Not yet. Almost. Just a little bit more.

"Stevie? Are you here?"

Simon's voice carries down the stairs and into my body like a second wind.

My throat rips open with my scream. "Simon! Help!"

It's all I can manage before a hand clasps over my mouth, silencing me. The pain that follows is sharp when the needle plunges into my neck.

What We Do in Secret

CHAPTER

FORTY-SIX

Karla's grip is steel against my skin. My scream tears out raw, more animal than human. She's stronger than she looks.

"Simon!" I thrash against her, biting down hard enough to taste blood.

She gasps, pulling away. I use that sliver of opportunity to rear my head forward and slam it back, straight into her face. Bone on bone.

Karla stumbles, hissing like a feral animal, one heel skidding on the floor, the other clicking uselessly.

Impractical-ass shoes.

The tape on my wrists is slick with sweat and blood. I dig my nails in, brace my bum wrist against the weak side of the tape, and rip as hard as I can. It feels like some of the skin on my hands goes with it, but I'm free.

Not all the way. Not yet. My legs. I need my legs.

I bend, clawing at the duct tape like it's alive, biting at it with my teeth, spit mixing with sweat, eyes stinging.

The door shudders again behind us. Another pound. Louder.

Simon desperately trying to get in. Trying to save me. There is rage in every slam of his fist...until the sound shifts.

He's using something now. A crowbar? A pipe? I don't know. I don't care. As long as he gets me the hell out of here.

Then I feel her. A weight crashing into my body. Karla tackles me from the side, and we tumble. My shoulder hits the base of the stairs with a crunch. Her hands are on my throat, thumbs pressing into my neck like claws. Her face, twisted into something like madness and grief.

"You're ruining everything!" she screams, but I shove her off with my newly freed hands. She loses balance in those ridiculous shoes again and crashes backward.

My legs are still bound, but I drag myself away, fingers tearing at the tape like my life depends on it.

Because it does.

Another slam. Another scream. Simon's voice, savage and real and shaking with something I've never heard from him before.

Rage.

I didn't know he had so much of it in him.

But I don't realize Karla has moved until it is too late.

She's at the base of the staircase, silent, controlled, knife in hand, just out of sight from the door. The blood drains from my face. Her intention is clear. She's going to ambush him.

"No," I whisper. "No, no, no—"

I double down on the tape, biting and pulling and sobbing, while the sticky film fights me back. The tape is soaked, my mouth is bleeding, but I'm almost there.

Then Karla calls out to him, steady and cold.

"Simon, it's over. I've already given her a lethal dose of insulin. It won't take long. I'm just trying to do what's right by Bodhi."

Simon doesn't hesitate. "You crazy bitch. I'm going to kill you!"

Another blow to the door. The hinges cry out.

Karla's voice is sharper now. "Kill me? Like you killed Heather?"

Silence.

She keeps going. "Are you finally ready to confess? Or do you really want to die with this on your conscience?"

More silence, stretching out like wire pulled too tightly. Then, Simon's voice, low and dangerous.

"The only one dying today is you, you crazy fucking bitch."

Simon's assault on the door resumes, louder this time. Heavier.

He's using something big now. The impact makes the entire staircase vibrate.

"And trust me," he bellows, "it's not going to be *anything* like when Melissa killed that whore, Heather. I'm going to take my time with you."

Everything freezes.

The tape drops from my hands. I look up. So does Karla. Shock flickers between us like a struck match.

Simon hits the door again. This time, the wood splinters, and a ray of light leaks through.

It reminds me of that scene in *The Shining*. Darling. Love of my life. I'm not gonna hurt you. But he did. Or at least, he tried to hurt them.

Before tonight I couldn't see Simon being violent, but this person...This person isn't the Simon I know. This is a completely different man. Or maybe this has been him all along and I was just too blind in love to notice.

"You want the goddamn truth?" he screams. "She was a gold-digging gutter slut looking for a payday and thought I was it. Melissa knew what had to be done. So, she took care of it."

Another slam.

"And now I'm going to take care of you!"

The door buckles. One more hit. One more breath. One more second.

I'm on my feet now, my legs shaky but free of the tape I don't even remember getting off. Everything is beginning to blur around me.

Karla. Simon. The photos. Heather. Melissa. And Bodhi, stuck somewhere in the middle of the storm, just needing someone solid to hold onto.

Something cold brushes my palm.

Karla is standing dangerously close for someone who has probably already killed me. She's got a look in her eye I don't quite understand.

I glance down at our hands and realize what she's doing.

She's giving me the knife.

CHAPTER

FORTY-SEVEN

Simon bursts through the door like a gunshot, and before I can react, his hands are around my throat.

There is no time. No plea, no scream, no breath. Just the impact, my back slamming into the wall, hard enough that the edges of everything blur and scatter like marbles spilled on tile.

His fingers dig in deep, merciless, almost ravenous. His eyes are wild but not unrecognizable. I see the man I once knew, who smiled sinfully while he offered me a drink. The one who kissed every part of me in his van that night. The one who wanted me to surprise him.

There are crumbs of that man here still, but he's mostly gone now. What's inside him is something else. Something that has always been there, maybe, buried like bone beneath the dirt.

This is it. The last thing I'll ever see. Simon's face contorted with rage. This is how I'll leave the world, pinned like a moth, breathless and burning against the source of my obsession.

What did Heather see? It's a passive thought, but I cling to it. Better there than here.

Did she call out for him? Did she beg, thinking he'd protect her? Did he smile at her like everything was fine, right up until it wasn't? Did Heather see the betrayal in stereo, from two people she trusted like family?

My stomach turns. I watch the scene play out in my head while my vision begins to fade in soft, stuttering flashes. The terror on Heather's face. The confusion. The heartbreak.

And Bodhi.

He was there. Bodhi witnessed it. His tiny hands clutching something soft. A blanket. A toy. Anything but understanding what was happening.

That poor baby, his brain still forming, still trying to make sense of colors and letters and faces and space and people. Instead, he was forced to watch something no child should ever have to watch.

My lungs scream. I can't draw air, can't even swallow. There's a wetness in my mouth that doesn't belong. Blood, I think. My blood. My heartbeat hammers somewhere far away, in my ears or in the walls. I can't tell anymore. My legs are giving out. I am a rag doll.

Simon is draining the life out of me, second by second.

But then his grip falters.

His grip falters.

The rage disappears from his eyes like someone pulled a plug inside him, and it all drains out in one long, slow spiral. His eyes widen, not with anger this time, but with something more terrifying.

Understanding.

He opens his mouth, and I brace myself for what's coming, no matter what that is. But there's nothing.

No words come from his lips. Just a wet, gurgling sound. Warmth splashes across my face.

Blood. It's in my mouth. In my hair.

The world moves in slow, uneven frames as he stumbles backward, mouth still open in stunned silence, hands clutching at the nothing in front of him until he collapses.

Behind him, Stevie stands, her chest heaving. The knife I gave her still clutched in her fist, her knuckles white around the handle.

What We Do in Secret

CHAPTER

FORTY-EIGHT

Simon is dead.

There's blood soaking into the dirt of the basement floor, his eyes frozen open, wide and gazing at nothing. His mouth is still parted in that silent, smug little gasp, like he can't believe someone other than him pulled the final string.

I'm slumped on the ground, my back against the cold brick wall, my hand clamped over my throat where he just tried to kill me. And he would have succeeded if it weren't for...

Across from me, Stevie stares at Simon's body. Her entire body is shaking. The knife falls heavily beside her feet. She stumbles like she's drunk, her arm shooting out to the photo developing table to support herself.

"Stevie," I say, but it comes out hoarse. Too soft.

She doesn't look at me. Stevie is pale, gray almost, and swaying like a gust of air might take her out. The glaze is creeping into her eyes.

My heart drops to the filthy, grout-speckled floor.

The insulin.

"Stevie," I say again, louder this time, crawling toward her on shaking arms. "It's okay. It's okay. I'm going to help you, okay? I-I messed up, but I can fix it, I swear."

I stand, taking her face in my hands, forcing her to look at me, but her eyes are already beginning to flutter.

"I'm so sorry," I whisper. "I'll get something upstairs. Chocolate, honey, whatever I have. I can reverse it. You're gonna be okay. Please, don't die. Please."

I turn toward the stairs and begin to take them two at a time. Then I feel it.

My scalp is yanked back so hard it snaps my neck. A scream tears from my mouth. I am dragged down to the ground again. And then she's on top of me.

But it's not the girl I've been trying to save. This is something else. A ghost wearing her skin.

She wails, high and cracked, like a dying animal, and her hands come down on my face, clawing, flailing. Not hard, not sharp, but enough to sting. Enough to tell me she still has just a little bit of strength left, and she's using every last drop to punish me.

"You should've left us alone!" she sobs, her voice splitting down the middle. "We were fine until you came! You ruined it. You ruined everything."

I shield my face, squinting up at her blurred figure. "I'm sorry. I didn't know. I was trying to help! Please, Stevie, we need to hurry!"

"No!" she screams. Her body crumples forward onto mine. She is barely holding herself up now. Her words are wet and broken, slurring together like her mouth can't keep up. "I deserve to die after what I did."

"What you...?" I pause, breath catching. "What are you talking about?"

Stevie stops hitting. Stops moving entirely. Her head lolls beside mine. Our cheeks are nearly touching now.

I don't try to escape. I just listen.

"She was just a kid...someone's baby," she mumbles. "I can't believe I did that. I can't believe I..."

Her voice breaks off again.

"...Melissa said she'd make it go away. Make her go away. But you can't make death go away..."

There's a beat of silence, and then she whispers.

"...it grows roots in you." A sob wracks her thin frame.

"Are you...Are you saying *you* killed Heather?" My voice cracks. "Not Melissa?"

But she doesn't answer.

"She's killing me now. Every day. Every single day. Just let me go. Please. Let me go. I deserve—I..."

Her hand rises to her throat, like she's clawing at something growing inside.

"I deserve..."

She exhales and goes silent.

I sit up slowly, carefully moving her to the floor beside me. Her chest doesn't rise again.

I wait.

Still nothing.

"Stevie?" I place a finger on her pulse point beneath her ear, but it's still.

She's dead.

I sit there, frozen in the center of the darkroom, with Simon's corpse and Stevie's confession thick as the blood beneath my nails.

I should cry. Scream. Do something. But all I feel is...hollow, like something inside me has been scooped out.

No, *burned* out.

I look at Stevie's face, peaceful now, and brush a strand of her hair behind her ear. But I can't stop thinking about what she said.

You can't make death go away.

That's true. Death lingers like a ghost in the room, no matter how hard you try to conceal it. But I can still do what I came here to do.

Stevie's story may have ended here tonight, but mine doesn't have to. Mine is far from finished. And I deserve a happy ending.

With that, I grab the gas can from the photo table.

EPILOGUE

Nothing is more cleansing than fire.

The orange glow shrinks in my rearview mirror the farther we drive from New Haven. By the time we reach the next town, there may be nothing left of my old life at all. That thought is kind of comforting.

A familiar silver car with a logo I recognize speeds past me in the opposite direction as I merge onto the highway.

Dr. McCoy.

She's probably on her way to the scene by now, where someone will tell her my body is still inside the burning house. She'll feel guilty. Maybe she'll wonder if she could've saved me. She'll replay it again and again in her head, asking what she missed.

But the truth is, she didn't miss a thing.

I'm exactly where I'm meant to be. Headed west on I-22, with Bodhi, my son. I glance at his face in the rearview. He still won't look at me, but that's okay. We've got time. A whole new life ahead of us. One without lies, without violence, without betrayal.

I'm going to be a good mother.

No.

I'm going to be a *great* mother.

I flip on the oldies station. Joey Quinones croons "It Was Only a Dream" through the speakers, soft and haunting. That's exactly right.

I'm going to give him the childhood I never had. Soon, it'll be like our old lives never happened. Like it was just some nightmare, fading fast, half-forgotten by the time our feet hit the floor.

He'll come around.

And I'll be here when he does.

As a small publisher collaborating with an indie horror author, we make an incredible team. But we wouldn't be able to do what we so love without you. Thank you for taking the time to read *Hidden Children*, by C. S. Magnuson.

It would mean the world to us if you would take a quick moment and leave a review on any book-purchasing platform, especially our direct website, so other readers might take a chance on us too.

Don't forget to subscribe to our newsletter for the latest horror community book news and grab your free copy of *HORRORSMITH:The Magazine* from our website: www.horrorsmithpublishing.com

ACKNOWLEDGMENTS

It takes a cult to write a book. That's always been true, and it's just as true this time around. I'll forever be grateful for mine.

To my precious husband, Adam. I know I went a little crazy with this one. Thank you for your patience, your unwavering support, and for not locking me in the basement (though let's be honest, I might've finished faster if you had). I love you endlessly.

To my beautiful children, Gabriel, Mila, and Isla. You will always be my reason for everything.

To my girlfriends, this story exists in part because of you. Thank you for reminding me how radiant and healing female friendship can be when it's free of toxicity.

To my baby reader group, The Gravediggers (I swear I'll make that name official soon!), The Psychological Thriller Readers Group, and the Killer Thrillers Reading Group...thank you for your enthusiasm, your encouragement, and your love not just for my work, but for thrillers in general. You make this journey worthwhile.

And to the entire Horrorsmith team, authors included, thank you for being such a vital part of this process. Lyndsey, you are a force. I honestly don't know how you manage to do it all. Your passion, insight, and relentless dedication make every project better. You're building something real here. Something with heart and integrity. You deserve all the praise.

Now...on to the next chapter.

ALSO BY CHRISTINA GRAVES

Still, Dark Places

ALSO BY HORRORSMITH PUBLISHING

The Devil Came Down the Mountain
Still, Dark Places
Dark Things Crawl Out
What We Do in Secret
Lake of Secrets
Haint Blue
The Taste of Tiny Bones
A Light on the Bayou
Haunted Halls
Their Hearses
Three Garden Village
Hidden Children
Angie Baby
Crepuscular
Blood Ground
His Shrill Song

AUTHOR OF WHAT WE DO IN SECRET
CHRISTINA GRAVES
STILL, DARK PLACES
A PSYCHOLOGICAL THRILLER NOVEL

ABOUT THE AUTHOR

Christina Graves is a digital artist and author currently living in the deep south with her husband and three children.

When she isn't writing, she can be found binging horror films, making her way through her ever-growing to-read list, and spending time with her family.

Stalk her on social media @christinagravesauthor while she works on her next novel.

More Titles from
HORRORSMITH PUBLISHING

LISTEN CLOSELY...
THE DEAD MIGHT SPEAK...

THE
DEVIL
CAME DOWN
THE
MOUNTAIN

CHRISTOPHER BOND

THE DEVIL CAME DOWN THE MOUNTAIN
BY CHRISTOPHER BOND

For almost a hundred years, locals have proclaimed a portion of the Uinta Mountains in Utah to be cursed. They call the area the Murmuring Caves, the site of the historic Yangguang Massacre, where distortions and reverberations beneath the earth's surface create something very akin to human voices.

And if you listen long enough...you might just hear the dead...

Josh Bridges, an experienced dark tourist, has finally convinced his three best friends to accompany him in search of the Murmuring Caves. But they only agreed because of the tragedy Josh just lived through, which seems to have broken him. They'd do anything for their friend...

Even descend into darkness...

But when they call out for help, what answers them might not be safe...

It might not even be alive.

Will Josh and his friends—Trey, Mandy, and Amber—make it down the mountain?

If these walls could talk...
they'd speak of death...

THEIR HEARSES

E.L. GILES

THEIR HEARSES
BY E.L. GILES

Years ago, John Berryman was responsible for the deaths of his two children and their nanny. But John Berryman was never seen or heard from again. He simply...vanished.

Now, decades later, someone has finally purchased John Berryman's rambling old house.

Marc Larose is no stranger to loss. He hopes to bring the decaying structure to its former glory, a warm place where his family can heal and begin anew, but if these walks could talk, they'd speed of death. Only, Marc isn't listening.

Something vengeful still lingers in the shadows of the old willow, and it has its eyes set on Marc. It isn't long before he is caught in the tangles of mystery, fear, and deceit, where forces beyond his control are vying for his very soul.

Will Marc figure out who...or what...is haunting his new home before he becomes its next victim?

CHRISTINA GRAVES

STILL, DARK PLACES

A PSYCHOLOGICAL THRILLER NOVEL

STILL, DARK PLACES
BY CHRISTINA GRAVES

The Seven Sisters of Still Water. Missing but not forgotten. Memorialized in graveyard stone...

Nora Gray, true crime podcast host, is being called back to her hometown over a decade later by a desperate mother. Another daughter, gone. And Nora knows more than anyone realizes, more than even she remembers.

They call it Skull House, this home back in the woods, rundown, abandoned. And for as long as Nora can recall, the local kids have dared each other to climb the stairs to the top, to brave the ghost of Helaena Barker, who they say waits in the attic behind the door...

But Skull House hides more than tales of ghosts, and it clings tightly to its secrets. Nora is convinced it also holds the missing clues to the Seven Sisters' disappearances and why Nora herself woke up in a field near the house, covered in blood, all those years ago.

While Nora investigates the missing girls, will she be able to trust anyone around her? Will she even be able to trust herself?

YOUR BEDTIME STORIES WILL NEVER BE THE SAME...

THE TASTE OF TINY BONES

VINCENT HESELWOOD

THE TASTE OF TINY BONES
BY VINCENT HESELWOOD

No one knows where he came from...He's what lingers in the shadows behind you when you turn off the lights and race up the stairs...The darkness beneath the bed that keeps your feet tucked tightly under the covers...The Bogeyman...

But Evie "Creepy" Mortenson has unknowingly found a way to make him something more than what he was, something much more vicious, something much more hungry...

A simple blog post causes new nightmares to start, new fears that give him new life, and now, something is very, very wrong.

She's lost control of the monster she created, and children are starting to die.

Will she and Detective Ezra Dean find a way to stop him before he goes viral?

You thought you were afraid of the Boogeyman before...Just wait...

Children were never supposed to go inside...

HAUNTED HALLS

W. A. ROBERTS

HAUNTED HALLS
BY W. A. ROBERTS

It's every mother's worst fear: Kasey's young son, Max, has gone missing. Except, Kasey is convinced he never left the house...

Under the scrutiny of local law enforcement in a town focused on her past, Kasey must navigate the hidden passageways of her home with a boyfriend she no longer knows if she can trust and a neighbor keeping something from Kasey she desperately needs to remember.

Will Kasey discover the neighborhood's secrets before it's too late and her son is lost to the house forever?

FROM THE AUTHOR OF HALLOWS EVE
WILLIAM OSWALD
HAINT
BLUE
What do you do if the Boo Hag is already inside?

HAINT BLUE
BY WILLIAM OSWALD

When their father commits suicide, Louis Lattimore and his sister, Ruby, are forced to move across the country at the behest of their mother, to a secret family estate tucked away among the sea islands of South Carolina.

Louis is soon befriended by his two new neighbors and learns his new home is nothing like his old one in upstate New York. But it's not just culture shock Louis is wrestling. The locals seem convinced the family mansion is haunted.

According to the local Gullah people, the manor is possessed by an insatiable spirit dubbed the Boo-hag. At the insistence of his new friends, Louis reluctantly seeks help from Auntie Caroline, an elderly member of the Gullah community revered to an almost supernatural status, and with good reason.

Is she the only person who can help save Louis and Ruby from the Boo-hag?

CASSANDRA O'SULLIVAN SACHAR

LAKE OF SECRETS

LAKE OF SECRETS
BY CASSANDRA O'SULLIVAN SACHAR

*Seventeen-year-old Callie Quinn's vacation is off to a terrible start. Her parents have forced her to spend the summer before her s
enior year of high school with an elderly aunt in Deerville, Pennsylvania, where there's nothing to do but watch old Westerns on TV and read the classics.*

But soon, a mystery catches Callie's attention: the drowning suicide of a pregnant teen during the 1940s. Haunted by dreams of the girl, it doesn't take much digging before Callie realizes that the story isn't what it appears to be. Why would a teen bent on suicide make a blanket for a baby who wouldn't survive?

For help, she turns to her only friend in Deerville, another outsider named Brian. Little by little, he and Callie get closer to the mystery of the girl's death, following a path that leads them deep into the prejudices of the 1940s. They also become closer with each other.

As Callie begins to open up about her past to Brian, she is forced to face hard truths—not only about a murderer who has been hiding in plain sight, but also the turbulent personal events that led to Callie's exile to Deerville in the first place.

HUSHED HORROR SERIES BOOK ONE
THE STILL
BELLA DEAN JOYNER

THE STILL
BY BELLA DEAN JOYNER

Lana Wellington and Derek Armary individually find themselves seeking fresh starts in Edelleen, Colorado, located along the calm banks of the South Platte River. But within the shadows of the town's historic mill, something evil stirs, something vengeful.

When the first dead body is discovered in the woods, followed by a second, Sheriff Curtis Haines believes he's on the trail of a serial killer. But by the time his own deputies begin to report sightings of a strange, robed figure, Haines remembers rumors of a
decades-old murder and wonders if something more supernatural has fallen upon Edelleen.

With a failing marriage and small-town politics hampering his efforts, Haines leans heavily on the rest of the force and the citizens to find answers about what happened at the old mill all those years ago.

The creature crawling from the stagnant waters near the old mill has set its sights on Lana and Derek, who now must help Haines figure out who or what is responsible for calling it forth into Edelleen, and why.

But will they die trying?

A. A. PFAU

CREPUSCULAR

Don't trust
anybody...

CREPUSCULAR
BY A. A. PFAU

Thirteen-year-old Dylan Fisher and his classmates are returning to their sleepy coastal town after a week-long camp and an abnormal summer storm.

But before they even make it back into town, something stops them in the road.

Something hungry...

Knowing the bus is no longer safe, the teens attempt to make it back into town on foot, only to find everything deserted. Their loved ones are gone.

Or are they?

Don't trust anybody...

LUXURY APARTMENTS WORTH DYING OVER

THREE GARDEN
VILLAGE
LANCE REEDINGER

THREE GARDEN VILLAGE
BY LANCE REEDINGER

Three Garden Village. Luxury apartments, all the amenities, all the style. But the residents are leaving in body bags...

Zoe and the other employees at The Garden suspect something sinister is stalking the property, but local law enforcement and the complex's upper management simply attempt to explain the deaths away.

When the blood starts flowing over the once serene property, will anyone make it out alive?

Better lock your doors...